Hell's Angel

A Lew Travis Mystery

Charles Dayton

Published by Foothill Associates
Nevada City, CA 95959

First Edition, 2018
Imprint of Record – Create Space

Also by Charles Dayton

In the Lew Travis Mystery Series:

Come Hell or High Water

Hell Hath No Fury

Hell to Pay

Time Passages: Ten Stories

There But For Fortune: A Novel

For more information about the author
and his books:

charlesdayton.net

1

Tuesday

I was in a deep sleep, dreaming about my old motorcycle, which somehow had maintained itself in spite of the fact it hadn't been out in years. I was taking a long relaxed ride through the countryside, fresh air blowing through my hair, trees and meadows floating by. When the irritating sound of a telephone intruded.

I groped for the phone, reaching from under the covers, trying to rouse myself, knocking it off the recharger, and watching as it fell to the floor and bounced. Twice.

The message machine kicked on downstairs. A male voice was leaving a message, but I couldn't make out whose it was. Probably a robo call. Why the hell did I even keep the damn landline?

I looked at the clock on the bed stand: nine-oh-five. I blinked to try to gain a fuller grasp on consciousness, staring up at the ceiling. Okay, nine-oh-five wasn't an uncivilized hour to call. Unless you hadn't gotten to sleep until nearly four. Happens when you're seventy-two. And sometimes drink a little too much. And let your mind go to thoughts better left alone.

I felt a paw against my cheek and looked into a yellow feline eye, up close; my huge black cat, Earl.

"Hey, bud." I reached out and gave him a stroke.

He pawed me again, this time on the side of the nose.

"Okay, okay. Give me a minute."

Sighing, I threw back the covers and swung my feet over the side of the bed, sitting there for a minute to let the blood reach my head. I had to be careful these days, standing up too fast. Damn body.

When my head felt clear enough I hoisted my six-foot frame up and made my way into the bathroom, going through the usual morning routine—peeing, brushing my teeth, splashing cold water on my face—and glanced at myself in the mirror. Same old age lines around my eyes, same thin white hair, same grey whiskers. It wasn't getting better.

I plodded over to the closet and put on a robe and slippers, then headed for the stairs in my little cedar-sided bungalow, trying to clear the cobwebs. The half-story upstairs was comprised of my bedroom and the 'master' bathroom. Downstairs was larger, with a living room, dining room, kitchen, and den/office, plus another bathroom. I trudged through the living room to the front door, unlocked it and pulled it open, and looked out through my front porch at the front yard and pretty spring morning. The sun was up, the sky blue, the air fresh. I tried to ignore the lawn, which as usual needed mowing.

I took in a deep lungful of fresh air, then reached down and picked up the morning paper, feeling a touch of light-headedness. It was the local rag, the *Sienna Sentinel*, which I didn't think much of, despite of the fact I worked there, at least on an occasional basis. 'Part-time investigative reporter'—that was my official title. Mostly it let me snoop into various and sundry matters, whatever appealed to my curiosity and might be of interest to readers, sometimes of a possible criminal nature. It wasn't entirely clear to me why I kept doing it. There must be better ways to spend your time once you don't actually have to work. But what the hell, it kept me in contact with the world, and people I pretty much liked at the paper. One I really liked.

I turned back inside and headed for the kitchen, then remembered the phone call. I stopped and punched the message button.

"Lew. You alive, old man? I thought guys your age got up early? Give me a call when your brain kicks in. I've got something I need to tell you." Aside from the typical insult, his tone sounded somber.

Tim Royce was my young friend at the paper, now an assistant editor after just three years. He was maybe five foot nine, a hundred and fifty pounds, with dark curly hair, penetrating dark eyes, and a quick mind. His rapid rise there may have been influenced by the fact there weren't a lot of people at the *Sentinel* like him, with degrees from prestigious eastern colleges and an openness to trying new things. It still stumped me why an urban kid who had grown up in New York City wanted to live in an old gold mining town in the foothills of the Sierra Nevada Mountains of Northern California.

I resumed my journey to the kitchen and put some water on for coffee. Earl preceded me, meowing his expectations vociferously. I reached for his kibble and shook a generous helping into his bowl. He smelled it briefly, apparently to be sure it met his standards—which his girth suggested weren't all that high—and began crunching away.

I sat down at my old wooden kitchen table and studied the front page. An accident on the road up from Sacramento, a head-on with one driver killed and the other in critical condition. A man shot on the middle fork of the Yuba, apparently a fight over a woman. A drug bust out in the countryside at a cabin where they'd apparently been cooking meth. It was pretty much the same with this small town rag as every other: if it bled, it led.

The teakettle began whistling. I got up and poured hot water through the cone filter, smelling the first aromatic tinges of coffee. As the water seeped through I refilled it, then sat down and turned to the sports section. The Giants baseball season had just opened; they were playing the Padres in San Diego in the second game of the year. They were already down a game in the standings, having lost yesterday. On the other hand, the Warriors had beaten the Nuggets in Denver, their fifth road win in a row. Looked like they'd make the playoffs again easily.

I got up and removed the coffee cone and grounds, carrying my old ceramic mug back to the kitchen table, blowing on the surface before taking a sip. Thank God for coffee. The nearly-empty bottle of gin, still there from last night, sat on the counter. My twin nectars. Even the research of late had been reassuring: both alcohol and coffee were actually good for you. In limited amounts, of course. I felt it was important to view "limited" flexibly. Having rigid boundaries seemed like a personality flaw.

There was little of interest in the rest of the paper. Even the crossword wasn't much fun on Tuesday; it was still too easy. As the coffee began to kick in, I sighed and reached for the phone. Might as well see what was up.

"Sienna Sentinel." A soft female voice.

"Violet?"

A brief pause. "Hi, Lew."

"I thought you'd been promoted."

"Becky is out sick. Just filling in. What's up?"

"Tim called. Said there was something he wanted to tell me."

"He mentioned that on his way in. Shall I put you through?"

"Before you do, you good?"

She hesitated. "I'm okay." There was a pause. "It's been a while." Spoken with a slightly hurt tone.

I sighed. "Yeah; sorry. Been one of those stretches. I'm tying to get past it. You busy tonight?"

"That was abrupt."

"This weekend better?"

"Let me check my calendar." There was a brief pause. "Well, I'll have to rearrange a couple things, but I think I can make tonight work."

"A *couple* things? You have multiple conflicts on a Tuesday night?"

"I do have other interests, Lew. You haven't exactly been attentive of late."

Another sigh. "Yeah. Apologies?"

She hesitated. "Sure." She didn't sound convincing.

"What time is good for you?"

"Six?"

"I'll pick you up then. And, Violet…thanks."

"Sure. Here's Tim."

There were some clicks and a male voice came on the line. "Don't tell me you're up. I wasn't sure when we were going to hear from you again."

"Yeah, sorry. It's been one of those times."

He paused. "I'm afraid what I need to tell you isn't going to help."

I waited.

"It's about Jim Pearson." Spoken in a tone of voice that said more than the words.

A sense of dread came over me. Jim was an old colleague and friend.

"He'd been hospitalized for pneumonia. Apparently something went south." Tim paused, letting this sink in. "The service is this afternoon."

"The service? My god."

"I thought you'd want to go."

I rubbed my eyes, trying to make it seem real. "Jesus. Jim Pearson?"

"It's at two o'clock, Mortensen's Funeral Home."

I tried to make sense of this. "How can that be? He was still a young man."

"Forty-eight." Tim paused. "I didn't mean to shock you. I know you guys were pretty close?"

"I've kind of lost touch with him since he left the paper. But yes. Jim was...." I didn't know how to finish the sentence. How do you put into words the loss of someone you valued and loved, almost like a brother. Or son.

"Well, hey. I've got someone here waiting to see me." He hesitated. "Are you okay?"

"Yeah, sure, Tim. Thanks for letting me know."

"Sure."

We hung up and I sat there, dazed. Memories flooded in. Jim had grown up in a little farming town in the valley, and his Dad had died when he was fourteen. He'd gotten a part-time job and had taken on the burden of supporting his mother and two younger sisters until they got back on their feet. In college he'd fallen in love with the head cheerleader and married her after graduation. They'd had two daughters, to whom he'd been deeply devoted. He was a regular churchgoer, gave generously in its support, and contributed to a number of community projects. There was simply no one who didn't like Jim Pearson.

We'd worked together on a series of stories about the homeless problem in Sienna a few years back. He'd become deeply troubled, so much so he'd started giving regularly to the local food bank and made weekly deliveries to some of the local homeless camps. He'd become widely respected in that community, both among the officials who administered the programs and the homeless people themselves.

It was just one of those friendships that clicked, and then kept getting better. He'd sought my advice when troubled; I'd done the same with him, and come to trust him implicitly. He was always thoughtful and reasoned. One of those people on whom nature had bestowed true wisdom.

Jim Pearson, dead. It didn't seem possible.

2

I arrived at Mortensen's Funeral Home at one fifty-eight. A man with a long ragged beard and old but clean clothes handed me a program as I entered. The grief was evident in his eyes as we exchanged glances. I nodded my thanks and found my way to a seat at the back, surveying the eighty or so people sitting in front of me.

As my eyes roamed to the front of the room I noticed Jill, Jim's wife, sitting in the first row, holding a handkerchief over her nose. Next to her were their daughters: Rebecca, a sophomore in college, and Adele, a high school senior. Next to them was a large man with dark hair who had his arm around an attractive younger woman, neither of whom I recognized. He was patting her shoulder. Off to one side was a table covered with pictures of Jim at various ages, mostly taken with his family around him. A small dais stood in front on a slightly raised platform.

The program indicated that a Presbyterian minister would be officiating, with remarks by Jim's older daughter, Rebecca, and his business partner, Bruce Canton. Jim had left the *Sentinel* three years ago to become a partner in an insurance business. Even though he'd loved the newspaper work, he'd felt the need to make more money to support his family and cover his daughters' college educations. To my regret, I'd gradually lost touch with him.

The minister stepped to the dais and offered a solemn

greeting, bowed his head and said a prayer, and made some remarks about what a fine man James Pearson had been. He'd been a regular member of the combined Methodist-Presbyterian congregation for twenty years, since moving to Sienna, and had taught Sunday school to children there. The minister commented on how sad it was when someone left this world before their time, looking sympathetically at Jim's wife and daughters.

This was followed by a hymn, then brief remarks by Rebecca, touching on what a wonderful father he'd been, always attentive to the girls' needs and moods, always trying to support them. She broke down twice in tears, but bravely managed to finish. There was another hymn, and the minister introduced the business partner, who turned out to be the big man in the front row with his arm around the attractive younger woman: Bruce Canton. He looked even bigger when he stood, maybe 6'4" and 220 pounds. He strode to the dais and looked out over the audience, clearing his throat.

"Hard to know where to start with Jim. You all knew him, so I don't have to tell you what a terrific guy he was. We were partners for three years. Three wonderful years. Together we built our little insurance firm into one of the biggest in the area." He paused, looking around. "By the way, we have some terrific policies if any of you need one." He smiled, holding up his hands. "Just kidding, of course."

"I'm not going to say a lot, I just wanted to acknowledge how much we appreciated Jim at the firm. He had the highest of standards. He always marched to his own inner voice, one that told him to do the right thing. Actually, he became the conscience of the firm; he never tried to sell anyone a policy they didn't need." He paused. "Used to drive us crazy." A ripple of quiet laughter echoed through the room.

"Seriously, he's a huge loss to us all, and I want to offer my deepest condolences to Jill and the girls." He looked at them with a sad expression, shaking his head. "Even when things weren't at their best, I know he always cared. You guys were his whole life." He stood there for a moment, as though unsure what else to say, then nodded. "Thanks for giving me a chance to speak." He quietly stepped down and returned to his seat.

The minister made a few concluding remarks and offered a benediction. Then there was a final hymn, and the service ended. Everyone was invited to join the reception in the church's all-purpose room.

I got up and wandered over to the table with the pictures, glancing at the ones from Jim's youth, where he had been a high school star, graduating as valedictorian of his class, president of the national honor society, and captain of the basketball and tennis teams. There were also pictures from his college graduation, wedding, several with Jill in exotic settings, and his daughters at various stages of childhood. The family was an attractive one: Jill, who was still youthfully cute in her late forties, had short stylish blond hair, and the daughters, both verging on movie star beauty, were also blond but with longer hair.

As I stood there looking from picture to picture Jill came over and stood beside me. I hadn't known her well, Jim had kept his personal life pretty much to himself. But I had met her once or twice and knew how much he'd loved her. She was looking at the pictures with a sad expression. Not knowing what to say, I waited.

"Hard to believe, isn't it?" she said.

"Really hard. I'm sorry he left the paper."

She nodded. "Me too."

I looked at her inquiringly. "Really? Why?"

She looked me in the eye, a strange look I couldn't decipher, then back at the pictures. "It might have worked out differently."

Unsure how to respond, I said, "I can't begin to tell you how much I thought of Jim. Everybody did. It's hard to imagine what you're going through."

She shrugged in what seemed like a slightly dismissive way. "Life can be strange," she said. "I used to think I knew him."

I frowned. "I'm not sure..."

She looked directly at me. "You're Lew, right?"

"Yes. Lew Travis."

"Jim used to talk about you."

"Well, in my defense..."

She smiled. "It was the homelessness stories, wasn't it? The ones you worked on with him?"

"Good memory."

"I remember him saying how much he liked working with you. Said you were a shrewd old curmudgeon."

I leaned back. "Well, I..."

She touched my shoulder. "I didn't mean that like it came out. Jim really valued intelligence. And he liked"...she seemed to be searching for the right word..."mature people." She tipped her head, as though asking if I understood.

"I happen to agree with him on both counts."

She smiled. "I should probably get over to the reception. Are you coming?"

"Hadn't decided."

"Well, if you decide to come, maybe I can introduce you to Jim's daughters?"

"That would be nice."

***

11

I passed the refreshments table as I entered the room, picking up a glass of punch and a cookie and surveying the gathering. Virtually everyone who had been at the service was there. Jill was in one corner, her daughters next to her, in effect forming a reception line as people came by to offer their condolences. The business partner, Bruce Canton, stood across the room from them, his arm around the shoulder of the woman who had sat next to him at the service. She was dabbing at her eyes with a tissue as he leaned toward her, whispering something in her ear. She shook her head almost imperceptibly.

I quietly wound my way through the crowd until I happened on a middle-aged man I vaguely recognized from the *Sentinel*. I stopped and nodded toward him.

He nodded back. "Lew Travis?"

I struggled to recall his name, came up empty. "Do I remember you work in the ad department?"

He held out his hand. "Good memory. Harold Morgan."

"So you knew Jim?"

"He used to bring us Danish he bought on the way to work."

"Sounds like Jim. Nice service, eh?"

Harold shrugged noncommittally.

"No?"

"I could have done without the reference to Jim's marital problems."

I looked at him inquiringly. "Did I miss something?"

"That comment his partner made about 'when things weren't at their best'. Wasn't really necessary."

"I guess I didn't get the reference."

"Jim was separated from Jill when he died. They'd hit a rough patch. Didn't seem appropriate for a funeral service."

"I didn't know."

"That's about all *I* know," Harold said. "But we all

have our rough patches. Jim was a great guy."

"So are you still at the paper?"

"Yep. Still doing the same 'ol thing. Getting those ads out. That's what pays for the news. We're the invisible supports that keep the old rag going."

"An essential role."

Harold nodded. "What are *you* working on these days?"

I hesitated. There were times when the depression got bad enough that I didn't work on anything. It had been a few weeks. "Nothing at the moment."

"I like your articles. You have a nice touch with the mother tongue."

"Thanks. Good to know someone actually reads them."

"Well, we do get a little bored down there sometimes…" A twinkle appeared in his eyes.

I smiled, then held up my empty glass. "Good to see you, Harold. I should get a refill."

He nodded. "Good to see you, Lew."

As I headed toward the refreshments table, I walked past Bruce Canton and the young woman with him, catching a fragment of their conversation.

"We're all crushed, Karen, but we have to get past it. We have to move on."

She dabbed at her eyes, nodding unconvincingly.

I passed out of hearing range but glanced back and noticed him giving her another squeeze, then patting her hair and nudging her closer.

I poured myself another glass of punch and took another cookie, nibbling on it as I looked around. There was no one else I recognized, and several people were waiting in a line near Jill and the girls to add their condolences. It struck there might be better times to meet the daughters, and since I'd already touched base with Jill, I decided maybe it was a good time to leave. I finished the cookie and punch and headed for the exit.

The minister stood by the door saying goodbye to folks as they left. He held out his hand as I approached. "Thank you for coming." I nodded and shook hands, then started through the door. "God be with you," he said in a benevolent tone as I did so.

As I sensed the fresh outdoor air and started down the sidewalk, I wondered where God had been when Jim was dying. And why people always seemed to give him credit when things went well, but never blame when they didn't. I'd heard a hundred athletes thank God after a win; I'd never heard one blame him after a loss.

It was a pretty spring afternoon, the sky blue, the trees light green with their newly minted leaves, the smell of grass in the air. A bird landed in a branch above me and a squirrel scampered up a tree trunk as I approached. The signs of another renewal; spring was in the air. And Jim Pearson was dead.

Maybe there were things we weren't supposed to understand, a plan we weren't given to know. Given the day's events, that seemed doubtful to me, but even were it true, it seemed a little cruel. Why give us the intelligence to wonder, and then leave us in the dark?

Jim Pearson had been a good man. The kind we need more of. His death shouldn't have happened. I wondered how it had. What had Tim said: something had gone south at the hospital? I wondered what.

3

Violet was waiting when I rang her doorbell. She was dressed in comfortable slacks and a lovely teal angora sweater, her shoulder-length brown hair shining in the early evening light. Her eyebrows were raised as she glanced at her watch.

"Six-ten. Not bad, Lew."

"Fashionably late. Didn't want to get here ahead of time."

"Have you ever been early?"

I closed one eye, trying to remember. "I think I was early once to a basketball game. Had to wait for them to open the doors."

"Figures. A sports event."

"Hey, you watch the Warriors lately? They're great. Hasn't been a team this much fun to watch in a long time."

"Is that fencing or wrestling?"

I shook my head. "So, you ready?"

She nodded, stepped out, and pulled the door shut behind her.

As we started down the street in my old blue Honda Accord, she said, "So, where we going?"

"Your favorite place."

Her eyes widened. "Le Plus Delicieux?"

"Okay, your second favorite place."

"Oh. When are you going to take me to my favorite

place?"

"Don't you want something to look forward to?"

"I *have* something to look forward to. I've been looking forward to it for a long time."

I looked away. "One day." I guess my tone gave me away.

"So, it's been another of those times? Seemed like you were maybe gaining." In that soft, sympathetic voice.

"You know she died about this time of year. It gets me down a little each time it rolls around."

"Lew, that was ten years ago."

I nodded. "Yeah." I sighed, then glanced at her. "I'm trying, Violet. Really."

We were quiet the rest of the drive.

***

Valentino's is a classic old Italian restaurant, with red-checkered tablecloths and candles. We were seated at a table near the back. A young man with long blond hair arrived, announcing he'd be our waiter for tonight. It was a common practice, but always made me wonder: did they think we couldn't tell? I nodded politely and ordered a bottle of Chianti.

"So, how was the service?" Violet asked as the waiter left.

"Painful. Aren't they all? The passing of another person you knew and liked. Isn't God wise? Letting the best of us expire before our time."

She looked at me with her head cocked, frowning. "Lew." The tone conveyed a gentle warning.

I sighed. "Sorry. I'm just not fond of death. Maybe it has something to do with the fact I'm old."

"At least the service was for a person you liked."

16

I nodded reluctantly. "Did you know he'd been separated?"

Violet looked away, as though trying to remember. "I think there were rumors a couple years back—after he'd left the paper—that they were having their problems. As I recall it had something to do with conflicts over raising the girls. They were always the apples of Jim's eye; I suspect he spoiled them pretty rotten. I think Jill had a little"...she hesitated, searching for the right words..."firmer ideas about raising them. At least that was the rumor."

"Makes sense. I remember he couldn't wait to get home at the end of the day to see them."

The waiter returned with a basket of bread and the bottle of Chianti. He poured out a small portion for me to sample. Another silly tradition, but I complied and nodded my approval. He poured us each a generous glass, then took our orders. Violet opted for the ravioli in a mushroom cream sauce; I ordered the seafood linguini in a marinara sauce.

"The separation must have been hard on him," Violet said as the waiter left.

I nodded. "Do you know anything about Bruce Canton, his business partner?"

"I know he tried to sell the newspaper a policy, using Jim as the conduit. I think we already had one we were happy with, so it didn't materialize. As I recall, Jim was embarrassed to be put in the position he was. But he was a good soldier. Came back a couple times with different offers. I don't think the *Sentinel* ever bought one."

"Apparently their insurance business did well?"

Violet nodded. "They ran an aggressive advertising campaign, including in the paper. They offered to undercut anyone else on any policy. I think they did quite well."

"You don't happen to know anything about a young

woman Jim might have known, do you? I think her name is Karen. Didn't get her last name. She was at the service with Canton. He was trying to comfort her. She seemed pretty broken up."

Violet frowned. "No. Why?"

I shrugged. "No idea. It just seemed a little curious; she seemed more broken up by Jim's passing than his wife did."

Violet's eyebrows narrowed. "Leeww? That sounds a little suspicious."

I frowned, not responding.

Violet was staring directly at me. "You suspect foul play, don't you?"

"I don't know enough to suspect anything." I paused. "Not yet, anyway."

Violet's eyebrows were raised, as though she were intrigued. "You're going to look into this, aren't you?"

I shrugged noncommittally.

"Well, good. I don't know if you'll get anywhere, but maybe it will help pull you out of your funk."

The food arrived and we began eating. I noticed Violet glancing at me surreptitiously once or twice, as though she was weighing something. I wondered what was going through her mind.

When the check arrived, Violet reached for it; I gently grasped her wrist before she could pick it up. "I'm too much of a traditionalist for that. I can handle this."

"You know that's a little outmoded, Lew. We ladies like to keep things on an even footing."

"I'm already way in the hole with you, given the last few weeks. This is just a down payment."

She smiled coyly. "Would you have any interest in coming over to do a little more leveling of things?"

I contemplated her pretty face, hesitating. "I don't

deserve you, Violet. You do know I know that?"

"Why don't you let me decide that?"

I shook my head, staring at her. "You are beautiful. Have I told you that lately?"

She frowned. "I'm fifty-two. No woman is beautiful at fifty-two. We're past our prime."

"If that's the case, I'm glad I didn't know you in your prime. I couldn't have handled someone that gorgeous."

She scowled. "You old flatterer."

"It's true. For an old codger like me, you're a dream come true. I don't know how I got so lucky."

"Well, for one thing, the pickings are a little slim for us older single ladies. You men keep dropping off."

"So it's desperation?"

She frowned, as though considering this, then nodded. "Pretty much. Which reminds me, you get a checkup lately?"

"For what?"

"You know they don't recommend more than two drinks a day for men, Lew." She was staring at my empty wine glass.

"I follow that rule."

She looked at me skeptically. "*Really?*"

I nodded. "Absolutely. I just use a big glass."

She rolled her eyes. "So what about my invitation?"

I looked away, then back, grimacing. "Can I take a rain check? I'm just not quite there yet. But I'm working on it. I promise."

She sighed. "Okay. But you know, when there's a drought, any rain is welcome."

I frowned. "What does that mean?"

She glanced away with a coy expression.

***

We pulled up to the curb outside Violet's condo. I looked at her warmly. Then I leaned over and kissed her. When I leaned back I looked into her eyes. "I've missed you."

She stared back, looking at me quizzically.

"Is the weekend still a possibility?" I asked.

"For?"

"Another get together?"

She frowned. "Can I check my calendar? Get back to you tomorrow?" I sensed a change in tone.

I nodded. "Sure."

She opened the door and got out, then looked back in, her eyes earnest. "Good night, Lew." She quietly closed the door and headed through the gate.

I sat there and watched until she had opened her door, stepped through, and closed it behind her. Then I slowly pulled away from the curb, shaking my head.

"You're a damn fool," I said to myself.

***

I lay in bed, staring at the ceiling, Earl curled up at my feet. A half-empty glass of gin sat on the bed stand, next to a stack of books. I glanced at the pictures on the other side of the bed. Mary's side. The kids, small and innocent. Mary with that warm playful look in her eyes. So beautiful. For thirty-seven years, my whole life.

It had happened ten years ago, almost to the day. There had been a warm spring storm, a nasty one, with thunder and lightning, and heavy downpours. But Mary had insisted on going to visit her friend who lived out in the countryside and tended to get lonely. On a narrow rural road with no shoulders. In her little Toyota.

The head-on had been devastating. The huge late-model Lincoln Continental had been almost completely on Mary's side. The skid marks suggested it had been going well over the speed limit. With that arrogant SOB at the wheel, three sheets to the wind. Who hadn't even bothered to call 911, with his minor injuries, while she was bleeding to death behind the wheel. Said he was too confused, when it was obvious he just didn't want anyone to find out how drunk he was.

I'd found her myself when she hadn't made it home as expected. I'd called her friend and learned she'd left an hour earlier. I knew the route, drove out there. I still have nightmares about it, those terrible images.

The attorney he hired was good. Pointed out that the weather was a major factor. It had happened on a curve, with little time for either driver to react. He noted that when the breath test was taken—several hours later—it was below the legal limit, if barely. He offered his condolences to me and the kids, and to pay for the damages. The only problem was there was no way to pay for the only damage that mattered.

Ten long years. It had gotten a little better the last few. But there were still times when gin was the only thing that helped. I'd always managed to come out of it eventually. Knowing Violet had helped. But I wasn't sure anyone could really fill that void. Or when it got bad, make me want to keep trying.

4

Wednesday

The next morning brought the usual: a throbbing hangover. It's not like I have a cast iron stomach; there is a price to pay. It's a matter of balancing two needs: the more gin, the less emotional pain; the less gin, the less physical pain. It's not like Mary would have liked this. I need to move on. But god, it's hard. I was on my third cup of coffee, which was just beginning to help.

I had managed to get the paper, where there was a short piece about Jim, apparently written by someone who knew him when he worked there. It touched on his move to the insurance firm; his wife and daughters; and his membership in the church and involvement in community causes. It ended by touching on something I'd forgotten: his collection of local Indian artifacts. I wondered if maybe Harve had been the author.

Harve is Tim's office mate. He's a Maidu, the Indian language group that dwelt in the northern Sierra Nevada foothills, and more precisely a Nisenan, the tribe that lived in and around what became Sienna before the gold rush. He's a big man, broad in the shoulders and muscular, with straight black hair, a strong nose and jaw, and a handsome visage.

Harve's ancestors were mostly wiped out in about a twenty-year span between the beginning of the gold rush and 1870, partly from the diseases the white man brought, against which they had no defenses, and partly by the fact they were viewed as subhuman. There were bounty hunters who, for five dollars apiece, had made collections of their scalps, which they proudly displayed. Harve was among the few descendants who were still around. His full Indian name was Walter "White Cloud" Harvey. Everyone called him Harve. He was in his thirties now, and still unmarried.

It struck me a call to Harve might be worth a shot. I dialed the *Sentinel*. A young female voice answered.

"Sienna Sentinel, your best source of local news." Becky. I liked Becky. She was a kid; this was her first job. Short dark hair, a tasteful tattoo of a butterfly on her forearm, a tiny diamond nose pin, and a languid attitude. I especially liked the fact she put up with my impudence.

"How do you determine what's best?" I asked.

"I'm sorry?"

"That's a big claim. There are a lot of other sources of local news."

Her voice was tentative. "Is this…?"

She had a nasal twang from the cold. "You don't sound all that much better. Shouldn't you be home resting?"

"How did you…?"

"Just one of those alternative local news sources."

"Mr. Travis! Of course."

"Lew, remember? Unless you want me to call you by your last name? I think we've been over that?"

Her voice became relaxed, and took on a tolerant tone, like she was speaking to an amusing if annoying friend. "Hi, Lew. What can I do for you?"

"Am I going to have to talk to your higher ups again about this silly advertising thing? You know we all have sensitive BS detectors these days. We all form our own opinions about the best source of news. Seems like credibility ought to be at the top of a newspaper's agenda. And why are you at work if you're still sick?"

"It gets boring lying around the house all day."

"Okay, I can buy that. Just don't push yourself too hard."

"Thank you, Lew. How can I be of service?"

"Is Harve around?"

"Yeah, I saw him come in a while ago. Shall I put you through?"

"Please. Thanks."

There were some clicks on the line, then a familiar voice. "Back from the dead, old man?"

"That's a hell of a greeting."

"Tim filled me in. Sounds like it fits."

"It happens. I'm gaining. That aside, could we try to keep the word 'dead' out of the conversation? We old people get nervous around it."

"What can I do for you, Lew?"

"Did you write the piece about Jim in this morning's paper?"

"As a matter of fact."

"What else do you know about it? Anything you couldn't put in the paper?"

"Just like that? You're not going to offer to buy me lunch, or even a cup of coffee? You just want my inside information?"

"I'd be happy to buy you lunch, Harve? I know what a cheap SOB you are."

He hesitated. "You're seeking my help while proffering insults? Has your old brain deteriorated even further?"

"Well?"

"Actually, I'm a little busy today. What do you want to know?"

"I'll be brief. I'm wondering if you have any insights

into how Jim actually died. The paper never said, and nothing came out at his funeral. Just that he was fighting a case of pneumonia."

Harve sighed. "It's unclear. The pneumonia was nasty; he'd been put on a ventilator. I'm told they're actually doing an autopsy on him. I don't know where that stands."

"How did you find that out?"

"My contacts at the hospital."

"Could you link me to one of them? Someone I could talk to there?"

"With what excuse?"

"The usual. I'm putting together a longer piece on Jim, trying to collect as many details as I can? You wouldn't have to mention the 'investigative' part of my moniker. Just a reporter doing a retrospective on a local citizen."

"Why are you interested in this?" Harve asked.

"I'm not sure I am. But I'd like to learn a little more."

"You sniffing foul play here, Lew?"

"Let's just say Jim was a guy I thought a lot of. I'd like to learn a little more about why he isn't still with us."

There was a momentary pause. "My best source is probably one of the nurses who was attending Jim. Her name is Jennifer Sanchez. She's a sweetie. I'll give her a call, see what I can do."

"Thanks, Harve. And I owe you a lunch. When your demanding schedule lets up."

"I do a favor for you, and what do I get in return? Sarcasm."

"I thought you liked sarcasm."

"At least it suggests your brain is still functioning."

***

I'd just started to write down the questions I wanted to

25

ask Jennifer Sanchez when the phone rang. I looked at the caller ID: Sienna Memorial Hospital.

Frowning, I picked up and answered tentatively. "Hello?"

"Mr. Travis?"

"Yes."

"This is Jennifer Sanchez. Mr. Harvey said you wanted to talk to me?"

"That was fast."

"He just called, and I happen to be on a break. What can I do for you?"

"Did Mr. Harvey explain why I wanted to talk with you?"

"He said you were doing a retrospective piece on Mr. Pearson?"

"Yes. Jim was a friend of mine. I'm a part-time reporter for the paper. I thought it would be a nice thing to do a background article about his life."

"That's a nice idea. How can I help?"

"Well, one of the things I'm interested in, although it probably won't be a feature of the article, is just how he died. I know he had pneumonia. Can you tell me anything beyond that?"

There was a pause. Then she spoke in a quieter voice. "This is kind of a sensitive matter."

"How so?"

"It's true when anyone dies here. People have strong feelings about that. And it's not unusual for hospitals to be sued. They're actually conducting an autopsy on Mr. Pearson's body to determine the exact cause of death." Her tone was somber.

"Harve mentioned that. And a lawsuit is the furthest thing from my mind. I'm just a concerned friend."

"Well, I can tell you that he had a severe case of

26

pneumonia."

"And?"

"Pneumonia interferes with a person's breathing. That's the big danger. It attacks the lungs."

"How was he being treated?"

"With intravenous antibiotics. And he was intubated. He was on a respirator."

"Was this the case when he died?"

She spoke slowly. "Yes."

"Is that typical?"

A pause. "Actually, it's kind of unusual for a patient to die while intubated."

"Because?"

"They're being helped with the thing they're having the most difficulty with—breathing."

"But somehow it didn't work in this case?"

A sigh. "No."

I hesitated. I needed more, but I sensed Jennifer didn't know more, or couldn't say more, at least until the results of the autopsy were available. I decided to shift gears.

"Well, can you tell me what he was like? As a patient? Don't nurses form opinions about patients? Whether they're cooperative or belligerent?"

"We try to treat everyone equally, but you can't help liking some patients more than others. Everyone here loved Jim—Mr. Pearson."

"So you were on a first name basis with him? How long was he there?"

"Only a few days, and I shouldn't have said that. But yes, he was a lovely person. He was hurting, sometimes gasping for air—until we got him on the ventilator—but he was still friendly. He liked to tease us about which doctors we thought were the cutest."

"*No.*" In my best shocked tone.

27

A slight giggle.

"Aren't some of the docs women these days?"

"Sure. And some of the nurses are men. He teased us in either case."

"Did you learn anything about his personal life that might be good in an article?"

"Like what?"

"Well, who came to see him in the hospital?"

"Well, there was his wife and daughters, of course."

"They came often?"

"His daughters were here quite a bit. His wife came by once or twice."

"Who else?"

"His minister stopped by a couple of times. And his business partner."

"Anyone else?"

"There was another woman. I'm not sure what her relationship was. She was pretty young—older than his daughters, but younger than his wife—who came by two or three times."

"Did you happen to get her name?"

A pause. "Kathy, maybe? Or…"

"Karen?"

"That's it."

"Do you happen to know her last name?"

"Nooo."

"Is there any way to find out?"

"Well…"

"It's confidential?"

"Yes. But visitors have to sign in." She hesitated. "If you could promise I didn't tell you."

"Of course. That would be great. I'd like to flesh out the story with as many perspectives as possible."

"Sure, Mr. Travis."

"By the way, you can just call me Lew."

She hesitated. "Okay…. Hey, my break's ending. I have to get back on duty. Can we finish this later?"

"Why don't you just call when it's convenient for you? If I'm not here, just let me know a good time to call back."

"Okay."

I hung up and scribbled some notes to myself. I didn't know much about ventilators, how they worked. A better understanding might be helpful. And I should probably talk to Jim's wife; that cryptic comment she'd made at the funeral kind of stuck in my brain, how she used to think she knew Jim, but wasn't so sure any more. What could that mean? And Karen. Definitely Karen.

5

It was ten a.m. and the hangover was beginning to clear; thank god for coffee. Earl was off on one of his regular neighborhood jaunts. Who knew where a wily old tomcat liked to spend his time? All I knew was that he always came back for dinner. Often several times a day.

I decided to crank up the old Mac and do a little online searching. Much as I resented the influence of the Internet, it made certain kinds of information gathering easier. I hit the browser icon and typed Bruce Canton Insurance in the search box. Up popped the website, complete with his picture, that of a woman about the same age, a shot of his office, and the address and phone number. I jotted down the address and entered it into Google maps. It was just a mile away, on Cedar Street. Well, what did I have to lose?

A glance out the kitchen window revealed a bright mid-morning sun and deep blue sky. A lovely day. I threw on a windbreaker, grabbed my car keys from their hook inside the back door, and headed out to the garage. The garage door, the old kind that lifts up in an arc, was slightly stuck, as usual; it was getting harder and harder to pull up, but after several hard tugs it finally gave way. There was Old Blue, my timeworn Honda Accord, waiting faithfully as always. After twenty years and two hundred thousand miles, a car comes to feel like a friend.

I backed out of the gravel driveway and headed off to

the business section of town. Not that this took very long. Sienna isn't exactly a major metropolis, with just a few blocks of downtown streets, surrounded by a mixture of housing, some old and elegant, some new and not. Cedar Street was one of the downtown streets, a block off the main drag and running parallel to it.

I drove slowly along it, checking for numbers, passing a little grocery, a wine tasting room, a yoga studio. Sure enough, there it was, a one-story wood-framed structure set back from the street, with a big sign in front that read:

Canton Insurance
Best Bet in Sienna

At least the sign was honest: that's what insurance was, a bet. An insurance policy was a bet against your own good fortune. You were paying money to wager something bad might happen to you. If nothing did, you still paid your money; you just got nothing in return. Why do we all feel such a need to protect ourselves?

I pulled into the little parking lot in front of the building and got out, then made my way toward the entry, glancing through the large windows in front. There were two desks, one on each side of the room, and a door behind each, presumably leading to offices in back. The glass-paneled door swung open easily. A middle-aged woman at one of the desks looked up.

She was the woman I'd seen in the picture on the website, although in person she was a bit less attractive. She was stocky, to use a kind term, wearing beige slacks and a yellow top, neither of which hid her girth. Also a gaudy necklace and earrings, not that I was much of an expert in these matters. Her narrow reading glasses hung from a chain around her neck.

"Good morning," she said in a robust cheery voice.

I didn't do all that well with cheeriness, especially when my hangover hadn't quite lifted. I nodded and said hello.

"What can I do for you?" Still cheery.

"I was looking for Bruce Canton. Isn't he the owner?"

"He's one of the owners," she said. "It's a partnership." She smiled.

"Ah. With James Pearson, if I'm not mistaken."

"Well, actually, that's not quite right. Mr. Pearson was technically an employee of the firm. My husband and I are the actual partners."

"Oh. So you must be…Mrs. Canton?"

"Indeed. Roberta Eileen Canton." She reached out her hand. "And you are…?"

"Lew Travis." We briefly shook; she had a serious grip.

"Are you here to…?" Her eyebrows were raised expectantly; I sensed she was hoping to sell me an insurance policy.

"I'm a reporter with the *Sentinel*. I'm putting together a retrospective piece on Jim Pearson's life. I thought since he and Mr. Canton were partners—well, worked together for the last three years—perhaps I could talk to him for a bit and fill in some details of his work life."

"Oh." The cheeriness had dissipated. "Could *I* maybe be of help? We did all work as a team."

"Well, sure, I suppose."

"Have a seat, Mr. Travis. Would you like some coffee?" The cheeriness was back.

"Coffee would be great."

Roberta Eileen Canton got up and poured me a cup from the Mr. Coffee pot on a table to the side, set it down on the front edge of her desk, and motioned to one of the two plush chairs there. Then she sat down behind her desk, leaned back, and smiled.

"What would you like to know?"

"How about we start with the roles each of you had in the firm?"

"Sure. Let's see. Bruce and I started the firm about ten years ago. He's kind of the people person. Seems to have a knack that way. He handles most of the interactions with our clients. I'm what I guess you might call the quiet one behind the scenes. I handle the paperwork end of things—getting out the new policies, doing the billing, arranging legal matters, that sort of thing."

"Where did Jim fit into this?"

"We were feeling a little overwhelmed when he came on board, so we took him on to help with whatever felt most out of control. He did a little bit of everything. He was good with clients, so that was part of it, meeting with new folks. When I got overwhelmed, he helped with the billing. Sometimes he manned the office when neither Bruce nor I could be here."

"How do you feel he worked out?"

"Like a hand in a glove. He was a huge help. Everybody liked him. He made sure things didn't slip through the cracks. Helped when there were complaints. I don't know what we're going to do without him."

"If it's not too indelicate to ask, can you say anything about how he did financially?"

She frowned. "Are you asking how much he was paid?"

I frowned. "Not exactly, just…"

"Well, in this business a lot of your income is based on commissions. He of course had a base salary, but as time went by the commissions comprised the majority of his income. He did quite well, if that's what you're asking. I'm not at liberty to give you exact figures, but he joined us in the hope of improving his income, and I don't think he was disappointed. We've almost doubled in size since he came on board."

"What kind of hours did he work?"

"It varied. There are gluts, and there are slow times. You never know. It's been pretty fast and furious of late. He had been putting in long hours."

"Until he got sick?"

She nodded sadly. "Yeah. It's hard to believe. Who could have predicted anything like this? Have you had your pneumonia shots, Mr. Travis?"

I ignored the question; I avoided medical procedures that weren't forced on me. "How about the personal side. Can you think of any particular quirks Jim had, things that might endear him to readers?"

She looked away, thinking. "He was a generous man."

"How so?"

"He didn't like to push clients who were late on payments. He'd sometimes work out extended deadlines for them." She rolled her eyes; it was hard to tell whether this was friendly teasing or she was genuinely annoyed. "He gave to several good causes. Food banks, shelters, things of that sort. He was a religious guy, always went to church. I think he actually tithed. You don't see that too often these days."

I jotted notes as she spoke, looking up when she'd finished. "That's helpful. Anything else come to mind?"

"Well, I suppose you could say it wasn't only with respect to money he was generous. He cared about people. When he saw someone having a tough time, he'd talk to them, listen, try to help. He hated suffering."

"Can you think of an example?"

She frowned. "I suppose you could say his relationship with…" She shook her head. "No, I think I shouldn't mention that. It's a little too personal."

"Can you describe it in a non-personal way?"

"It was someone going through a rough patch. Jim was trying to be there for her." She stopped and scowled. "Well, okay, it was a her. But I don't think it was more than that. He *was* separated." Again she stopped, waving her hand. "Scratch both of those comments. Let's just say it was Jim being Jim. He was a lovely man."

I nodded. "Okay. Well, all that is helpful. Thanks." I put my notebook away.

"Do you want me to have Bruce get in touch with you when he gets back?"

"That would be great." I handed her my *Sentinel* business card.

She looked at it, scowling. "You're an *investigative* reporter?"

"That just means I do in-depth stories. I'm not a regular writer for the paper."

She looked at me a bit askance, as though trying to make a judgment. "So you're not *investigating* anything?" Her head was cocked to the side.

I looked at her skeptical expression. "Just collecting information for the retrospective."

"Ah." She seemed to relax. "You don't need an insurance policy, do you?"

I smiled. "No. I don't have much need that way."

She held out her hand. "Well, if you change your mind, you know where to find us. Can't be too careful, you know. Burglaries, fires, water damage. Lot of things can go wrong with a house."

I resisted rolling my eyes, we shook briefly, and I headed back out and climbed into Old Blue, making a few mental notes as I did so. So Jim wasn't actually a partner. And had perhaps annoyed the two partners with his generosity. I remembered Bruce's comment at the funeral, about how he never sold anyone a policy they didn't need.

Then there was the fact that in spite of Bruce Canton's behavior toward the young woman he was with at the funeral, it seems he had a wife who was his partner, who he clearly wasn't divorced from, and who for some reason didn't come to the funeral, even though, in her own words, they all "worked as a team". How did this relate to the young woman Canton was there with? Did Bruce arrange things so Roberta wouldn't be there? Did she just not care? What did this mean about the young woman herself, 'Karen' something? Was she the one Jim had been providing "support" to? And just what kind of support might that have been?

More things to unravel. I started up the car and headed for home.

***

When I got back the answering machine was flashing. I punched the button. The message was spoken in a soft whisper.

> Hi, Mr. Travis. This is Jennifer Sanchez from the hospital. I did check down at the front desk. I think the young woman who visited Mr. Pearson was a Karen Black. At least there are three times that name comes up on the list while he was here, and they all indicate she was visiting Jim. Hope that helps.

Help indeed. And quick. Jennifer Sanchez was turning out to be an obliging font of information. I made a mental

36

note to thank Harve. And to try to track down contact information for Karen Black. I was curious about her relationships with both Jim Pearson and Bruce Canton.

However, before I did anything else, my stomach was reminding me that, as usual, I had eaten no breakfast. Coffee only went so far. I opened the door to my pantry—all right, cupboard—all right, shelf. As usual, the pickings were slim. I had more cat food in the house than people food. Which might make Earl happy, but it was a discrepancy that needed addressing. Even at my advanced age, food remained something of a necessity.

A perusal of the refrigerator revealed that things weren't in any better shape there. Stuffed at the back was a plastic container which, when I pried off the cover, revealed something green growing inside it. Jesus. This was beneath even me.

Okay, another trip was indicated. It had become pleasantly warm, so I left my windbreaker on its hook, grabbed my keys, and headed off to the nearest fast food joint. The glamorous life of the small town sleuth.

6

I scarfed down the hamburger—the cheap version with no cheese, lettuce, tomato, or onion—washing it down with a cup of black coffee. This had gotten better of late with all the competition from the expensive coffee shops. Not that it mattered a lot to me; I was happy with pretty much anything that had enough caffeine in it.

I took the last swig and reluctantly decided on a trip to my favorite grocery store. Which was not part of any chain: it was a locally-owned supermarket that specialized in locally-grown produce and meats. It was a bit more expensive than the chain stores, but seemed worth it. I headed there in Old Blue.

Sienna looks a lot like most other modest-sized towns if you keep your eyes focused on the immediate surroundings: the usual assortment of grocery stores, banks, gas stations, clothing stores, and real estate offices. It also has its share of little specialty shops; lots of Bay Area and Sacramento folks liked to come up for a weekend getaway. Where it differs is the more distant view. If you look up at the horizon from almost anywhere all you see is green, a backdrop of mountains and a seemingly endless panorama of trees.

If you head west, meaning down toward the Sacramento Valley, deciduous trees predominate, with broad stretches of grass-covered rolling hills and oak trees.

As you head east, up the mountain, evergreens predominate, cedars and pines and firs. The Tahoe National Forest begins not all that far up the mountain. It is an outdoor person's paradise.

I reached the supermarket and parked in its spacious lot. As I entered through the electric doors I noticed the quiet, typical of midday on a Wednesday. The shopping went quickly: bottle of inexpensive gin, pound of inexpensive coffee, and some lesser essentials—loaf of my favorite sourdough bread, jar of peanut butter, package of cheese, couple cans of soup, some bananas and apples. I didn't see anyone I knew—until I got to the checkout line.

Standing in front of me was my old friend Emmett. Emmett is a big guy, tall and 'full-bodied', a semi-retired real estate agent who gets a lot of pleasure out of life, at whatever the cost might be. He eats more than he should, especially the kinds of things he shouldn't. I glanced at his cart: two six packs of beer, two packages of Twinkies, a cherry pie, and a half gallon of mint chip ice cream.

"You planning to die early?" I said, pushing my cart in behind him.

He turned and looked at me. "Well, if it isn't Sherlock Holmes. You come out of your hibernation?"

"How'd you know about that?" I asked.

"You don't remember my messages? I called you twice last week to see if your lazy ass would like to engage in a game of chess. Either you don't listen to your messages or you were in one of your deep sleeps."

"The last time we talked about chess you said you were tired of losing."

"Yeah, well, that's one of my New Year's resolutions. Hope springs eternal."

"Sorry about not responding. Kind of a tough time of year for me."

39

"Yeah. I remember. Sorry. You doing better?"

I nodded. "A little."

"We late-inning bachelors have to keep our efforts up, you know. We don't have all that much time left." Emmett had gone through two marriages, both ending in divorce. He was great at parties and with real estate clients, but not so good when it came to keeping wives happy. Apparently he liked novelty in his life.

"Speak for yourself, Emmett."

"You working on any stories?"

"Might be."

"Pray tell."

"Too early to know yet. What are *you* up to?"

"Work, work, work. You know me."

"Lot of real estate action these days?"

"Real estate?"

"To what were you referring?"

"You name it. Keeping up with the news. Watching my favorite TV shows. Hitting the movies. Trying out new restaurants. Oh, and I followed up on another of my New Year's resolutions."

"That's a heavy schedule. What resolution?"

"To get out and about more. Develop some new romantic possibilities."

"Are you telling me you got a date, Emmett?"

He nodded, puffing out his expansive chest.

"You going to tell me with whom?"

He shook his head. "You'll find out eventually, if things go like I'm planning."

"How does she feel about good eating habits?" I nodded toward his cart.

"Got to enjoy the time we have left, Lew. You never know when it will all end."

"Looks like you're trying to hurry things along."

The lady in front of Emmett finished paying and he moved his cart ahead as the clerk began to ring him up. "Rather enjoy myself for ten years than torture myself for twenty," he said over his shoulder. "God didn't make ice cream so we'd eat brussel sprouts."

"Good to see you're hanging on to your religious convictions," I said, lifting my purchases onto the belt.

He paid his bill and picked up the bags. "Let me know when you're feeling brave enough to take me on in chess."

I nodded, wondering how long I'd have him around to spar with. I also wondered whom he had that date with.

***

I needed to thank Jennifer for her quick and helpful information. And since I didn't have a number for her, other than the hospital's general number, I decided a trip to the hospital might prove useful.

As I approached the entrance, it came to me that I wasn't sure how to find her. I was also afraid the receptionist wouldn't react kindly to a request to see a nurse, as opposed to a patient. I decided my best strategy was to play dumb.

I stepped up to the desk and started to sign in.

"Who are you visiting today?" the lady in red and white stripes said sweetly.

"Jim Pearson."

She looked at me in slight horror. "You're not aware…?"

I put on my most convincing confused expression. "What?" I said, in a concerned tone.

"I'm afraid…were you close to Mr. Pearson?"

I nodded. "A mutual friend told me he was hospitalized here. Just thought I should stop by and say hi." Hey, I'm an

41

investigative reporter. Lying comes easy.

"Well, I'm afraid I have sad news for you, Mr. ..."

"Travis. Lew Travis."

She looked at me with a pained expression. "Mr. Pearson died three days ago."

I stepped back. "*No!*"

She nodded sadly. "I'm so sorry."

"He was still a young man."

She nodded again. "It was tragic, yes. I'm so sorry. Is there anything I can offer you? A tissue?" She held out a box.

I took one, thanking her. "How did it happen?"

"I don't think they know exactly. But he did have a nasty case of pneumonia. That can be deadly."

I nodded in agreement. "Is there anyone here I could talk with who was attending him before he died? So I could maybe get a little closure." I'd read closure was big in psychological circles.

"Well, let me think. I suppose there might be a nurse who was on his wing."

"That would be great. Thank you so much. Where would that be?"

"On the second floor, B wing. It should be easy to find. Let me put in a call to the nurses station up there, let them know you're coming."

"You're a Godsend." I nodded with a deeply appreciative expression as I left, heading for the elevator.

By the time I found the second floor B wing they were indeed waiting for me. A pretty young nurse with brown eyes and long dark hair, dressed in a light blue set of hospital scrubs, stood as I approached.

"You must be Mr. Travis?"

Her voice sounded familiar. "Jennifer?"

She nodded and held out her hand. "Good to meet you

in person, Mr. Travis."

"I wanted to say thanks for the help. You got back to me really quickly."

"Wasn't hard; it's a small hospital."

"It's appreciated. I haven't tracked Karen Black down yet, but I will. Meanwhile, I thought it might be good to get a look at where Jim spent his last days. Sometimes little things come out that can add meaning to an article."

"Sure." I thought I detected a slightly doubtful tone.

"If this isn't a good time…"

"No, it's fine."

I hesitated. "Is there something wrong, Jennifer. You sound a little…uncertain."

She sighed, and her expression darkened. "I'm not sure. Maybe." She looked away, as though weighing what to say, then down. "I probably shouldn't say anything."

I waited, not knowing how to encourage her.

"Well, I suppose it's going to come out anyway, if it happens."

I cocked my head in a listening gesture.

"I'm afraid they're going to accuse me of being responsible for Mr. Pearson's death."

"*What?* Why?"

"I was on duty that day, and it was my responsibility to monitor the patients on this floor. And I was the one who found him dead."

I looked at her in confusion, noticing that her eyes were moist. She was shaking her head.

"They're right; I was responsible. But I swear I was paying attention. There was no alert. If he'd rung for me, I would have been there in a heartbeat. There was no alarm from his ventilator not working properly. Nothing."

"Jeez."

"They actually don't know yet exactly how it happened.

But regardless, he was my responsibility. I'm afraid I somehow screwed up." She was looking down at the floor.

"That seems kind of unfair, Jennifer, especially if they don't even know yet exactly how he died."

She shrugged sadly.

"Would you mind if I took a look at the room he was in?"

She looked down at a chart on the desk next to her and leafed through a few pages. "Two-oh-seven. It's just down the hall. Looks like it's empty at the moment." She took a step in that direction and nodded for me to follow her.

It was a standard hospital room. Metal bed you could crank up on one end. Metal tray on wheels to one side. TV high on the wall at the foot of the bed, with a remote on the tray. A plastic chair for visitors. A window from which you could see the mountains in the distance.

"So it was a single-patient room?" I asked.

"Yes. We only have a few, but the ICU was full, and we only use ventilators in these single rooms."

"How does a ventilator work? I've never actually seen one."

"There are two types, one with a mask that goes over a patient's mouth and nose, and the other with a tube that goes down the patient's throat and into the windpipe. It's called an endotracheal tube. Jim had the latter type. By the time he got here, his breathing was so strained the doctors figured that was safest. That's called intubation."

"So the tube comes out of his mouth and goes into a machine that pumps in air?"

"In and out. If you're having trouble breathing, you need help in both directions. There's a cuff outside the mouth, a connecting device. The tubes from the ventilator fit into that connector."

"How are they held in place?"

"They slide together. There can't be any air leaking out or it doesn't work right. This was an old one with straps of Velcro that went around the joints between the ventilator tubes and the cuff, and the endotracheal tube from the mouth. Newer ones have these tubes sealed in place.

"How do you know how much air to pump in?"

"The doctors determine that. There are several adjustments: volume, pressure, rate. Also, in some cases, the mixture has more than the normal amount of oxygen."

"How do you know it's all working like it should?"

"Once it's set up they measure the patient's blood oxygen level. As long as that is where it should be, they know it's working right."

"What if something goes wrong?"

"There's an alarm if anything goes wrong; we'd hear it at the nurses' station and come in and check."

"What do you check for?"

"The most common problem is aspiration. The patient has a lot of phlegm when they have pneumonia, and it can block the air passages."

"Amazing. Modern medicine."

"Yeah. It's just unfortunate when it doesn't help," she said sadly.

I waited a moment, then asked: "Do *you* have any idea what happened in Jim's case, Jennifer?"

She frowned, shaking her head. "I'm baffled. I'm hoping the autopsy will provide a clue."

I looked at her, hoping she'd say something more. Apparently she sensed this.

"It's not really my place to say anything more."

"But if you could…?" I said softly.

She looked down, crease lines in her forehead, then back up at me. "Can you promise it won't go any further if I do?"

45

I made a zipping motion on my lips. "Mum's the word."

She hesitated. "When I found him, Jim's skin was blue. I don't think there's much doubt that he suffocated."

"While on the respirator?"

She nodded. "It should never happen."

"There was no alarm?"

"No." Her tone was firm.

"And the ventilator was working okay?"

"It seemed fine. It was running just like it was supposed to. Pumping air in and out. All the settings were right. And Jim was dead."

"No idea what could have happened?"

She shrugged. "Machines aren't perfect; they're checking every part of it. Maybe the alarm didn't work. There were no power outages, so it couldn't have been that. All the fittings seemed okay. The hospital is pretty worried. It's the kind of thing they can get sued for. But right now, it's pretty much a mystery."

Jennifer's pain was apparent. Nurses are trained to save lives. Something like this violates everything they try to prevent. This was evident in her woeful expression.

"Who else was around when it happened?"

She looked at me inquiringly. "You mean hospital staff?"

"Hospital staff, other patients, visitors."

Her brows furrowed. "Well, let's see. There was one other nurse. I know she has no idea; we've talked about it. There were no docs on the floor at the time. There were a couple other patients in adjoining rooms. I don't know if they had any visitors."

"Do you remember who was in the adjoining rooms?"

She frowned, thinking. "Things were a little light at the time. We had several empty rooms." She hesitated. "Oh, there was a mom with a little kid with her in the room a couple doors away." She smiled. "Cutest kid you can imagine. I think he was about eight. She was a single mom, and he was really worried about her. We all loved the little guy. She turned out to be fine; she had an infected laceration on her leg from a car accident. They kept her here until they were sure the infection was under control. That kid never left her side; he even spent nights here. I think his name was Jeremy." She was smiling at the memory.

"Any way to find out her name?"

She winced. "I don't know. That's kind of a no-no with patients. You know, confidentiality."

I nodded. "Of course. I just thought maybe she'd seen something. But I understand."

"Well…"

I put my hands up defensively. "I don't want to get you in any more trouble, Jennifer."

We made our way back to the nurses' station and I thanked her again. I turned and headed for the elevator. As I did so, I heard a soft "Lew".

I turned back. She handed me a little piece of paper with something written on it. "I didn't give you this," she said. She was rolling her eyes.

I glanced down at it. It was the name and address of a woman.

"You didn't have to…"

She touched me on the forearm. "Just don't tell anyone."

"Of course. You're being a huge help."

I headed back to the elevator and downstairs. The red-and-white-striped lady smiled at me as I passed her desk. "Find them okay?"

"I did. Thanks for your help."

"You have a good day, Mr. Travis."

"You too."

I headed out the door, trying to remember where I'd parked Old Blue.

7

When I got home I checked my email, cranking up the old Mac and clicking the icon. I liked email, but I was uncomfortable with all the other stuff going on, the social media and blogs and all. I steadfastly refused to sign up with any of them, including Facebook and Twitter. I knew some people swore by them, and claimed they enriched their lives. And perhaps for some they had. But they seemed to me to have become the bane of actual conversation among real people in real time.

However, I did need to be able to learn everything I could online that related to a story, so given my lack of expertise in this regard, I had managed to ferret out a consultant. One who was enough younger than me to have grown up with this stuff: seventeen, to be precise. He was a high school kid who seemed to know everything there was to know about computers and what they could do: Zane.

I'd met Zane a couple years ago by accident, when we'd both been in a café having coffee, and he was banging away on his computer. He had long hair and sloppy clothes, both of which made me like him. I'd been positioned so I could look over his shoulder, and couldn't help noticing the speed with which he zoomed from one thing to the next. As he got up to leave, I half-jokingly asked him if he took clients. He looked at me skeptically, then shrugged. One thing had led to another, and it had become a regular arrangement. It had worked out well for both of us: he needed the pocket money and I needed the help.

I made a mental note to get in touch with Zane. Meanwhile, I looked at what messages had arrived. There were two:

```
Hi, Lew,
    Checked  my  calendar  for  the
weekend.  I  can  see  you  Friday  or
Sunday;  I'm  afraid  Saturday  is
out. Either of those work for you?
    Violet
```

Tied up on Saturday? What did that mean? I knew I wasn't doing right by Violet, but I had to admit, that brought me up a bit short.

The second email was from Tim:

```
    lew, what's  up?  haven't  heard
back from you. anything brewing?
why don't you swing by? tim
```

It occurred to me maybe a visit to the *Sentinel* could kill a couple of birds: touch base with Tim and Harve, and maybe see Violet. I glanced at my watch: just shy of three. What the hell?

Becky greeted me at the front desk, nose pin and all. "Hi…Lew. Still having a hard time calling you that."

"Because I'm so old?"

She frowned. "I didn't say that."

"But you were thinking it. You know, we're all pretty much the same inside. We just look a little different."

"No, you *are* a little different." This from a voice behind the counter.

I glanced back there. "Hi, Violet."

She nodded. "Just don't want to give our young folks a false picture. Why are you here, Lew?" Her voice held genuine curiosity.

I wanted to say something like, 'Because I thought I might catch you in', but it seemed too blunt. "Tim invited me to stop by?"

"Oh. Must be a slow day." With that subtle slyness in her tone.

"Is the kid around?"

"I believe he goes by something other than 'the kid'."

"My apologies." I looked back at Becky. "Is the esteemed assistant editor in residence?"

Becky rolled her eyes. "Let me check." She dialed a number and spoke briefly to someone, then looked up. "The boss awaits you."

I nodded my thanks and made my way past the counter and down a hallway toward the back. As usual Tim's office was a mess. Stacks of paper everywhere. A sign above his desk read: "A disorganized desk is the sign of a disorganized mind." He lifted a stack of papers off a chair next to his desk and nudged it in my direction with his foot. "Have a seat, Lew. Good to see you out and about."

I sat down and looked at him. "Thank you, esteemed Assistant Editor. How are things in the world of management?"

Tim stared at me, frowning. "You seem to have your usual level of sarcasm working. Does that mean you're feeling better?"

"What makes you think I was feeling bad?"

"Not hearing from you for weeks. And one of our employees seems to track this. I'm not sure why."

"Yeah, Harve is a sweetheart."

He shook his head slowly. "I sometimes wonder why we put up with you."

I raised my eyebrows. "The quality of my writing?"

"It's certainly not the quantity."

I shrugged. "Sometimes you have to choose: quality or quantity."

"Which brings us to the topic at hand. How's progress on Jim's story?"

"It's coming. Actually, I've gotten kind of interested in it."

"Good. He was quite a guy."

"That's one reason."

He frowned. "There's another?"

"Might be."

"Which is?"

I hesitated. "There may be some suspicious circumstances regarding exactly how he died."

"*What*? What are you talking about?"

I filled him in on what I'd learned.

"Wow."

"Yeah. Nothing that I'd call solid evidence, but it looks a little suspicious."

"Who do you suspect?"

"Just getting started, Tim. Don't even know what happened yet. I need to talk to some more folks. Especially the people who visited him in the hospital."

"Who were?"

"His wife. His daughters. His business partner. And a young lady whose relationship to him I have yet to discern."

He raised his eyebrows in interest. "Sounds like you have your work cut out for you."

"I could use a bit of help, now that you mention it."

"Help?"

"There is an autopsy being conducted on Jim's body to determine the cause of death. While I've been given unofficial information that would seem to provide the answer, it would be helpful to have the official word. With your established contacts there I thought perhaps you could put me in touch with the hospital's pathology department. Or make the inquiry yourself. Given your high status with the paper."

"You want me to find out the official cause of death?" He sounded skeptical.

"You're quick, Tim. For such a young person."

"What makes you think anyone at the hospital is going to tell a newspaper person *anything* that might implicate them in possible criminal action? People don't as a rule offer that kind of information to newspapers."

"Your trusted contacts there, assurance this information will be held in the highest of confidence, and personal charm."

He shook his head and looked out the window. "God."

"Is that a yes?"

He sighed and rolled his eyes. "I can ask, but don't expect an answer."

"Great. So where is your crack office mate?"

"I believe Harve is out actually working on a story. Do you need to reach him for some reason?"

"I'd like to offer him my gratitude, and ask him a couple follow-up questions. He was the one who gave me the lead for most of what I've learned so far."

"Harve was?"

"Is your hearing causing problems, Tim?"

He rolled his eyes. "I'll let him know. Anything *else* I can do for you?"

I frowned, as though thinking. "I don't believe we've talked about a raise for awhile."

He scowled. "I'm trying to think. What do people usually get raises for? Oh, yeah. Good performance."

"This story may be a whopper."

"If and when that turns out to be the case might be the time to discuss this?"

I shook my head. "You're a hard man, Tim. I guess that's what management does to a person."

"Yeah."

"I want you to picture an old man trying to scrape together enough to buy his next meal."

"At the moment I'm picturing an old man leaving my office."

I stood and started for the door, stopping briefly to look at him. "Could you try to get on those things as soon as possible?"

There was an exasperated sigh as I stepped out into the hall. I strode past the front desk, nodding to Becky.

"Goodbye, Lew." She said it with panache.

"I like your style, kid. Maybe you can give this old crew lessons."

I glanced behind her but Violet was nowhere to be seen.

***

I checked my watch as I left the building: not quite four. Too early to start thinking about dinner. I remembered the note Jennifer had given me, the name and address of the woman with the infected laceration who had been a couple rooms down from Jim's at the hospital, and her little boy. I felt in my pocket, pulled out the note: Nancy Wilson, along with her address. It occurred to me I should try to track down her phone number and give her a call first. But that would give her the option to say no; not shrewd from a strategic standpoint.

As I pulled up in front of her house I conducted a quick

appraisal: a little one-story matchbox, painted beige, set back from the street, with a low-pitched roof and a one-car garage to one side. I parked and walked slowly up to the front door, glancing at the scrub tree, brown grass, and small bicycle lying in the front yard. There was a button for the doorbell, the cheap kind that developers used to use. I pushed it and heard a chime sound inside. There was no response. I tried again. Still nothing.

I turned and headed back out to Old Blue. As I started to climb in, an old beat up Honda Civic with a crunched-in fender pulled into the driveway and stopped in front of the garage. A fortyish woman got out from the driver's side, and a boy about the age that Jeremy had been described, roughly eight, got out from the passenger side. He had a mop of brown hair and was carrying a backpack.

I swung the door shut and walked back toward the front door to intercept them. The mom saw me coming and put her arm around the boy.

I put my hands up defensively. "Not here to do you any harm. I'm a reporter with the *Sentinel*. Just wondered if I could ask you a couple questions?"

She frowned. "About what?"

I explained the situation. She continued to frown. "I don't understand," she said. "How are we going to help? We didn't even know that guy."

I put my hands out in a gesture of 'Who knows?' "I'm not sure you can. So this might be very short. But you never know." The boy was looking at me quizzically.

What is your name again, she asked.

"Lew Travis." I pulled out a business card and handed it to her. She studied it for a minute.

"How did you find us?"

I hesitated. "A very nice nurse at the hospital thought you might be helpful. I'm sorry if I'm intruding."

She stared at me, clearly weighing how to respond.

"How's the leg doing?" I asked.

She hesitated, still gauging what to do. "Better, thanks." She glanced at the card again, then shrugged. "I guess we could give you a few minutes, Mr. Travis." She looked down at Jeremy, who was tugging on her arm to go inside. She pulled out a key and opened the front door.

I followed them into a small living room. It was clean and neat, but basic, with just a small TV, a couch covered with a blanket, a plastic-laminated coffee table, and one old easy chair. She motioned to the chair for me to sit down.

"Do you need Jeremy for this?" she asked.

"If that's okay. You never know what a different pair of eyes might see."

"Okay." She sat down on the couch and patted the cushion next to her for Jeremy to sit. He was looking at me with a squint, as though sizing me up.

"What grade are you in, Jeremy?"

He glanced at his Mom before answering. "Third."

"Let's see. If I remember, you're reading quite a bit, and learning arithmetic?"

He frowned. "Sort of. We have calculators."

I glanced at Nancy, rolling my eyes. "Things have changed since my time, I guess."

"Me too," she said. "Hard to keep up. So, what is it you want to ask us?"

"The fellow I'm interested in was two rooms away from yours. He was a friend, and unfortunately died under circumstances that have the hospital people a little confused. I just wondered if you might have seen anyone hanging around in the hallway, or going into his room?"

She furrowed her brows. "You mean they suspect something?"

"It's not clear. They'll probably know more when they

get the autopsy results. For now I'm just trying to determine if there is any reason even to be suspicious."

"I didn't actually leave the room much. I was hooked up to an IV with antibiotics. Jeremy wandered around more than me." She looked at the boy. "Did you see anyone, Jeremy?"

He was looking away; I couldn't tell if he was even listening, but then he turned back and said, "Which room?"

I did my best to describe the relationship of his Mom's room to Jim's, two doors away. He would have had to pass Jim's to get to the bathroom or elevator.

He avoided my gaze, but responded. "Was that the room with the whooshing noise?"

"Whooshing noise?" I said.

"There was a room with a whooshing noise. It wasn't very loud, but I noticed it when I went to the bathroom."

"Oh, of course, yes. That was Jim's ventilator. He was on a breathing support system. That's the room."

Jeremy nodded.

"Did you see anyone go in there to visit?" I asked.

He shook his head, scowling.

I looked at Nancy, with my eyebrows raised, to ask whether she sensed anything there.

"Jeremy, it's just to be helpful. You didn't see anyone around there when you went to the bathroom, did you?" Nancy asked.

His scowl deepened, as though he was withdrawing into himself. He shook his head in a tight little no.

Nancy looked at me. "He's been a little withdrawn lately. I'm not sure why. Might be he was kind of freaked out with me in the hospital." She glanced toward the hallway. "It's just the two of us. My husband died in Iraq."

"Oh, I'm sorry."

"It's been hard. But we have each other."

Not knowing what else to say, I sighed and said, "Well, that's really all I came to ask about. I don't need to take up more of your time."

She nodded. "Okay. Sorry we weren't any help." She looked again at Jeremy, who was still frowning.

"No problem. Much appreciate you letting me ask my questions."

She accompanied me to the door and held it open for me. "Good luck."

"Thanks. You have my number there," I said, pointing to the business card she still held, "if anything else occurs to you."

"Right."

8

By the time I got back to the house it was nearly five. I still had the groceries in the back seat, so after pulling into the garage I grabbed them and headed for the back door. A large black furry object greeted me there.

"Hello, Earl. How was your day?"

He responded with a distinct meow. Earl had good diction for a cat, none of those mealy-mouthed half meows.

"I don't suppose I could interest you in a little dinner?"

Another distinct meow, as though this was enough talk, let's get on with it.

I pulled open the door and he scurried in ahead of me. By the time I'd set the grocery bags on the table he was standing over his food dish, meowing repeatedly.

"Okay, okay. Give me a minute."

He looked up with a scowl. Earl didn't take many prisoners. When he was hungry, he wanted action.

I pulled out his bag of kibble and half-filled his bowl. He went to work immediately.

I emptied my few purchases, putting the cheese and apples in the refrigerator. Then I pulled down a glass from the cupboard, threw in some ice cubes, and poured myself half a glass of gin. It wasn't quite five, but it was part of my effort to maintain some elasticity in my life, to view time limits as well as quantities flexibly.

Sipping on the gin, I wandered into the living room and

checked the message machine, which was flashing; I hit the button. Two messages.

The first voice was Harve's.

```
Hey, Sherlock. Watson here. Tim
said you wanted to talk to me.
Give me a call when you get back
from aimlessly wandering the
streets.
```

The second was a female voice I didn't at first recognize.

```
Hello, Mr. Travis. This is
Jennifer from the hospital? I had
another thought that might be of
interest. Can you give me a call
later on? I get off at six.
```

She left her home number. I did need to thank Harve. I dialed his number at the paper.

"Mr. Harvey's extension. Can I take a message?" Becky's voice.

"He makes you call him *Mr.* Harvey? And what are you doing still there? Don't they let you go home for dinner?"

"Hi, Lew. It's not quite five. That's when we quit."

"What about the Mr. part?"

"That's the newspaper's policy."

"Seems a little traditional. Who is *Mr.* Harvey jabbering with?"

"I think it's…."

A male voice cut into the line. "Is he bothering you again, Becky?"

"Well, well, if it isn't *Mr.* Harvey himself. You make your lovely receptionist call you *Mr.* Harvey?"

There was a pause. "Is there some reason for this call beyond trying to cause trouble?"

"I'm returning your call, *Mr.* Harvey."

There was a click on the line.

"Harve?"

"That was our lovely receptionist, apparently deciding she had better things to do than listen to your drivel."

"So what have you got?"

"A headache. It just came on."

I waited.

"Okay. It's about Jim."

"Speaking of which, I owe you one. Jennifer Sanchez is a godsend. Thanks for the contact."

"She's good with old people. I think they train them for that."

"Maybe she could give you some training?"

After a pause: "What did she tell you, Lew?"

"All kinds of things. Most of which I can't share at the moment."

"If it's a memory problem, I can wait."

I decided not to dignify that with a response.

"Okay, okay. *Why* can't you tell me?"

"If I explained that, you'd know what I can't tell you. What's the new information you have?"

He sighed. "I'm not sure why I bother, but okay. There are two people still here who Jim worked with on several stories. They both really liked him and have been forthcoming. Did you know he was separated from his wife?"

"Yeah, I picked that up."

"And he was apparently depressed about it."

"That makes sense."

"I mean, *really* depressed."

"As in…?"

61

"Well, let's hope not. It doesn't seem like he'd go that far, he loved those girls so much. But sometimes when you get really down, you lose perspective."

I had no argument on this point; I knew it all too well. "Are you suggesting this might be an explanation for his departure from the living?" I asked.

"It's really just idle speculation until we know more."

"Was he seeing someone about the depression?"

"Apparently he'd joined a support group. And had become friends with a young woman in the group. Rumor has it they were having an extended series of verbal exchanges."

"Verbal exchanges?"

"Is your hearing going too, Lew?"

I waited.

"That's generally how conversations work, Lew. One person says something while the other is listening, then they reverse roles, and so on."

I spoke with a tone of indulgent tolerance. "And that's all you meant by 'verbal exchanges'? That's kind of strange phrasing, for someone as literate as yourself."

"Apparently she had some problems of her own. From what I've been able to glean, they were trying to help each other over rough patches."

"Was the young woman's name Karen Black by any chance?"

The line went quiet for a moment. "How the hell did you know that?"

"What have you learned about her?"

"Apparently no more than you."

"If you'll be kind enough to tell me, I'll be able to determine that."

A brief pause. "Okay. Karen Black has quite a history. She apparently had a rough childhood: broken home, abusive father, boyfriends who wanted her for the wrong reasons. She's apparently quite attractive."

"Yes, she is."

"You've *met* her?"

"I've seen her."

"Where?"

"Where your partner in crime sent me yesterday. Jim's funeral."

"Oh. Well, was she alone?"

"No. She was with Jim's business partner, Bruce Canton. Although it turns out Jim wasn't actually a partner in the firm."

"Really?"

"Not according to Mrs. Canton. Who apparently is a partner."

"How did you find *that* out?"

"It's called research, Harve. I can try to explain it in simple language if you'd like?"

"So Bruce Canton brought Karen to the funeral rather than his wife?"

"Is *your* hearing okay?"

"I wonder how Mrs. Canton feels about that?"

"She didn't seem all that upset."

"How do you know that?"

"Sometimes if you watch people's reactions, they provide clues about...."

He interrupted me. "So why did you call me, if you already know all that?"

"You said you had some new information."

"I thought I did."

"Well, I'll give you partial credit. I didn't know about Karen Black's troubled background. Do you know what she does for a living?"

"She's a cosmetologist."

"There. See? You are sometimes a little help."

He sighed, pointedly.

"So I could presumably find her at her shop?"

"If you *researched* her hours, I suppose. It's called Tress of the d'Urbervilles."

"Wow. A literary cosmetologist."

"Apparently she's a bright young lady, has a BA in English. Just does this to make ends meet."

"Bright *and* beautiful. No wonder Jim was attracted to her."

"So now that I've bestowed the benefit of my generosity on you, can we stop this exchange? Because it's now after five and time for me to go home and have a beer."

"Sure, Harve. Wouldn't want to interfere with a man's bad habits." I rattled the ice in my glass so he could hear it. "And once again, I owe you a debt of gratitude. I'm going to actually have to find a way to repay you."

"I have some thoughts about that."

"Why don't you write them down so you don't forget them?"

There was a click.

"Goodbye, Harve."

***

Having restocked my larder I heated up a can of soup, threw together a cheese sandwich, and settled down in front of the TV, Earl curled up next to me on the couch. The six o'clock news was about as uplifting as usual: the non-functioning of Washington, a natural disaster, man's idiocy played out in various ways. I tried to limit my viewing to PBS; unlike the network broadcasts, it doesn't scream 'be afraid' every other sentence, and fill the advertising time with drug ads aimed at old people. But even on PBS, the events of most days seem boring in retrospect. The future is always a bit scary; it's unknown. Which is what the news is until we've watched it. But having watched it, it becomes the past, which is usually pretty much the same old stuff.

When the news hour ended at seven, it occurred to me it might be a good time to call Jennifer back. I dialed her number.

"Hello?"

"Hi, Jennifer. This is Lew Travis. You left a message that you had another thought you wanted to share? Is this a good time to talk?"

"Oh, hi Mr. Travis. Yeah, give me a minute."

I heard her shout something to someone, but couldn't make out what. Then she came back on the line.

"I wasn't sure I should even mention this…it's probably nothing. But it kind of stuck in my mind."

"Okay."

"There was this guy at the hospital on a couple of the days Mr. Pearson was intubated. He was kind of strange. Not a doctor or nurse or anything, and he didn't seem to be there to visit any particular patient."

"Why *was* he there?"

"I think he might have been…how do you put it…a few cards short of a full deck?"

"How so?"

"Well, he wasn't dressed all that strangely. In fact, he had on a tie and jacket. But they were old and kind of dirty, his hair was disheveled and needed a shampoo, and he was acting kind of strange."

"How do you mean?"

"He was going around from room to room, standing outside the door of each, putting his hands up in a prayer gesture. You know, with the palms together. And then he would say something under his breath."

"Hmm."

"I don't think he was dangerous. He seemed respectful of anyone he encountered. But when we asked what he was doing there, he'd just say, "The Lord's work.""

"A Jesus freak?"

"I guess. He might have been homeless; he had that feel about him. And I think he maybe had one of those messiah complexes? You know, where someone thinks they're actually God. Or the son of God."

"Crazy, in other words?"

"Yeah, I suppose."

"Can you describe him?"

"He was tall and thin. His hair was almost white and flyaway. He had a white beard, also unkempt. His cheeks were kind of hollow. And he didn't smell all that good."

"How old was he?"

"Pretty old. Maybe sixty."

I refrained from pointing out this was only old from certain perspectives. "What kind of jacket was it?"

"Checkered, brown and yellow as I recall. His shirt was white, but like I said, not very clean."

"That's a pretty good description."

"He was there on two different days. I think they finally had to escort him out of the hospital and not let him back in. I suppose, if he was homeless, maybe he was just trying to stay warm. And who knows, maybe he was stealing food. I never saw him do that, but who knows. Anyway..."

"It can't hurt to check it out. Thanks for the lead."

"Okay. Sorry if this is just a wild goose chase. But when I tried to remember details of what was going on while Jim was there, this came to mind."

"I wonder if anyone got his name?"

"I guess I could check at the front desk; he must have

signed in.

"That would be helpful. And thanks. You're being a big help. I don't know where any of this will lead, but I'll see what I can find out."

"Sure. You have a good evening, Mr....Lew."

"You too, Jennifer."

I hung up and leaned back on the couch, reflecting on the story Jim and I had worked on together, about the homeless camps in the area. He had been deeply troubled by them, had actually gone out and spent several nights living in one of them, talking with people there and learning what their needs were. We'd talked about this while we worked on the story, the problems that led to homelessness. There was a pretty high correlation between that and mental illness, as well as alcohol and drug abuse. Where did you start in dealing with all this?

There were debates about how best to do this. One view was that it belonged in the legal realm: these people were squatting on either private or public land, they were doing drugs illegally, littering, presenting a fire danger, and they needed to be rousted out and charged with appropriate crimes. An opposing view was that it was a social issue: what homeless people needed was help, they had no choice but to sleep wherever they could since they couldn't afford housing, and we needed to provide more food, clothing and shelter to help them get back on their feet.

Jim had been in the latter camp. But even given that bent, it had been hard to know how best to provide assistance. Food and shelter programs were helpful, but they didn't solve the underlying problem, they just treated the symptoms. And the symptoms fed on each other. If you didn't have a job, or enough money, how did you get health insurance? If you didn't have health insurance, how did you get help for alcohol or drug dependency? Or for that matter, if you couldn't afford housing, you probably couldn't afford decent clothing either, which would be needed if you were lucky enough to find a job? If fact, if you didn't have a place to live, how could you keep yourself clean, or together enough to hold down a job? Or stay healthy even without drug and alcohol problems? Sleeping outside on cold wet nights was not a recipe for anything positive.

Jim had done what he could. He'd worked in the local homeless shelter and helped to raise funds to feed and clothe its residents. He'd also made weekly visits to deliver food to the camps. But he'd never felt that he'd done enough. I wondered whether he'd had contact with the gentleman Jennifer had described.

***

I pulled out my growing body of notes, jotting down the new information from Jennifer and trying to decide what to focus on the next day. I wanted to talk to Bruce Canton, the owner of the insurance company. And I needed to decide whether this made more sense in the presence of his wife and business partner, Roberta Eileen, or by himself. I hoped Tim would put me in touch with someone who could give me the official autopsy report on the cause of Jim's death, as clear as that already seemed to be. I needed to talk with Jill again, Jim's wife, to learn more about his depression and how likely a suicide might have been, not to mention her cryptic comment at the funeral, wondering 'if she really knew Jim of late'. Then there was the "other woman", Karen Black, who'd apparently had relationships with both Jim and Bruce. Learning the nature of these relationships would be useful. And now I needed to figure out who the strange man was who had gone around praying for patients at the hospital. If he was as crazy as he sounded, who knows what he might have been capable of? The list of questions kept growing.

However, there was little I could do this evening, and I knew I wasn't at my best after half a glass of gin anyway. So I wandered out to the kitchen and poured myself a refill, then ambled into the den and checked email. There was nothing new, but I saw Violet's message there, about picking either Friday or Sunday for a get together. Was the fact she was busy on a Saturday night something I should be worried about? But then, what right did I have to be worried about anything she did, given my own hibernation over the past few weeks?

As I sipped slowly on the gin and pondered a response to Violet, another email popped up.

> Hi, Dad,
> How are you doing up there? Haven't heard from you for a while. I have spring break coming up. I'm thinking of driving up and spending a few days with you? I need a break from all the little monsters I have this year; they're a handful. Although I have some very cute ones.
> I know this is a tough time of year for you. Are you getting past it okay? You know it's tough for me too. I miss Mom more than I can tell you. But we do still have each other. And I may have some kind of exciting news to share.
> Let me know how you are and whether a visit would be welcome.
> Love, Kate

Sweet girl, no question. I was lucky that way. And she was right; we needed to stay in touch. I knew I wasn't keeping up my end of things well. I took another sip and tried to think how to respond. Did I want a visit? Would that just make Mary's memory more painful? Maybe I'd sleep on it, see how I felt in the morning.

I closed down the computer and meandered into the living room, where Earl was happily ensconced on one end of the couch. He was actually snoring, and not all that quietly. I sat down next to him and petted him lightly. He stirred slightly, adjusting his position enough so the snoring stopped, while not actually opening his eyes. His deep regular breathing made me jealous. Why did humans have to make so many decisions when cats only had to think about their stomachs and having a warm place to sleep?

9

Thursday

It was a restless night, full of strange dreams, weird people doing odd things. A witch-like old hag picking through a garbage can in an alley, apparently looking for food. An old man rowing a small boat through a body of water with limbs hanging over him, a snake hanging down from a branch above his head. A pair of vultures flying overhead, landing in the same tree, and the snake pulling itself up and slithering away.

I finally woke up around seven-thirty, feeling unrested and grumpy. I could tell I wasn't going to sleep anymore, so I stumbled out of bed and went through the morning routine, winding up in the kitchen sipping on a cup of coffee, rubbing my head and looking for something worth reading in the paper. When the phone rang.

I looked at the ID window: Sienna Memorial Hospital. At eight in the morning? I punched the answer button.

"Hello?"

"Lew?"

"Yeah."

"Sorry to call so early. This is Jennifer. I'm about to go on duty, but I did check for the name of that funny guy I told you about, and I don't think it's going to be much help. I think he signed in as 'Jesus'."

"Jesus?"

"Yeah."

Charles Dayton

"Well, that kind of confirms our diagnosis, doesn't it?"
She chuckled. "Yeah."
"Thanks, Jennifer. You're a treasure."
"Sure."

I hung up and took another slug of coffee, reflecting on the notes I'd been accumulating. I remembered visiting a couple of the homeless camps myself when I'd worked on the story with Jim. Might they still be there, and if so, might I learn something about this strange character if I paid them a visit? Then it occurred to me there was also a local shelter. Might he be staying there?

I slugged down the rest of the coffee and headed back upstairs. I needed a shower and some clean clothes. Not that the style was going to change. In the summer, it was inexpensive blue jeans and pullover shirts; in the winter, inexpensive blue jeans and flannel shirts. Since it was spring, I had to judge on a day-by-day basis; today it was inexpensive blue jeans and a dark red pullover. And comfortable walking shoes year around. No point in messing with what worked.

When I came back down Earl was meowing at the back door. "Sorry, pal. Didn't mean to hold up your day's adventures." I opened the door and he squeezed through and made off toward the neighbor's fence, which he knew how to get under in spite of his considerable girth. I hoped the feline ladies in the neighborhood were ready. But then they probably had long since figured him out.

I toasted a piece of bread, spread on some peanut butter, poured myself another cup of coffee, and consumed them slowly, waiting for the hangover to lift, and continuing to look for something interesting to read in the paper. Thank God for the sports section. The Giants had won last night and evened their record. And the Warriors had nailed down a playoff berth.

72

Around nine I finally faced up to the fact it was time to start doing something. I took my windbreaker and keys off their hooks and headed out the back door. It made sense to try the shelter first, since there was staff there that I could talk with that might provide a lead. It was located at the edge of town in a large old wood-frame two-story building. I parked in the small lot in front and found my way in.

There was a central hallway, with separate rooms for the men and women/children to the left and right respectively. The offices were in back. I made my way there and knocked on the door marked "Executive Director". Might as well go right to the top.

"Come in." A female voice. I'd read in the paper that it was mostly women who worked here. That nurturing trait so many of them seemed to have. And these days, unlike the hobo days of the depression, there were almost as many women and children who needed help as men. I pushed open the door and stepped in.

A middle-aged lady with a round face, gold wire-framed glasses, a colorful blouse, and a desk plate that read "Shirley Clinton, Director" looked up. "Good morning. What can I do for you?"

I introduced myself and explained the situation, sketching 'Jesus' as Jennifer had described him.

She squinted as she listened. "I think I do remember a man like that," she said. "He hasn't been here in several weeks, but he did spend time here this winter. I don't know where he might be now, but I seem to recall he'd been in one of the local camps when he came in. He was in rough shape, but we managed to get him cleaned up and fed while he was here. He liked to wear a jacket and tie."

"Do you remember how he was mentally?"

She frowned. "Now that you mention it, he did like to go around and say little prayers to others staying here. He

73

wasn't obnoxious about it, people were pretty accepting, but I think some of the other guests got to calling him the 'Reverend'."

"The Reverend?"

She nodded. "Let me see if I can find his name here." She pulled up a list on her computer screen and started scanning through it, running the cursor down one column of names after another. Finally she stopped and looked up.

"You know, I'm not sure, but I think this might be it. This is about the time he came in." She nodded for me to step around her desk and have a look.

I studied the long list of names, having no clue. "Which one is it?"

She looked up at me with a wry smile. She pointed to the single name, which stood out as soon as I saw it: "Jesus".

"That's him. It's how he signed in at the hospital."

"We don't try to challenge people when they come in, we just take the name they give us. We're here to help, not judge."

"So he probably was a little...?"

"We do have medical services, and he must have been checked out for basic things, but there are so many mental challenges among our guests we really can't provide in-depth psychological services."

"No. Of course not. It's great you do what you do."

"Is he in trouble?"

"I have no way of knowing at this point. I'm just beginning to look into it. But this helps. It confirms what I'd suspected about his lack of residence."

"Good luck tracking him down."

I stood to leave, when a thought occurred. "You don't think any of your current guests might remember him, do you?"

Her eyebrows lifted in contemplation. "Well, maybe. You want to check? It would have to be on the men's side, he wouldn't have been allowed on the women's. And I'm not sure how many would still be here when he was. We have a lot of turnover."

"If you don't mind?"

"Sure. Want me to come with you?"

"That would be great."

We made our way out to the hallway and into the men's sleeping area. There were eight or ten bunk beds spread around the walls of a large room, with a few in the middle as well. Most were unoccupied. While this was a shelter that provided twenty-four-hour residency, apparently on a pretty spring morning like this most opted for an outing.

I turned to her. "How should I proceed?"

"Why don't you let me give it a shot?"

"Thanks."

She stood up straight and took in a deep breath, then spoke in a loud voice. "Guests, this is Shirley. We have a gentleman here looking for the fellow who went by the name Jesus, with the nickname The Reverend. Did any of you happen to know him?"

The half-dozen men in the room looked at us, some with more interest than others. An old fellow in one corner raised his hand. He was on a bottom bunk, wearing an old red and black flannel shirt, blue jeans, and slippers. He was thin and wizened.

We walked over and Shirley spoke to him. "Hi. You are…?"

"Ralph Jefferson." His voice was weak and scratchy. I wondered what it must be like to reach such an age with nowhere to go but a homeless shelter.

"Yes, of course; Ralph. You help with serving dinner, don't you?"

He nodded.

"And you knew The Reverend?"

"He was on the bunk above me for awhile."

"Ah. What was he like?"

He rolled his eyes. "Crazy. Thought he was Jesus. Wanted to save us all."

She smiled. "That's what I thought. Do you have any idea where he went?"

He shrugged. "Not really."

I jumped in. "Did he like to wear jackets and ties?"

He nodded. "Yeah, I guess it was part of his act. Thought it made him look more legitimate."

"Act?"

He waved his hand. "Whatever you call it. His alter ego?"

"Did you ever see him not in this alter ego?"

He frowned. "You know, that's a good question. Sometimes at night he would lay up there and mumble to himself. I usually ignored him, but occasionally I tried to understand what he was saying. And sometimes he sounded like he was not all that crazy."

"How do you mean?"

"He would plan his next day's activities. Like he would say after breakfast he was going to visit this place or that."

"And he would follow the plan?"

"I can't say. I never actually followed him around."

"What kind of emotions did he exhibit?"

He paused, thinking. "He always sounded calm when he was bestowing his blessings on us during the day. But at night he sometimes sounded angry. He used to talk about God's vengeance."

"Did he ever do anything that frightened you?"

"One time he wanted to get the guy at McDonald's. Thought he was trying to poison him."

"Did he ever carry out any such threats?"

"Not that I know of. But I was glad when he left." He coughed, pulled out a dirty handkerchief, and blew his nose.

The thought occurred to me that maybe delivering food to shelters and homeless camps was how Jim had contracted the pneumonia. They tended to be breeding grounds for infections most people avoided.

I nodded. "Well, thanks. That's helpful."

"Did he do something?" Ralph asked.

"That's what I'm trying to find out."

He looked at me skeptically. "You a cop?"

"No. I'm with the *Sentinel*. The local paper? Just collecting background information for a story."

"What kind of story?"

"A retrospective on a man's life. A friend who recently died."

"And you think The Reverend might have...had something to do with that?"

I held up my hands defensively. "I'm no where near reaching that conclusion. I'm just trying to track down clues. It might well have been from natural causes."

Ralph nodded.

I thanked him and turned to leave. Shirley had been taking all this in, standing back a bit. As I turned she nodded for me to join her in the hallway. When we got there, she looked at me with a sober expression. "Ralph is a pretty sane guy," she said. "I think you can take what he said in there seriously."

"I had that sense," I said.

"But if you do find The Reverend is somehow implicated in some criminal act, could you maybe not mention his association with the shelter? We get enough bad publicity as it is. You know, the NIMBYs? The folks who don't want a facility like this nearby."

"Sure."

She held out her hand. "Good luck, Mr. Travis. Let me know what happens."

I nodded, shaking her hand and thanking her, and headed out to the parking lot, realizing I needed to track down The Reverend.

10

When I got back to the house, there was an email from Tim.

```
    hey, lew. i did manage to make a
contact   at   the   hospital.   wasn't
easy; they're  not  fond  of  talking
to    newspaper    people    about
sensitive  topics.  but  I  got  you  a
contact  to  follow  up  with.  i  know
the  guy,  he's  solid,  and  i  gave
him   an   ironclad   promise   there
would  be  no  mention  of  anything
related  to  the  autopsy  in  the
paper.  give  me  a  call.  tim
```

I did so, to his direct line. I usually avoided doing this, as Becky was likely to know where Tim or Harve were if they didn't pick up. And then there was always the possibility Violet might be the one to answer.

"Sentinel. Royce speaking."

"I got through directly to the Assistant Managing Editor?" My tone held amazement.

"Hello, Methuselah."

"So you have a hospital contact for me?"

"No 'Thanks, Tim'? No 'Nice work, Mr. Assistant

Editor'?"

"I need to find out if the contact is any good first."

There was a pause. "You making any progress?" In a skeptical tone.

"I have some things I'm looking into."

"That doesn't really sound like progress."

"I'm an *investigative* reporter, Tim. Investigations take time. If you're at all thorough about them."

"Uh huh. Is Harve still lending you a hand?"

"Harve has been a wonder. Now *his* contact…."

Another pause. "You want the name?"

"That would be a good next step. Names are actually less useful when you don't know them."

"Are you sitting down?"

I waited.

"I talked to the Chief Medical Officer at the hospital. That's as high as it gets. His name is Gustave Bennigan. He's a friend. We play squash."

"Squash? I didn't know you played squash. Isn't that kind of an upper-class sport?"

"There's a lot you don't know about me, Lew."

"Yeah. People with criminal records often don't like to talk about their past. Was that the reason for your early departure from New York City to a remote old gold mining town in the Sierra Nevada Mountains?"

He sighed. "I'm really not sure why I put up with you."

"I think we've touched on this. Something to do with the level of journalistic excellence."

"You want Gus's number?"

"My pen stands ready."

He gave me the phone number, then added: "He's a busy guy. I gave him *your* number as well, and suggested he call you at *his* convenience. You just need to let him know what works for you."

"Oh, well. That could make it difficult."

"Because of your tight schedule?" His tone dripped with sarcasm.

I made some paper rustling noises. "Let me see. I have a brief slot open tomorrow afternoon. And…maybe again Friday morning."

"A *paper* calendar, Lew?"

"It saves losing data when there's the inevitable crash."

Tim sighed. "Okay, I've done you my favor for the day. Keep me apprised."

"You mean I get another one tomorrow?"

There was a brief silence, then a dial tone.

I put in a call to the number Tim had provided and got an answering machine. I explained who I was, left my number, and suggested some times to call.

***

It was mid-morning and I was feeling better. I might actually be making a little headway in this investigation. I dug out my list of musings and pondered the options. There was one person in particular I had not made contact with, and who struck me as of particular interest. I conducted a brief search on the Internet, jotted down an address, and headed out to Old Blue.

Tress of the d'Ubervilles was located in a slightly dodgy part of town, in a row of little shops between a large industrial building and a tire and auto service garage. I parked in front and got out slowly, looking in through the bay window of the salon.

There were two chairs, but just one was occupied, with a wispy white-haired head emerging from a black cloak. A young woman with long auburn hair, a pair of tight-fitting blue jeans covering a shapely body, and a loose-fitting

81

blouse was snipping away at the white wisps. I pushed in through the glass-paneled door. They both looked at me with inquisitive glances.

I nodded. "Hi."

The young woman responded. "Hello. You looking for a haircut? We don't take walk-ins, but I'd be happy to schedule an appointment." Her tone was friendly.

"Actually, I was just hoping to talk to…" I pulled out my little notebook and looked at it, as though I was unsure of the name…"Ms. Black? Is there a Karen Black working here?"

"I'm Karen Black."

"Ah. Well, you're the person, then. When might be a time we could chat?"

She frowned. "About…?"

"I'm with the *Sentinel*? We're doing a series of stories on local businesses that seem to have particularly good ratings on Yelp? Which your salon is an example of? I was wondering if I could get some details on the business that we could use in such a story?" I hesitated. "Assuming that would be of interest?"

She looked at me skeptically. "Who did you say you were?"

"Lew Travis." I pulled out one of my business cards and handed it to her.

She studied it for a moment, then stepped over to a desk and looked through an appointment book. "Actually, I have a little break after this appointment. And we're almost done. Would you like to wait?"

"That would be great. Thanks."

I sat in one of the two waiting chairs and lifted the morning paper from a little side table. Having already exhausted everything I might possibly be interested in in the paper, I used the time to quietly make observations. My attention quickly went to Karen. She was a beautiful woman, no question. In addition to her well-endowed body, she had classical features, strong facial bones and beautiful green eyes, with smooth glowing skin. Her auburn hair cascaded down over her shoulders, and her voice was soft and inviting. I had trouble keeping my eyes off her.

She was as good as her word, and within a few minutes was removing the cloak from the lady and shaking it out, then helping her on with her jacket and holding the door for her.

"See you next time, Gladys," she said, turning back to me.

She eyed me with a questioning look. "I didn't know I had any Yelp reviews," she said. "Not many folks up here use Yelp."

I nodded. "You have me dead to rights. I'm actually here for a different purpose."

Her questioning look turned dark. "Who are you then?"

"The card is legitimate. I am with the paper. I'm actually gathering background information on Jim Pearson. He's an old friend of mine. And if my information is correct, of yours also? I just didn't want to share that with your customer. I thought maybe you'd prefer it be private."

"I knew Jim. What kind of information are you after?"

"I'm putting together a retrospective on his life. I'm trying to fill in the gaps in my knowledge. I knew him several years ago, but after he left the paper, I didn't keep up with him. I understand you knew him more recently?"

She continued to stand, her expression skeptical.

"Would you like to sit down?" I nodded toward the other chair.

She did so reluctantly, keeping her eyes on me.

"As you know, Jim died a few days ago. You probably didn't see me, but I was at the funeral. As I noticed you

83

were."

She frowned. "Okay."

"I was there at the suggestion of the *Sentinel's* assistant editor. He thought I'd want to attend because Jim and I had worked together and become friends."

She nodded.

"But it may be a little more complicated than that." I stopped as she looked at me inquiringly. "There may be some questions surrounding Jim's death. I have no firm evidence yet, but I'm trying to learn more."

A concerned expression crossed her face. "What kind of questions?"

"There is a chance Jim died under suspicious circumstances."

She blanched. "*What?*"

"Given your friendship with him, I thought it made sense to learn what I could from you. It may help to resolve my questions."

"You think Jim was…?" she said haltingly.

"That's not clear; it's what I'm trying to find out."

She looked away. Her face had turned ashen. "Wow." I waited for her to recover. Finally she looked back at me.

"So…what do you want to know?"

"Let's start with when you and Jim met."

She frowned. "How is that relevant? You're not suggesting…?" She let the question hang there.

"No. I'm not suggesting anything. As I said, I'm just trying to learn what I can about the recent events of his life. I'm curious how long you've known him."

"We met in a support group about six months ago."

"A support group?"

"It's run by a couple of local psychologists. They take turns leading weekly sessions for people who need help getting through something. Jim and I happened to go to a couple of the same meetings, and got to talking after one of them."

"Can you tell me anything about why Jim was seeking support?"

"That's kind of a private matter."

I paused, nodding to acknowledge the point, and did my best to speak gently. "I know he was separated from his wife. So I'm guessing it had something to do with that?"

She nodded. "Yes."

"Do you know what his feelings were in that regard?"

She hesitated. "His separation? He was troubled by it. He loved his two girls, hated being separated from them."

I nodded. "That makes sense. When I worked with him he often talked about how wonderful they were. I know he dreaded having them graduate and leave home."

"He felt terrible about what had happened to him and his wife."

"Do you have any insight in that regard? What their problems were?"

She frowned. "I think Jill was troubled herself. I'm not sure exactly why, Jim didn't like to talk about it. But there were apparently some underlying problems. He wasn't happy about it. It's why he'd come to the support group."

"Do you have any sense why he was reluctant to talk about it?"

"He was a private kind of guy. He felt this was a matter between him and his wife." Her tone had turned soft.

I nodded. "Okay. That certainly jibes with the man I knew."

"You knew him when?"

"A few years ago. When he worked at the paper. We worked on a couple stories together."

"Before his separation?"

"Yes. He always looked forward to getting home after

85

work. My sense was that he was a devoted family man."

Karen nodded. "Yeah." Spoken wistfully.

"So, if I could ask you a little about things at the end?"

Her eyes narrowed and her expression became guarded.

"He had pneumonia when he was admitted to the hospital?"

She nodded.

"And he was on a respirator there?"

"Yes. A ventilator, actually."

"There's a difference?"

"A respirator is a mask that filters air. A ventilator actually helps with breathing. A lot of people use the terms interchangeably." She shrugged, suggesting it was a trivial point.

I nodded, impressed. "Did you visit him at the hospital?"

"Yes."

"Was he conscious?"

"Yes."

"Did he talk to you?"

"While being intubated? He had a tube down his throat." Her tone held a slight element of annoyance. I sensed she didn't suffer fools lightly.

"Do you know if anyone else visited him?"

"His daughters were there some of the time."

"Anyone else?"

"Not while I was there."

"Did his daughters talk to you?"

She frowned. "A little."

I cocked my head to one side, waiting for clarification.

"It was a little complicated. I didn't really know his daughters. And I don't know what they thought of me."

"His wife Jill never came while you were at the hospital?"

She shook her head. "I don't know when she came. Or if." Her tone had turned hard.

I scribbled some notes, then looked up. "Can I ask you about one other thing?"

She glanced at her watch. "If it's brief. I have another client in a few minutes."

"Jim had a partner. Bruce Canton."

Her eyes narrowed. "Yes."

"Can you tell me anything about their relationship?"

"What do you want to know?"

"Did Jim talk about it? Was it a positive relationship? From his standpoint?"

Her brow became furrowed. "They were business partners."

"Well, okay. Was it a *friendly* business relationship?"

She hesitated. "They were different, Jim and Bruce. I think they got along as much as the business required. I don't know that it went beyond that."

"Did you know Bruce yourself?"

She leaned away from me with a skeptical expression. "Yes."

I spoke softly. "I don't mean to pry. I was just wondering if you and Mr. Canton had any kind of relationship."

"We know each other."

"How did you meet *him*?"

"I had an insurance policy with his firm."

"So you knew him before meeting Jim?"

She nodded. "How is this relevant to Jim?" There was an edge in her voice.

I shrugged. "Maybe it isn't. I'm just trying to understand the relationships in Jim's life when he...."

"Jim was a friend. Bruce Canton was my insurance agent."

It struck me he might have been more than that, given their behavior at the funeral, but I could tell this was a sensitive topic so decided to drop it, much as I was curious.

"Okay. Just to summarize, if I'm understanding you, your sense is that Jim and Bruce were not exactly friends, it was pretty much a business relationship?"

"Yes."

I shrugged. "Actually, I suppose that makes sense. As I understand it, Jim wasn't actually a partner in the firm. Bruce and his wife were the legal partners."

She nodded.

"Any idea how Jim felt about that?"

She hesitated. "Bruce is a businessman. He's good at what he does. I don't think Jim had quite the same motives."

I gave her my innocent inquiring look.

"I think you have to take a person for who they are. Some men know how to make money. Some are less concerned with that. Both are fine. They're just different." She said this as though that was the end of the matter.

Which, I realized, it probably needed to be. I nodded, putting away my notebook. "Okay. Well, I should let you get back to work. Thanks for your time."

"So, what's next?"

"I'm sorry?"

"In your gathering of information."

"I'm not sure. This gives me some insights I didn't have. Let me ponder them. Can I get back to you if other questions occur?"

"Sure, Mr. Travis." Her tone was businesslike.

I stood and headed for the door, pushing through and making it out to Old Blue. I glanced back at the shop as I got in. She was staring at me through the glass door, with an expression I had trouble interpreting.

11

I felt my stomach growling as I drove away. Damn thing required a lot of attention. Why did we have to constantly put in more fuel? Wouldn't it be nicer if we had a bigger gas tank so we could focus on other things longer when we felt like it? Another example of bad engineering. Who designed this thing?

I considered the options, using my usual set of criteria. Actually, there was mainly one criterion: I wanted something now. If it was more than ten minutes away, it didn't qualify.

I pulled into the local taco joint and ordered a couple chicken tacos and a cup of black coffee. The girl in the window was young and cheery. I felt old and uncheery, but did my best to be civil. She handed me the order and my change and wished me a nice day. I mumbled something back.

I hate the nice day business. Seems so artificial, and ultimately false. She was a nice enough girl, but let's be honest, she didn't give a damn how nice my day was. Nor I hers. Couldn't we just say 'thanks' and leave it at that? Isn't language used best when things are clear and straightforward? We need less euphemism and more honesty. In my grumpy considered opinion.

There was a little park just a couple blocks away, with picnic tables. I drove there and pulled up, still feeling irritable, and noticed what looked like two homeless people sitting on one of the park benches. The kind that broke your heart: a mom and her daughter. How did we get to the point where one of the largest categories of poverty-stricken people in the country was single mothers and their kids? Why was no one doing anything about this?

Now feeling even grouchier, I found my way to one of the picnic tables and began eating a taco, sipping on the coffee between bites and studying the mom and little girl. There was a grocery cart next to them piled high with what were probably all their worldly possessions. The mom was reading a wrinkled newspaper that must have been left on the bench, and occasionally pointing out something to the little girl. The girl was twirling a pigtail around a finger over and over, and humming a little tune to herself. A thought occurred.

I finished the taco. Then I got up and walked over, taking my second taco. I stopped in front of them. They looked up at me with worried expressions, the kind that come with being constantly unwanted and hassled.

"Hi. I bought these two tacos, but you know, I just ate one and I'm full. Would you like the other?"

The mom shrugged. "Sure. Thanks."

I handed it to her, mustering up a little smile. She studied it for a moment, then broke it in half, handing half to the girl, who looked at me inquiringly. Apparently this wasn't the kind of exchange they were accustomed to. I nodded to them and headed back to Old Blue. A pitiful contribution, but somehow it made me feel a little better.

**

I sat in the car watching them eat the taco for a bit, contemplating what my next venture should be. I needed to get home and check messages; that Chief Medical Officer might have called. But it was a warm pleasant spring day, the grass was fresh and thick, robins were hopping around, and I felt like staying out a while longer.

Karen's comments about Jim and his family stuck in my head. I knew where he'd lived—we'd met there a couple times while working on the story—and it occurred to me that one of the people on my list to talk with was Jill, his wife. I had no idea if she'd be there, but as usual I figured my chances of actually talking with her were better if I didn't ask permission in advance. I started up Old Blue and headed down the street toward their house.

They lived in a lovely two-story Victorian with dormers poking out in two directions and a detached two-car garage around in back. The front yard was surrounded by a white picket fence, with several maple trees just inside the fence, currently in the process of budding out.

I parked in front and found my way through the gate and up the stairs to the front door. There was a metal knocker, which I sounded twice. In a moment footsteps approached and there was a click as the door was unlocked. It swung open part way and there stood Jill.

She looked at me in confusion.

"Hi. I'm Lew Travis. We talked at the funeral?"

She nodded. "Yeah. I know who you are." Her tone was neutral.

I summoned my sympathetic tone. "I know it's a difficult time for you, but I wonder if I could borrow a few minutes of your time. I've decided to write a retrospective on Jim's life and I need to fill in some gaps?"

She stared at me, seemingly unsure.

"It won't take long," I added. "Maybe five minutes?" I'd learned that if you asked for something small, people were more likely to say yes, and once you'd gained their trust, they were usually okay with offering more.

Jill frowned, glancing at her watch. "Well, okay. I do have to leave in a little while."

"That's fine." I looked past her into the living room, trying to nudge her along.

She swung the door open wider and stepped back. I entered and found my way to one end of a couch. She sat on the other end and crossed her arms across her chest. She was dressed in khaki slacks and a blue cotton shirt. Her blond hair was cut short, and she wore tasteful gold earrings. She appeared to be in good shape, as though she worked out regularly.

"What kind of article are you talking about?" she asked.

"A retrospective on Jim's life. A bit on his childhood and education, but mostly on his life here in Sienna, his family, his work, ways in which he contributed to the community."

She frowned. "Can you be a little more specific?"

"Well, how about some background information first. Can you tell me how you met, and how you wound up in Sienna?"

It seems they had met in college, where Jill was a cheerleader and Jim was a starting guard for the basketball team. They had fallen in love their senior year, gotten married just after graduation, and lived for a few years in the San Francisco Bay Area. Jim had started out as a sports writer for a small local paper there, and had moved up to head sports writer, while Jill had been a fundraiser for a community foundation. They had grown tired of the expensive housing and crowded freeways in the Bay Area and decided to take a flyer on an old gold mining town in the Sierra Nevada foothills. They'd lived here now for nearly twenty years, since their older daughter was a baby. Their second daughter had been born here. Jill covered all this quickly and efficiently.

"Okay, thanks. Let's move to your lives here in Sienna. I know Jim caught on with the *Sentinel*. What did you do when you moved here?"

She frowned. "I was pretty tired of fund raising, and there weren't many opportunities for it up here anyway. So I found a job working for the county district attorney's office, first as a receptionist and eventually as their office manager."

"Are you still doing that?"

She nodded. "Part-time. I decided to throttle back when Jim got the insurance job and our financial situation improved."

"So you must have a good knowledge of the local law enforcement system?"

She frowned. "Mostly just the legal system. They're not the same."

I nodded in acknowledgment. "Interesting work?"

"Frankly, it's mostly depressing. You'd be surprised how much local crime there is, between the weed growers and the meth cookers and the wife beaters and the child molesters." She spoke as though this was understood among those who knew anything; it was just the natural order of things.

"Jeez."

"But that's got little to do with Jim. He didn't see it. He always looked at the good side of people." Her tone held sarcasm; this was an apparent point of disagreement between them.

I spoke carefully, not wanting to take sides. "I had that sense when I worked with Jim. Can you give me any examples of his community work?"

"Well, there was the homelessness thing. Fit right into his wheelhouse. He volunteered at the local shelter, helped

93

to manage the food support program." It was clear this was not *her* 'thing'.

"Anything else come to mind?"

"I suppose you could mention the church business. He was on a couple committees, sometimes served as the lay minister when our regular minister was away."

I sensed this was not her 'business' either.

I wasn't sure where to go next, but since we seemed to be surveying their differences, I figured I might as well touch on one I already knew of. "What about his role as father?"

She scowled. "That could take awhile. I guess you could say he was close to the girls." She rolled her eyes.

I cocked my head, waiting for her to say more.

"What?"

"You sound a little...skeptical?"

"Sorry." Spoken with sarcasm.

"So...there were problems there?"

She sighed, waving her hand dismissively. "No, no. He was the ideal father. Coached soccer when they were young, helped them with their homework when they were older." Her tone was not admiring.

"So Jim's passing must be particularly hard on them?"

"I'm sure it is." More sarcasm.

I waited for her to say more; she didn't. I weighed how hard to push this, but since I'd gone this far, I decided I might as well go for broke. "I understand the two of you had a falling out at some point?"

She stared at me, hard. "How is that relevant?"

"I just thought you might want to say something about it?"

She scowled. "Not really. Jim wasn't perfect. He had his downsides."

I nodded, trying to encourage her to continue.

"Do you have a specific question?"

"He must have been troubled by the separation? As you no doubt were?"

She shrugged. "Yeah."

"Can you give me any insights into why…?"

She looked aside, sighing, then back at me. "Let me try to put it positively. Maybe Jim had too high expectations of himself. Or for that matter, life. Sometimes you have to just accept that it's not all sweetness and light. Like the bumper sticker says: 'Life Is Hard; Then You Die'. I'm not sure he was very good at seeing that. He wanted things to be better. Which led to disappointments. And sometimes depression. Which can lead to other problems. And not just for that person. It can get hard on the people around you."

"Okay. I can see how that could be a problem."

She nodded. "We didn't part casually, Mr. Travis. There were real issues." She paused. "But don't put that in the article."

"No. Of course not."

She stared at me. "Anything else?" She glanced at her watch, then looked back, eyebrows raised.

I knew the cue. "No. You've been most helpful. Much appreciated." I put away my notebook and stood.

She held out her hand. "Good luck with the article. I look forward to reading it."

I headed for the door and let myself out. As I walked down the sidewalk toward the street, a phrase echoed in my head. *Hard woman.*

***

When I got back to the house I checked messages. Sure enough, Gustave Bennigan had left one:

Hello, Mr. Travis. This is
Gustave Bennigan, Chief Medical
Officer with the Sienna Memorial
Hospital. Timothy Royce at the
Sienna Sentinel suggested you'd
like to talk with me? Apparently
I've missed you. Just let me know
when is a good time for you.

Damn, I'd been afraid of that. I called back and left a
message, suggesting he call whenever was convenient after
his work hours ended, apologizing for missing him.

Then I checked email.

Hi, Lew,
Haven't heard back from you
about the weekend. Will either
Friday or Sunday work for you? If
you're tied up, just let me know;
we can look for another time.
Violet

I reread the message. 'Tied up?' She knew I was never
tied up. Depressed and unavailable maybe, but not because
of scheduling conflicts. Then it struck me: It wasn't that
she was worried *I* might be tied up. She had other plans to
make herself, and needed to know when she'd be free.
Which she'd already done for Saturday.

I sat there absorbing this. Violet had her own unhappy
history. She was a widow; her husband had died of a long
illness a few years back. She'd stuck with him until the
end, visiting the hospital every day, bringing him his
favorite treats. She had walked through her own lonely
valley of the shadow of death. She was trying to come out
the other end, establish a new life. And for some reason not

entirely clear to me, she seemed to like me. My periodic depressive disappearances weren't helping.

12

I was sipping on my half-glass of gin, watching the news while eating another exciting dinner comprised of a cheese sandwich and canned soup, when the phone rang. I looked at the ID window: Sienna Memorial Hospital. I punched the talk button.

"Hello."

"Hello. Is Mr. Travis in?"

"Speaking."

"Ah. Caught you."

"Dr. Bennigan? Sorry I missed your call earlier."

"Just got through my paperwork. Thought I'd try you before I headed home."

"Much appreciated."

"So, let's see, Tim said you wanted to talk to me about"…there was the sound of paper rustling…"ah, here it is, a Mr. Pearson?"

"Exactly."

"What did you want to ask me?" His tone was friendly.

I was frankly a little surprised he didn't know. But then, maybe Tim hadn't been specific. Or maybe he thought Dr. Bennigan would be more likely to call me if he didn't know the specifics involved. Being the shrewd newspaperman he was.

"Well, do you know about Mr. Pearson's case?"

More rustling. "Let's see, admitted for pneumonia,

intubated, patient recovering slowly, and then…" His voice trailed off. "Oh dear. One of our losses. I'm so sorry, Mr. Travis. Was he a friend?"

"Yes. However, that's not the reason for my call."

"Oh?"

"There seems to be some mystery concerning exactly *why* he died."

"I don't…oh, I see there's an autopsy report here also. I hadn't been tracking…"

"That's what I was hoping to learn about. I knew an autopsy was underway."

"Well, let me read this, it says…hmmm. The conclusion seems to be that he died…oh, my."

"Yes?"

"This is most unusual."

"This being…?"

"Well, goodness." There was an extended pause.

Finally I spoke. "I can tell you, doctor, that I talked with a nurse there who attended Jim, who was trying to be circumspect but was upset at what she discovered."

"Because?"

"She said Jim was blue when she found him?"

"Yes, well, that would be consistent with…" There was a pause. "Can I call you back, Mr. Travis? Perhaps tomorrow? I need to be sure I understand exactly what information we have here before I say more."

"Okay."

"And Tim assured me…you do know Mr. Royce?"

"Yes."

"Well, Mr. Royce assured me this would all be kept strictly confidential?"

"Yes, of course."

"Yes. Well. Let me do a little looking into this. I'll be back in touch."

"Okay, I'll look for your call tomorrow?"

"Yes."

"Thank you, doctor."

"Good night, Mr. Travis." There was a click.

I set the phone down and took another sip of gin. That wasn't exactly what you'd call an official autopsy report, but the picture was pretty clear. Jim had suffocated. And just how a person on a ventilator managed to suffocate seemed to be the question at hand.

I tried to play out the possibilities in my mind. Can ventilators fail? Perhaps due to a power outage? But hospitals have emergency generating systems. Were such emergency generating systems just for ORs and ICUs? Surely they must serve the whole hospital. Had there been such an outage in the first place? I didn't remember one affecting my own electricity recently. And Jennifer would have known about it in any event.

So, what other possibilities? Maybe the ventilator failed due to a malfunction of the machine itself? Might that explain why the alarm hadn't sounded? Although it seemed to me a ventilator should have a built-in fail-safe system. What other piece of equipment would be as critical to the survival of a patient?

If it wasn't the ventilator, what other explanations could there be? It seemed that Jim had been quite depressed when he contracted the pneumonia. Might he have 'pulled the plug' himself? From Jennifer's explanation of how ventilators worked, this seemed possible. He'd just have to undo the Velcro and pull the connector apart from his breathing tube. But as I thought about this theory, there was one fatal flaw. The unit had been working perfectly when he'd been discovered. Dead men don't plug connectors back together. So much for that idea.

But wait. Maybe he'd had a confidante who'd provided

assistance? Someone who saw his suffering, who he plotted with, a co-conspirator? Someone who loved him so much they'd do even this for him? I'd heard of husbands and wives, when the end was near, agreeing to help each other die. Could that be possible?

But there was also the question of the alarm. Jennifer had said there was an alarm if anything related to the ventilator's operation became disturbed. It had rate, volume, and pressure adjustments. If any of these were altered, a nurse would have known. Did that eliminate the suicide theory? Surely this would have gone off if the breathing tube had become disconnected.

Which led to another thought. And a darker theory. And a different kind of motivation.

Earl was curled up next to me on the couch, sleeping. I ran my fingers through the fur on his neck, scratching gently behind his ears, his favorite place. He moved slightly and began purring.

Reflecting on all this, one thing seemed clear: I needed more information. I thought about my notes: each new bit of information led to more questions. It was like an expanding balloon, with what I knew on the inside and what I didn't know on the outside. What was most important to focus on next?

Friday

It was another clear sunny day when I awoke, and nearly eight-thirty. I felt a momentary pang of guilt at the lateness of the hour. Which quickly passed. I'd resented having to get up to an alarm clock my entire working life, not to mention those seemingly endless years when the kids had to be at school at a ridiculous hour. Thank God researchers had finally determined it was bad for teenagers to be forced out of bed at the crack of dawn. Their bodies didn't work that way. Unfortunately, this 'discovery', which any casual glance at the typical teenager at seven-thirty on any given morning would make obvious, took until my days of school taxi driving were over.

Earl stretched and yawned, then lazily rolled over and hopped down from the bed, emitting a brief but distinct meow when he landed. He looked up at me, his message quite clear.

"Give me a few minutes, bud. You know the routine."

He turned as though acknowledging this and trotted toward the stairs while I headed into the bathroom.

Two cups of coffee and some kibble later I gave up trying to find anything of interest in the paper and let Earl out the back door. Then I checked email.

There was Violet's message still waiting for a response. It was already Friday, so I needed to get back to her. I felt increasingly consumed by the gathering mystery of how Jim had died. I was also curious about what her Saturday scheduling conflict was. It occurred to me I might be likelier to learn something about that after the occasion than before. I decided on Sunday for our get together, and sent her a brief email to that effect.

Then I looked over my list of questions, trying to think where I most needed more information. There was Gus, the Chief Medical Officer; but there the ball was in his court. I still hadn't talked to Bruce Canton, Jim's 'partner' at the insurance firm. I considered another swing by Tress of the d'Urbervilles to see if I could learn anything more from Karen Black. But what most stuck in my mind was that homeless character who'd been hanging around the hospital doing curious things. How had I let that drop?

People with messiah complexes give me the creeps, not

just because they're out of touch with reality, but because sometimes they're capable of heinous acts, which they justify by saying God told them to do it. They're just like many religious fundamentalists, who think their beliefs justify any act committed against those who don't happen to agree with them. It struck me that someone with a messiah complex needed to be tracked down and investigated.

However, my only clue as to his whereabouts was one of the local homeless camps. Well, what the hell. A little trek through the woods might be nice on a fresh spring morning. I threw on my windbreaker, lifted the car keys off their hook, and headed out the back door.

People living in homeless camps span a wide variety of personalities and attitudes. While many suffer from substance abuse—alcoholism or drugs—these can be the result of homelessness as much as the cause. Being disconnected from society, shunned by everyone, lacking any regular schedule or events to look forward to, people need escapes, and alcohol and drugs provide ready avenues. Most folks suffering from these problems aren't hostile; they're discouraged and depressed. While some resent outsiders, because they so often harass them, many welcome those who are trying to help. Of course there are exceptions, people who are naturally alienated by society or suffering from mental illness. And I wasn't going to be offering help; I was seeking it. Which made my reception in such communities uncertain.

I knew where a couple of the larger camps had been from the articles I'd worked on years ago. What I didn't know was whether they were still there. There seemed to be only one way to find out.

I decided to hit the closer one first, which was right at the edge of town, just a little way off the road, hidden by trees and thickets. I parked where the trail to the camp emerged from the trees and headed down the path.

Once I got a little way in there were tents scattered among the trees and bushes here and there, and about a hundred yards in was a clearing that represented the central square of this little community. There were a dozen or so tents circling this clearing, with logs providing seating places for perhaps fifteen or twenty people. Only half a dozen people were outside as this came into view, four men and two women, who seemed to be passing the time idly. They looked up skeptically as I approached.

I stopped as I reached the circle. "Good morning."

A couple nodded, the rest stared at me, waiting.

"I'm not here to bother you. I'm trying to find someone who I think is homeless."

One of the men, perhaps in his late twenties, with long hair and a beard, responded. "For what purpose?"

I realized I needed to be cautious. I couldn't say, for example, "He may have killed someone." I was pretty sure that would be the end of the conversation.

"I'm not a cop. I'm in no official capacity. He's just a guy who may need some help. He's been hanging around the hospital, and the people there are concerned about him."

The man with the beard said, "Is he sick?"

"Quite possibly." This of course was true, if you didn't mind a broad interpretation of "sick".

"So, describe him."

"He's an older guy, and often wears a jacket and tie."

Three of the others sitting there looked at me and rolled their eyes, shaking their heads. I wasn't sure how to interpret this.

Again the spokesperson for the group responded. "We know who you're talking about. He's not here."

"What do you know about him?" I asked.

"He's crazy. And a pain in the ass."

"Because…?"

"He thinks he's Jesus. He thinks he can save everyone. Drives us nuts when he's around."

"Do you have any idea where he is? Or what his name is?"

"He goes by 'The Reverend'." He made air quotation marks, rolling his eyes. He was here a few days ago. We finally threw him out. He's probably at one of the other camps."

I nodded. "Okay. Thanks. Can you tell me anything else about him?"

One of the women spoke. "I think he has a friend, or maybe just someone who's taken pity on him, who lets him stay at his place sometimes. I've seen him coming out of a house in town."

"Really? Where?"

"On that street where the animal shelter is. It's an old house, needs paint; it has a dilapidated front porch. On the right as you're leaving town."

"I know where that is."

"If you can get him admitted permanently, we'd be eternally grateful."

I smiled. "I'll see what I can do. Thanks."

"What's your name? Just in case he shows up."

"Lew Travis." I handed her my card.

She studied it, frowning. "What's 'investigative' mean? I thought you said you weren't in any official capacity."

"I work part-time for the newspaper. I'm doing a story on a guy who worked to alleviate homelessness. Jim Pearson."

"What's that got to do with The Reverend?"

I tried to think quickly. I didn't want to lie to these

people, but neither did I want to suggest anything involving possible criminal activity. I knew they had a skeptical view of police. "I think he might have known Jim. I just wanted to talk to him to see if he had anything to add to the story."

Another of the women said, "Did you say Jim Pearson?"

I nodded. "He was a friend of mine."

"Was? Did something happen to him?" She sounded like she knew him.

I nodded. "Yeah, unfortunately."

The original spokesperson said, "Jim was a friend to all of us. We wondered why we hadn't seen him for a while. What happened?"

I explained the developments as succinctly as I could, leaving out any reference to 'foul play' or 'criminal activity', in a tone that conveyed my own distress.

"That's awful. He wasn't very old. What happened?"

I shrugged. "No one seems to really know. That's what I'm trying to find out."

"And you think The Reverend might have had something to do with it?"

"I really have no idea. I just thought I should talk to him, since he'd been seen at the hospital when Jim was there."

They all nodded. "Yeah, really. Hey, good luck, man."

"Thanks." I nodded and turned to leave, when the woman spoke again. "You sure you have those directions clear? To that guy's house?"

I glanced back. "Yeah. I know the place."

"Okay. If we can help..."

"Thanks. Let me see what I can find out."

***

Hell's Angel

It didn't take me long to find my way there in Old Blue, and sure enough, the house was obvious. Not only did the front porch look like it was about to fall down, but an old fence out by the road had partially collapsed, and there was a swing hanging by one rope in a tree in front. I looked at the mailbox, which was cockeyed on its post: 919 Old Mine Road.

I parked and made my way through a creaky gate along a short stretch of broken concrete that passed for a sidewalk, and stepped up the two stairs to the rickety front porch. I knocked on the door; a ferocious bark erupted instantly from inside.

I took a step back, hoping whoever answered the door would be holding Cujo back.

Steps approached and the door creaked open a crack. A man with a dark ragged beard and long tangled hair peered out, doing his best to hold the dog inside. He shouted, "Shut up, shithead!" Then he looked up. "Yeah?"

I decided to approach this obliquely. "Hello. I'm with the Interfaith Food Service. We're doing a survey to determine who qualifies for a weekly delivery of free food."

"Free?"

I nodded. "Might you qualify?"

He scowled, conducting what appeared to be a search of his critical faculties to determine the answer to this apparently baffling question. Finally a response. "I don't need no free food." He began to close the door.

I spoke quickly. "Before you go, a neighbor mentioned he'd seen a man who appeared to be homeless here?"

The door opened a few inches again. "Yeah?"

"Is that someone who might need this service?"

"The Reverend, you mean?"

"Is that his name?"

"That's the one he goes by."

"Does he need food?"

"Might."

"Any idea how I'd find him?"

Again he appeared to search the further reaches of his mind. "I can tell him you're lookin' for him if you like."

"Is he staying here?"

"Did last night. Might come back."

"Any idea where he might be now?"

He scowled. "Mostly hangs around town. Free places. Mostly churches I think?"

"Does he have a favorite one?"

He squinted. "I think that big one over by the creek, maybe? Has two names. Methodist something."

"The Methodist-Presbyterian?"

"Yeah."

"Okay. Thanks. I'll see if I can find him there."

"What you want him for?"

"Like I said; to see if he qualifies for free food."

"Oh, right. He don't eat a lot, he's pretty scrawny."

"Nice of you let him stay here," I said.

"Yeah, well. He didn't ask the first time; I just found him out here on the porch. One of those cold nights. Just seemed like the decent thing to do, let him come inside. I don't really talk to him much."

"That's still nice of you."

"Yeah, well." He looked down at his feet, then back up. "Good luck." He nodded and closed the door.

I headed back out to Old Blue. Surprising where you sometimes found a bit of humanity.

I climbed back into Old Blue and headed over to the Methodist-Presbyterian church. This is a large modern building, with a worship hall that holds around two hundred people. It has a high vaulted ceiling and expansive windows, a broad raised altar, and an adjoining building for related activities: Sunday school, social events, whatever.

I parked in a lot at one side and walked up to the main entrance. You never knew whether a church would be locked or open. Different churches took different approaches to this, and with the growth of homelessness, more were keeping things locked. However, some took the opposite approach, in effect providing the homeless a shelter if they had nowhere else to go. I tried the door knob and it worked. I pushed through.

The door opened into a large vestibule with several coat hanger racks and a wooden counter on one side. Across the vestibule were double doors that opened into the nave. I walked quietly to these and again pushed through, into a large congregational hall.

There were natural wooden pews down both sides with an aisle in the middle. I glanced around the voluminous space, looking for any signs of life. It appeared to be entirely vacant. I made my way slowly up the central aisle, glancing left and right down the long pews. I was about to give up as I reached the front, when there he was.

He was lying down on the very first pew, curled up on his side, apparently asleep. He wore worn brown pants that had once been expensive wool slacks and a brown and yellow-checkered sport coat, pulled around his shoulders. Perhaps his most distinctive feature was his long blond-white hair, well over his shoulders, with strands of gray mixed in. This was accompanied by a long white beard. Both were wild and disheveled, almost like the pictures one often sees of Jesus, except for the color and obvious lack of attention to hygiene. There was also a distinctly unpleasant odor emanating from him.

As I stood staring at him he stirred, then opened his eyes and looked at me.

109

I nodded. "Hello."

He sat up, and as he did so, I could see that he was tall and thin. "Welcome, my son. Have you come seeking solace?"

I frowned. "I've come to see if I could find you."

He blinked. "And how may I be of service, my son. Jesus loves all his children, you know."

"And you are…?"

"People call me The Reverend. But I am…" He nodded benignly, with a slight bent of his head, as though acknowledging the obvious.

"May I sit down?"

He slid over, making room.

Suddenly I realized I was now on the spot. How does one approach a crazy person? As I sat down, my mind whirled. Then it came to me: if I was going to get him to talk, I needed to enter his world.

"I am troubled," I said. "I've lost a close friend."

"He put his hand on my shoulder. "God be with you. He is there to provide solace to the troubled."

I nodded. "You are kind."

He bowed slightly, graciously acknowledging my response. "We must all face hard times in this vale of tears. It is only when we enter the Kingdom of Heaven that pain will cease. But God can soften our pain."

Glancing toward the altar, I said, "Especially in His house of worship."

"It is one of the wonders of the world, how God provides for us places in which we may worship Him."

I waited a moment before deciding to try a new gambit. "Does He not also sometimes need to punish sinners?" I spoke as though I was personally concerned about such a possibility.

He leaned away from me, with a hard stare. "Have you

sinned, my son?"

"Perhaps; I know we all do sometimes. But that is not the reason I sought you out today. I need your counsel."

He frowned, waiting for me to say more.

"I find myself in a difficult position. Can you tell me: How do you distinguish good from evil?"

His eyes narrowed. "How do you mean, my son?"

"When you encounter sinners? How do you know they are sinners?"

"God is all wise. I listen to His voice. I am merely the vehicle of His wisdom."

"How do His messages come to you?"

"In various ways. Sometimes in my sleep. Sometimes through His voice. Sometimes through the contrails."

"The contrails?"

"Left by airplanes." He said this as though it was obvious.

"I don't understand."

"They begin as airplane exhaust. But they are in the sky, where God lives. There are messages in the contrails."

"How do you go about reading them?"

"I just know. God speaks in mysterious ways."

"So you listen to His messages, and then perform His wishes as he conveys them to you?"

He nodded benignly.

"And what does He tell you to do to the wicked?"

His face darkened and his voice became deeper. "We must inflict vengeance on those who do not know God and do not obey the gospel. So sayeth the Bible."

I nodded, waiting for him to continue.

"Do you not know of the great flood, of Sodom and Gomorrah, of the plagues cast upon Egypt? We must glory in God, as he demands. His will must be done." His voice rose in indignation.

"And you have had to face such wickedness?"

A cautious expression spread across his face. "The evil among us must be stamped out. It must face God's wrath. I must carry out the commandments of the Lord."

"How do you do this?"

His eyes narrowed, with a look that was distinctly creepy. His voice softened again. "We must not talk of such things, my son. We must always seek peace. That is the wish of the Almighty."

I nodded as he put his hand on my shoulder. I tried not to shudder.

"Can you tell me more of your sadness?" he asked.

"I lost a friend who had become ill and was hospitalized."

His expression took on a guarded look. "We must trust in the Lord when we are ill, not mere mortals."

"Well, doctors can sometimes help. But in this case medicine failed."

His voice grew strong again. "We must not put our trust in false Gods. There is but one true God. I will pray that your friend finds his way to a better place." He paused. "Had he accepted the Lord as his savior?"

"He was a regular church goer."

The Reverend looked up toward the ceiling. "Then his spirit may linger even here."

"Any help you can give him..."

"I cannot make judgments about any man's entry to heaven; only the Father can do that. But I will pray for him."

I nodded. "Thank you, Reverend." I began to stand up.

He put his hand on my forehead as I did so, closing his eyes and tilting his head upward. "Dear Father, allow this man the peace he seeks." He lowered his hand and looked at me beatifically.

I stood, nodded to him, and said "Thanks." Then I quietly walked back down the center aisle and outside. I climbed into Old Blue and leaned back, rubbing my face. Dealing with crazy people always drained me. But I sensed this would not be the last time I needed to talk with The Reverend.

13

When I got back to the house there was a message waiting for me from Gustave Bennigan, the hospital's Chief Medical Officer:

```
    Mr. Travis, I've looked into the
matter   we   discussed,   and   I'm
afraid I won't be able to comment
further. There is an investigation
underway,  and  until  the  findings
from that emerge it is best that I
not comment. Please be assured we
will do everything in our power to
uncover  the  facts  and  report  them
honestly.
```

The wording of that last sentence provoked in me a twinge of suspicion. Might this be a cover-up in the making? Jennifer had warned me that hospitals were sensitive about matters that might lead to lawsuits.

I wondered whether my friends at the *Sentinel* had learned anything new, given Tim's connection to Dr. Bennigan. I put in a call.

"Sienna Sentinel." A soft female voice.

"They've got you on the switchboard again?"

A brief pause. "Good morning, Lew."

"Good ear."
"You have a unique voice."
"Oh?"
"It's gravelly."
"Gravelly?"
"You know. Deep and kind of rough."
I made a growling sound.
Violet chuckled. "What can I do for you?"
"What did you have in mind?"
"You sound frisky."
"I miss you."
"You have me wondering sometimes."
"Yeah. Sorry about that. You do understand; it's not about you?"
"Sure." She didn't sound entirely convinced. "Who did you want to talk to?"
"Is Tim around?"
"I believe so. Shall I put you though?"
"Please." Spoken in the deepest, gravelliest voice I could muster.
After a couple clicks Tim's voice came on: "If it isn't the provocateur."
"I beg your pardon?"
"It seems you've managed to provoke a full-blown investigation. Apparently you scared the shit out of my doctor friend."
"He didn't seem to be much on top of things over there."
"He has a lot of things to be on top of."
"Well, you'd think a suspicious death might be somewhere near the top of the pile."
"It is now. He's got his whole legal department looking into this."
"Good. What have they learned?"

"Gus hasn't said. They're just getting started." There was a brief pause. "What have *you* learned?"

I hesitated. I realized I had learned very little that was more than speculation so far. "That there are some suspicious circumstances surrounding Jim's death."

"How shrewd. Could you elaborate?"

"I think we've been over this. I'm not at liberty to reveal my sources at this point."

"I didn't ask about your sources. What are the suspicious circumstances?"

"They're a little complex, actually. And as yet a bit muddy. I don't want to confuse you."

"That's exactly what you're doing. And did the last time I asked you that question."

"It's called consistency. That's what you get from dependable people."

"Dependably annoying. Is that all you have to say?"

"It's been lovely talking?"

There was a click.

***

I reflected on Tim's tidbit of information. The hospital was in an uproar. It seemed clear there were some disturbing findings the hospital had uncovered. But I could see little more to do on that front except wait to see what emerged from their investigation.

And there were a lot of other matters on which I needed more information. I still hadn't talked to Bruce Canton. Nor seen him with his wife, to get a read on their relationship. I had some more questions I wanted to ask Karen Black. Not to mention Jill Pearson. And I could use some more background on The Reverend.

It seemed like it was time to bring in my ace in the

hole: Zane. He's something of a genius on this count. If information is available in a public record, he can find it. And even if it isn't, he can often find it. I didn't know much about hacking, but as far as I could tell, Zane could break into the NSA and learn what the President's plans were for lunch. This ought to be a piece of cake for him.

The problem was, I wasn't sure how to suggest he begin such an inquiry. How do you track down information on a crazy person? Especially one who's real name you don't even know. But what the hell, I didn't have a better idea.

I decided an email might be better than a phone call. It would let Zane think about it, knowing the basics of the situation, so he could turn me down if he felt it was a wild goose chase. I opened my email and began pecking away.

```
Hi, Zane,
How are things over there? I'm
wondering if you could use a
little more cash to pad your
bankroll? I have a friend who died
recently      under    suspicious
circumstances, and I'm trying to
track down information about one
of the suspects. He's a homeless
guy who was seen wandering around
the hospital while my friend was
there.
    I just talked to him at the
Methodist-Presbyterian    Church,
where he likes to hang out. He
refers to himself as either The
Reverend, or 'Jesus', which
probably tells you all you need to
know about his mental state.
```

Except that, in addition to being
a full-blown loon, I sense he has
an angry streak. Or in his
parlance, a need to perform
vengeance on the wicked. In the
name of God, of course. He's been
in and out of the local shelter,
but to the degree he has a current
residence, is sleeping at the home
of a rustic gentleman over on Old
Mine Road, number 919. I didn't
get his name.

Any chance you could do a little
looking into this guy for me? Can
you give me a call?
Lew

I took a breath and pressed the send button. This might
be something of a test for Zane; there wasn't a whole lot
there to go on.

Then I decided on the next step in my information
gathering. I lifted my keys off their hook and headed out to
the garage. Who knew if I could catch Canton in, but it
couldn't hurt to try.

I pulled up in front of the insurance office and parked,
glancing in through the picture windows to see if anyone
was there. It appeared to be empty, but I figured as long as
I'd made this much of an effort I might as well at least
knock on the door. There was no answer, so I tried it and
found it open. I pushed in and called 'hello'.

A voice from the rear called back. "Just a minute." A
male voice. I sat down and waited, and sure enough, Bruce
Canton emerged. He glanced at me inquiringly.

"Hello." He paused. "Do I know you? You look
familiar." He smiled; his tone was warm and friendly. No

doubt a well-rehearsed response to any potential client.

"I attended the funeral for Jim Pearson, so you might have seen me there?"

The smile evaporated. "Ah. Okay." He held out his hand. "Bruce Canton. Which I guess you know."

I nodded. "Lew Travis."

"What can I do for you, Lew Travis?"

I handed him my card. "I'm with the *Sentinel*? We thought we'd do a retrospective on Jim's life, and since he worked here the last few years, I thought you might be willing to share a few thoughts about him?"

"Ah. Yes. Roberta mentioned you'd stopped by. Be glad to." He pointed me to a chair, which I eased into, sitting down across from him.

"Maybe we could start with why you hired Jim?" I said.

"Okay." He leaned back in his chair. "Jim had a great reputation, everyone spoke highly of him. He wanted a chance to make more money than he was making at the paper, which I thought we could offer. I believe he met that goal here," he said with a touch of pride.

"Was he a partner?"

He frowned. "Nooo. We already had a partnership in place, and it would have been complicated to modify that. You know: legally. Plus we wanted to make sure he'd be happy here before he got locked into the place."

"But you do have a partnership with your wife?"

"Yes."

"How long have the two of you been in business?"

He squinted in a thinking gesture. "I guess it's ten years now. Jim was with us the last three."

"What was his role here?"

"A little of everything. He did whatever we asked. And he never complained. He was the ideal colleague."

"Anything you can say about him that might make a

good quote for the article?"

"We miss him. We're deeply saddened by his departure. We extend our sympathies to his wife and daughters."

I waited for more, which wasn't forthcoming. I tried a prompt.

"While I probably wouldn't include this in the article, your wife mentioned that he was sometimes a bit...over generous with clients?"

Canton scowled. "Well, Jim was a generous guy. He didn't like to bug clients about late payments. And he didn't like to push policies on people who weren't sure they wanted one. I think I mentioned this at the funeral." He smiled. "Hope that came across as intended?" His eyebrows were raised in a questioning gesture.

I nodded. Just then the front door opened and in walked Roberta. She looked at us inquiringly.

"Hi, dear," Bruce said. "I believe you know Mr. Travis?"

She nodded, a wave of recognition crossing her face. "Yes. Of course. Hello." I nodded in response. "And you are here to...?" she asked.

"I just thought it would be good to have some quotes from your husband," I said. "For the article?"

There was no attempt at a smile. She was staring at Bruce with an expression that seemed pointed.

"I'm just saying nice things about Jim," he said defensively.

She nodded without replying and sat down at the desk on the other side, apparently needing to take care of something there.

I turned back toward Bruce. "So, where were we?"

He was glancing back and forth between his wife and me, seemingly unsure how to proceed. "Do you have more questions?"

"Well, I don't want to include anything inappropriate in the article, but I can't help but wonder. Did you notice anything about Jim that might have suggested he was depressed?"

He looked confused. "Depressed?"

Roberta's voice intruded. "He was dealing with a difficult situation at home, if that's what you're referring to?"

"So I understand. I just wondered if this manifested itself in his work in any way?"

"Not directly, at least not that I noticed," she said. "Bruce?"

"No. I didn't see any fall-off. He was a hard worker."

"Did you notice any evidence of him dealing with his marital issues outside the office?" I was fishing, but you never knew what might cause a bite.

"Well, he had made friends with another woman," Bruce said. "Not that that was a problem for us."

Again Roberta's voice chimed in. "What he did outside the office was his business."

I glanced down at my notes, thumbing back a few pages. "Would this have been...a Karen Black?"

Bruce's eyes widened. "As a matter of fact..."

"The young woman you were with at the funeral?" I was being deliberately provocative, wondering how Roberta would respond.

He cleared his throat. "Only to try to provide support for her. I knew the young lady; she was a client of ours. She had become somewhat attached to Jim. I was trying to give her a shoulder to lean on. So to speak."

I glanced at Roberta, whose face had darkened. She said nothing.

"Do you know the nature of this friendship?"

"How do you mean?"

"Well, not to be indelicate, but do you know just how close they were?"

Bruce leaned back in his chair, shaking his head. "Not really. Jim didn't discuss his private life with us. But I don't think they were really…an item."

I nodded, glancing at my little notebook.

"Apparently they met at a support group meeting?"

"Okay. I didn't know that."

"And were trying to support each other through some difficult times?"

"Makes sense."

"Suggesting Jim was perhaps struggling with depression?"

Again Roberta's voice intruded. "Mr. Travis, are you suggesting…how do I put this tactfully…that Jim might have participated in his own demise?" Her tone implied a kind of intrigue with this thought.

I shrugged, looking at her. "I'm not really suggesting anything. I'm just trying to get a sense for what might have happened. There seems to be some confusion on this point. At the hospital."

She frowned. "Well, I don't want to promote any kind of suspicion—we have no evidence in that direction—but given Jim's behavior here, it seems possible he might have been depressed enough to…well, you get my drift."

"Really?"

"Like I said, I'm only speculating."

"But you think that might really have been a possibility?"

She shrugged in a gesture suggesting 'anything's possible'.

I looked back at Bruce. "Was that your sense, also?"

He was frowning and nodding. "One never knows

about such things."

I waited for either of them to volunteer more, but neither did. I glanced again at Roberta, who was staring at Bruce in a way that people who know each other well sometimes communicate. But I couldn't read her thoughts.

I put my little notebook back in my pocket. "Well, I think that's the end of my questions. If you think of something else that might be good to include in the piece, you have my card. I nodded toward the desk where it lay.

"Right," Bruce said.

"We'll be looking forward to seeing the article," Roberta said.

I stood to leave. As I did so she spoke again. "By the way, I might mention that we've offered Jim's wife a little…condolence package? It's not a lot, just a gesture to let her know how much we valued him."

"That's generous of you."

"It seemed only right. She's a lovely woman. It's got to be crushing for her."

I nodded. "Well, thank you both."

I turned and pushed back out through the door, heading out to Old Blue.

14

By now my stomach rumblings were audible. Damn thing. Needs constant attention. Not that I don't like eating. I just wish when it had to be done was a little more under my direction. I was tired of fast food and feeling like a little nap anyway—it was, after all, afternoon now—so headed for home.

I threw together a tuna sandwich and took it into the living room. Not that there was anything on TV worth watching at this hour, but somehow it felt more comfortable than eating alone at the kitchen table. I took the paper with me; it wasn't great on national news, but it did keep you up on local things. Which, after all, was its main purpose.

I nibbled on the sandwich slowly as I looked through the paper, noticing the *New York Times* crossword, which was carried in the *Sentinel* a few weeks behind the *Times*. By Friday these had become challenging. I pulled out that page and folded it down, then pulled out a pen and started filling in a few words here and there. I could usually get most of it done, but sometimes got hung up when two obscure names crossed each other. I wished they'd ban clues that sought obscure names; there was no way to get around them. You either knew them or you didn't.

When I really got frustrated I'd resort to googling Rex Parker. I had a love-hate relationship with the guy. He did every New York Times crossword the moment it came out at midnight, electronically. Then he posted his solution on his website, with the time it had taken him to complete the puzzle, rating it from easy to challenging, and offering commentary on the clues. That could be fun to read after you'd spent hours struggling with some particularly difficult puzzle, except he usually completed them in about ten minutes. Always felt a little like bragging. I usually had to come back to the damn things several times before the various sections fell into place, and even then I was sometimes stumped. Comes with an old brain I guess. The information might be in there somewhere, but it gets lost in some blind canyon.

I got as far as I could on a first pass, maybe a dozen words, finishing my sandwich in the process, and lay down on the couch, feeling a little catnap coming on. I used to resist these, but they'd been coming on more frequently of late, and even a few minutes of dozing did wonders in terms of recharging my batteries. They also often helped to locate those words that were lost in the ozone.

The next thing I knew, the phone was ringing. I groggily sat up and reached for it, looking at the ID window. The number looked vaguely familiar; I couldn't remember who it was, but I didn't think it was a solicitation. I pushed the talk button.

"Hello?"

"Yo. Mr. T. How you doin'?"

"*Zane*. How are you? Been awhile."

"Yeah, I was getting worried about you."

"Because?"

"Ah…no reason. Good to hear your voice, though. What's up?"

I sketched the situation more fully than I had in the email, realizing again that I hadn't given him many points of reference with which to track down The Reverend.

"Jeez, Mr. T. That's going to take some work."

"That's what I figured. Do you think you can do anything?"

"Let me give it a shot. Can't promise anything. How soon you need this?"

"The sooner the better. You busy with other things?"

"Not really. School's a bore. I need to spend some time with my girlfriend over the weekend, but I'll see what I can do."

"How are things going in that regard? With your girlfriend?"

He hesitated. "Pretty good. She's a sweetie. But you know how it is with women, they require care and feeding."

I smiled. Sixteen and he'd already figured that out.

"Understood. Well, do what you can and let me know."

"You got it. The usual payment scheme?"

"Assuming your rates haven't gone up."

"Not for you, Mr. T."

"I'll look forward to seeing what you come up with. No problem if you can't pull it off; nothing ventured, nothing gained."

"I'm on it."

We hung up, and I leaned back on the couch. Jeez. Sixteen and he was talking about his 'woman' and had favorite clients. Or was clever enough to make them think that. I tried to remember what I'd been doing when I was sixteen. Wishing I had the courage to ask a girl out and wondering how I was going to get through an entire weekend with no plans.

It occurred to me I hadn't checked email since this morning. I pulled myself off the couch and wandered out to the den, firing up my email and clicking the inbox. There were Russian women who wanted to get to know me better;

incredible deals on one hundred magazines I didn't want; and two hotel chains offering free weekends in exotic locations just for signing up for their credit card.

And one from someone I knew: Harve. It was short and simple:

`Give me a call.`

I did so, to his direct line. He picked up on the fifth ring.

"Hello?" He sounded distracted.

"You *are* awake," I said. "I couldn't tell there, with all the rings."

There was a pause. "Is there a purpose for this call, other than annoying me? Because I'm actually kind of busy."

"Just responding to your request."

"Oh. Well, I actually do have a little news for you."

"About time. I thought I was going to have to find a new assistant."

Another pause. "I've been in touch with Jennifer again. Seems the autopsy has been completed."

"Ah ha."

"Her conclusions about Jim's cause of death have been confirmed. He suffocated. But with some complications."

"Such as?"

"It appears there may have been tampering with the ventilator."

"Whoa."

"The alarm was apparently somehow disarmed. They don't know exactly how, but it didn't go off at the time Jim apparently stopped getting air."

"Wow."

"Yeah. There's no longer much question: Jim did not

die of natural causes."

"What happens next?"

"They've brought in the Sienna Police Department."

"Of course," I said, groaning to myself. I had a somewhat strained relationship with the Sienna Police Department. There is a natural conflict between reporters who are trying to bring information to the public and the police who like to play things close to the vest. It probably doesn't help that I'm not particularly sensitive to their concerns, and the chief, John Christiansen, is a bit of a straight arrow.

"Looks like you're going to get an opportunity to renew some old friendships, Lew."

"Goddamn it."

"What did you expect?"

"I was hoping the hospital itself would figure it out."

"It seems to have gone beyond a medical investigation."

"Do you know if the boys in blue have learned anything yet?"

"They've just begun. I'll try to find out what I can as they get into it. For the moment they're trying to keep things quiet. In addition to the obvious sensitivity of this to the hospital's reputation, they don't want to alert whoever did this to the fact it's under investigation."

"I guess that makes sense."

"By the way, if anyone asks, I didn't tell you this. The last thing I need is to get Jennifer in more trouble."

"How does it come to be that she is so beholden to you, Harve? Do you have some incriminating evidence you're holding over her?"

There was no response.

"You're paying her for this information in large denomination bills?"

Again, no response.

"Well?"

"She trusts me, Lew. And she really liked Jim. She wants the truth to come out. And she's worried it never will if it's left up to the hospital and the cops."

"I can see why the hospital is concerned. This isn't exactly reassuring information for future patients, who have enough to worry about without fearing there are killers lurking around. But why do the cops want to hush it up?"

"Because the chances of their solving this are probably somewhere south of fifty-fifty? How many files do they have down there for unsolved cases? This isn't exactly a crack Scotland Yard crew we're talking about. They're good at small town stuff, but this looks like a professional operation."

"I guess that makes sense. Anyway, thanks for clueing me in. This confirms what was already pretty clear, but it's good to have official validation. If there was any doubt about the need to unravel this thing before, there isn't any more. You're doing okay, Watson."

There was a deep sigh on the line. "Sometimes I wonder why I help you, Travis. You do know you're a royal pain in the ass."

"Royal. I like that."

"You know, for reasons beyond my understanding, you seem to have a knack for this. You're kind of like an idiot savant. They can't tie their own shoes, but they can handle numbers like a high-end computer."

"Well, I'll buy half of that description."

"You're right. 'Savant' is putting it too…"

I hung up before he could finish.

***

I leaned back in my old desk chair. It wasn't that I was surprised by this news, but it provided official confirmation. One of the finest men I'd ever known, killed by a sophisticated murderer. Why? How? And more to the point, who? If there had been little doubt before; now there was none. I could sense my determination growing; this cur was not going to get away with it.

And it wasn't that I didn't welcome the involvement of the Sienna Police Department. If they could unravel this, more power to them. It was just that I had little confidence that would happen. I knew these guys. They were honest and well intentioned. But that wasn't usually enough.

I pulled out my notes and went over them again. As I sifted through the list of people I wanted to learn more about, one name popped out as perhaps the lynchpin: Karen Black. She'd had a close relationship with Jim. But I didn't know the precise nature of that relationship. And how did it relate to Bruce Canton, with whom she apparently also had a close relationship? I wasn't sure how much more I could learn from talking with her again—she'd seemed pretty guarded the last time. But there were a lot of things I needed to find out, and she seemed like a key source.

I drummed my fingers on the desk, trying to decide how best to approach her. Was there a way I might gain her confidence? Perhaps if I treated her as a confidante? Lead her to believe someone else was the main suspect?

I pulled out her business card and looked at the number, then picked up the phone and dialed.

She answered on the second ring. "Tress of the d'Urbervilles."

"Hi. Karen? This is Lew Travis."

There was a moment of silence. "Yes?"

"I'm wondering if we could talk again? I'm afraid my suspicions have been confirmed."

"Oh no."

"I have some theories about how it happened, but I could use your help to sort them out."

"How?" Her tone was guarded.

"As near as I can tell, you were the closest person to Jim when he was admitted to the hospital. I need to get a better sense of the things that were on his mind, and who the other people were he was talking with. I won't ask you about the personal side of things, that's your business. But I need your help in figuring out who might have had a motive to do him in."

There was a moment of silence. "What makes you think I can help?"

"To be honest, I don't really know. Maybe you can't. But can we at least talk so I can ask you what I need to?"

Another pause, and a sigh. "I suppose. But I don't know anything about his actual death."

"I know that. This is not about you." A lie, but my sole motive at the moment was to get her to talk.

"When did you want to meet?"

"How soon can you be available?"

"Just a minute."

I waited. It was half a minute before she came back on. "I'm booked solid until the end of the afternoon. I guess I could talk then."

"When do you get free?"

"Five-thirty."

"Can we meet then?"

"Where?"

"What works for you?"

"How about some place other than the shop. I need a break from this place."

"You name it."

"I sometimes have a glass of wine after work. Do you

know where One Mile Down is?"

One Mile Down was a bar that featured historical pictures of Sienna. In addition to the many old downtown brick buildings—added after the several fires that destroyed the town in its early days—there were hundreds of miles of underground tunnels at various levels below the surface, left over from Sienna's gold mining days, some as much as a mile down. The bar was a casual place with comfortable seating and a friendly barkeep. I sometimes frequented it myself. "Sure."

"I can meet you there at, say, five-forty-five?"

"See you then."

15

I arrived at One Mile Down a few minutes early and found a table near the back. The bartender was a man who had worked there for probably forty years. He was a sweet old guy who was always friendly and knew what I'd order. He brought me a gin and tonic without my asking.

"How you doin', Lew?" he said as he carefully set the overflowing glass down in front of me.

I nodded. "Okay, Slim. You?"

"Still waking up in the morning. All I ask."

"Louisa treating you okay?"

"She puts up with me. Can't ask a woman for more than that." He saluted me and headed back for the bar.

I smiled. Slim was a guy who didn't demand a lot of life, and was consequently pretty happy with what he got. Might be a lesson there for a lot of us.

I took a generous gulp and leaned back, just as Karen emerged through the door. She looked around the darkened room, then headed over and sat down across from me. She was wearing those tight jeans and a white cotton pullover shirt which accentuated her figure even more than usual. I noticed three guys at the bar staring at her as she made her way across the room.

Slim came back to take her order. "You know this guy?" he asked, nodding toward me.

She frowned. "Not really. What should I know?"

"He's with the paper," he said, rolling his eyes. "Don't say anything you don't want to see in print." Then he smiled. "What'll it be?"

"House chardonnay?"

He nodded and headed back to the bar.

Karen looked back at me. "I take it you're a regular here?"

"That's probably overstating it. But I come by often enough they know me."

She glanced at my drink. "Gin and tonic?"

I nodded.

"You know, wine is easier on your stomach."

"It's not my stomach I drink it for."

She smiled. Among her other attractions, she had perfect teeth. "So what did you want to talk to me about?"

"Like I suggested on the phone, is it okay if I treat you as a colleague here?"

She looked at me skeptically. "I'm not sure what that means, but I suppose."

"Let me tell you what I know, and we'll take it from there."

I filled her in on what Harve had conveyed, including the fact the local cops were now conducting an investigation. I figured she'd find this out on her own anyway, and I might gain her confidence by tipping her off. She took this in, listening and frowning. When I stopped, her frown became a scowl.

"I just don't understand it. Who would want to hurt someone as nice as Jim?"

"That's what we have to find out."

She nodded. "Okay. What do you want to know?"

"If I understood you correctly before, you and Jim did a fair amount of talking?"

She nodded. "Yeah."

"Can you tell me more about what was on his mind?"

She frowned. "I think I mentioned how upset he was about the separation, and not seeing his girls very often?"

"You did."

"So…?"

"What did he say about Jill?"

"About Jill? His wife?" Her jaw clenched, slightly but noticeably. "He couldn't understand how she could be so hostile toward him, not even let him see the girls. He thought she was being unfair."

"Why did they separate in the first place?"

"She threw him out." Her tone was hard.

"Why?"

"Said he was too difficult to live with anymore. She couldn't stand having someone so depressed around. She thought he should get help."

"Did he?"

Her tone softened. "He resisted that. He was like a lot of men; he thought he could handle his problems on his own."

"But he eventually did seek help? Isn't that how you met him?"

She nodded. "But that was a while after the separation."

"Did he talk to you about *why* he was so depressed before the separation?"

"I think it was the fact his girls were leaving. One was about to start college, and the other was a sophomore in high school. He was having trouble facing not having them around. And about the job."

"What about the job?"

She cocked her head a bit, as though considering this. "Jim was a sweet guy. He wasn't really cut out to be a salesman. Which is a lot of what being an insurance agent involves."

"He didn't like selling insurance?"

"He hated it."

"Why did he do it?"

"Because of the money. He needed to make more than he could at the paper. And Jill pushed him that way."

"She wanted him to make more?"

"Yeah." She rolled her eyes.

"Why was that so important to her?"

"Well, this is getting into territory where I'm not really an expert. Jim worked hard not to criticize her. But I got the sense she liked nice things."

"Such as?"

"Clothes, jewelry, that sort of thing."

"So he felt he had to keep selling insurance to keep her happy?"

"Yeah. But…"

I waited.

"The job entailed more than just selling. There were other parts he liked okay. Like helping people get together a claim after a loss. He felt good when he was helping someone."

"So he had mixed feelings, some good, some not?" I looked at her inquiringly.

She frowned. "More negative than positive. I don't think he was all that happy with…his colleagues."

"The Cantons?"

She nodded, taking a sizeable sip of wine.

I took another swig of my g & t. "Why not?"

"They were serious business people; they pushed people hard to buy policies. Even when, in Jim's view, they didn't always need them. They kept telling him that was how you made money. This wasn't a social service agency they were running, their goal was to make as much as they could."

136

"And Jim didn't like that?"

"No. Or the fact that…" She stopped, grimacing.

Again I waited.

She sighed. "I feel a little awkward telling you all this. Jim was a very private guy. He didn't like to talk about this stuff."

"That's exactly why I wanted to talk to you."

She nodded, acknowledging the point. "Okay. Well, I think he felt kind of tag-teamed by the two of them. They were the owners, and sometimes they apparently made that clear to him. There was a hierarchy there, they were on one level—the owners and partners, who had their way of doing things —and he was below them, just an employee. He felt that to keep the job he had no recourse but to do their bidding. And he wanted to keep the money flowing, to keep Jill happy, with the hope he could get back with his girls. He was caught between a rock and a hard place."

"So it was the job that brought him to the therapy group?"

"The job, and missing his girls. Plus he was pretty lonely. Jill wanted nothing to do with him. He felt abandoned and alone."

"Which is how you became friends with him?"

She nodded. "Yeah. He needed a friend. And I became that friend."

"Did you need one also?"

She scowled. "Is that relevant?"

"I'm just trying to understand the circumstances. Jim needed you to talk to about his situation. Did you have a situation you needed to talk to him about?"

"Well, yes. Why else would a person go to a therapy group?"

"Was he helping?"

"He was a good listener. No one could really solve my

problems. But being able to talk about them helped."

I hesitated. "I know it's none of my business, but I can't help being curious. Can you say anything about what your problems were?"

She frowned, sighing. "It's a little complicated. You'd have to understand my history."

I cocked my head in a listening position. A few moments passed; I could tell she was weighing what if anything to say.

"Okay. I'll give you a quick overview." She looked down, as though gathering herself, then back up. "I didn't have a great childhood."

"In what sense?"

"A lot of senses. My parents were poor. We lived on the wrong side of the tracks. I got made fun of at school for the clothes I wore."

"That's awful."

"And when I got a little older, there were other problems." Again I waited. "It gets a little personal. You might have noticed that nature was kind to me in certain ways." She rolled her eyes, as if dismissing this. "Which tended to bring the wrong kind of attention, especially at that age."

"What age do you mean?"

"Twelve. Thirteen."

"Boys in your class?"

"Yeah. But it was more the…men."

"Men?"

"One in particular. An uncle."

"Eeew."

"It wasn't pretty. He was a big guy, and he was a genius at coming by the house when my parents weren't there, like after school while they were still at work."

"Oh, god."

"I did my best to fight him off. But it was a losing battle."

"Jeez. Karen."

"It ended eventually. I fought him so hard one time that I got pretty beat up, cuts and bruises, and when I went to the emergency room to get treated, they asked me a lot of questions. I told them what was going on, and they got the guy locked up. But that didn't happen as soon as it should have." She paused and looked away, as though considering whether to continue, then back at me. "I learned early what having an abortion is like. I hated doing it, but the alternative was to have my uncle's baby."

"Aargh." I didn't know what else to say.

"They got me on birth control after that; just wish it had been earlier."

I sighed. "That's the kind of thing it's hard to hear about."

"And it didn't really end there. That taught me what men were after, and that I could attract them pretty much at will. So I began using that to get things I wanted."

"Like?"

"The things my parents couldn't afford. Clothes. Jewelry. Nice restaurants. All of which came with a price." She ran her hand across her face, where I noticed a bit of moisture on one cheek.

I waited for her to dry her eyes. "I'm sorry about all that, Karen. And thanks for being so open. You didn't have to tell me that. It's appreciated. It's great you found Jim's shoulder to lean on. It's hard for all of us who knew him to believe he's gone."

She nodded. I waited briefly to move on before asking: "Can I touch on one more thing?"

She pulled a tissue out of her pocket and blew her nose, then waited.

"I need to learn more about the Cantons. Can you give me any details of what Jim said about them?"

She frowned. "I've already pretty much told you. What kind of details?"

"What about their own relationship?"

"They were pretty tight, I think. Jim said he couldn't detect much light between them."

"In an emotional sense, or a business sense?"

"I think it was all about the business for them."

"So you don't think they were close...as a married couple?"

She considered this. "I didn't talk with Roberta much. I'd known Bruce previously. He used to come to me to get his hair cut. He was careful about what he said, but I think it was a difficult relationship."

"He stopped coming for his hair?"

"Yeah. I don't actually know why. But I figured that was his business."

"I got the sense, at the funeral, that you and Bruce were...?" I let the question hang there.

She rolled her eyes. "I figured you'd get around to that sooner or later." She sipped some more wine.

"And?"

"In some ways Bruce was a little like Jim. He needed more affection than he was getting at home."

"But you said he was focused on the business."

"He was. He definitely had that side. But he had another side also."

"And you were...?"

She scowled. "I guess I caught his fancy, like I usually do with men. I think he was jealous of Jim in that regard. I liked Jim; he could see that. We had become good friends. I think he envied that."

"And he was seeking your friendship also?"

She shrugged. "Yeah. Whatever that meant to him. Might be more than friendship."

"Thus all the touching…?"

She nodded. "Like a lot of men, he didn't know how to go about making friends."

"But with Jim…?"

She hesitated. "I thought this wasn't going to be personal?"

I shrugged. "Sorry. Forget it."

She stared at me, as though trying to make a decision. "Well, as long as I'm being open here, I might as well tell you. Jim and I were friends. That's it."

"He didn't want more than that?"

"I don't really know. He might have, at some level. But he was genuinely concerned about me as a person. He seemed to understand the trauma I'd been through, and that letting things go in that direction could demean what we had. He thought the best way to be helpful was to be my friend." She looked at me with a mixture of pain and warmth. "Which frankly, was pretty damn unusual for me. And I appreciated it."

I nodded. "Okay. Thanks for your honesty. That helps."

"How?"

"I'm not sure yet, but motivation is usually the key to solving these things. And this helps me understand some of the motivations involved."

Slim happened by and looked at our respective empty glasses. "Refills?"

I glanced at Karen. She shook her head. "I need to get home." She looked at me. "Assuming we're done?"

"Yeah. And…thanks."

16

When I got back to the house I poured myself a half-glass of gin over ice. Gin and tonics were nice, but they were slow. I needed to decompress. I jotted down some notes from what I'd learned: more confirmation about what a decent guy Jim was; some insights into Jill; information about the relationship between Bruce and Roberta Canton. And intriguing background on Karen Black.

There were no phone messages so I checked email: one from Zane.

```
    hi mr. t.  got some stuff for
you.  more to go, but call me if
you'd like a report on progress.
zane
```

I dialed his number.

"Yo. Mr. T."

"That was fast. We just talked this afternoon."

"I had a study hall last period at school."

"And no schoolwork?"

"Not that I felt like doing."

Same ol' Zane. He wasn't going to get into Harvard, but he might wind up making a fortune in Silicon Valley.

"So you've learned something already?'

"A little. Your friend Jesus, aka The Reverend, is

actually a guy named Zeke Zorias. He was born in Charleston, South Carolina in 1942. Never graduated from high school. Served a couple of tours in Vietnam, where he apparently suffered some brain damage in a landmine explosion. He's been variously diagnosed with PTSD, dissociative identity disorder, and schizophrenia. You have him right; he's a nut case."

"That's all you were able to learn in one afternoon?" I said ironically.

He ignored me. "He moved to California in 1990, has lived various places around the state, in LA for awhile, then the Valley—Bakersfield and Fresno—before making his way to San Jose in 2001. He first appeared in records up here about three years ago. Like you said, he's been homeless much of the time, in and out of three different local shelters. And you have his current residence correct, if you can call it that."

"That's a lot of information."

"He has a spotty criminal record—petty theft, breaking and entering, burglary—and has spent time in several county jails and a couple state prisons out here. These were mostly for nonviolent crimes, although one was for aggravated assault, just a couple years ago. So there may be a trend here; he may be going further around the bend as he ages. That can happen with brain damage."

I was shaking my head. "How did you learn all this, Zane?"

"Do you really want me to go into that?"

"Actually, no. You're amazing."

"I'm still digging."

"Well, while you're at it, can I add a second excavation project?"

"Sure."

"The Canton Insurance Agency. It's local. I'm just

wondering if there have ever been any complaints or suits brought against it. Also, what the owners are like, and if they have any criminal record. Bruce and Roberta Canton. That enough to go on?"

"More than. Should be an easy one."

"Great, and thanks!"

"No prob, Mr. T. Made my afternoon a little more interesting. Although I can't work on this tonight. Like I said, my girlfriend…"

"Understood, Zane. You have a good time."

"Thanks. Catch you tomorrow."

I hung up, wondering how young people knew how to do this stuff. Well, Zane at least. The kid had a talent, no question.

It seemed a little late in the day to pursue other lines of investigation. I added a few more jottings to my growing body of notes and put the notebook away. Time for some dinner.

I found myself wishing I'd picked Friday to see Violet; I had no idea what to prepare. In fact, 'prepare' was putting it a little elegantly; heat up? Or maybe not? Cold dinners weren't all that uncommon. I peered into the refrigerator. There was some of that great bread left. And cheese. More soup? I checked the cupboard: two cans, both tomato basil. At least that made the decision easy.

I opened one, plopped the contents into a saucepan, and fired up the burner. Then I ripped off a thick hunk of bread, added a chunk of cheese, and carried everything into the living room while the soup finished heating. I turned on the PBS news, which was just starting, and listened to the headlines before returning to the kitchen and pouring half the soup into a bowl. Another wild Friday night.

***

I had fallen asleep on the couch when the phone rang. Groggily I reached for it, knocking it on the floor. The message machine kicked in.

> Hey, old man. You there? I know figuring out how to answer one of those fancy talking devices is a challenge for you, but I have a little info I thought might be of interest. I'm around if you feel like talking. You know the number.

Tim at home on a Friday night? Was this syndrome catching? I called him back.

"Lew. That was quick."

"You caught me away from the phone."

"There's a thing called remotes now. They actually let you move them around."

I ignored him. "What are you doing in on a Friday night?"

"Relaxing at home?" His tone suggested this was a pretty dumb question.

"No date?"

"A couple of hot women tried to pry me out for the night, but I needed an evening to relax and recover."

"From?"

"A hard week of work, Lew. The newspaper business is pretty much nonstop. Plus it involved a lot of talking to you."

"Which brings us to the point. What have you got?"

"Well, first, I talked to Gus at the hospital again. Just to remind you, everything he tells me is strictly confidential. If one word gets out, my link is dead."

"Understood."

"They've made some progress in their internal investigation."

"To wit?"

"Several sets of fingerprints."

"Where? Whose?"

"First, there were some on the metal guardrails of the bed, and on the tray table."

"Still there? They hadn't sanitized the room?"

"They sealed it off as soon as the investigation began. Fortunately no one had used it since Jim."

"So, let me guess whose fingerprints: Jim's and some nurses."

"They've eliminated all the ones belonging to hospital staff."

"Then…who else's?"

"His daughters, both those places."

"That makes sense. And?"

"His wife's. No surprise there."

"Okay."

"But the curious part—this is where you might want to do a little sleuthing—is that there were three sets elsewhere."

"Stop teasing me."

"There were two sets *on* the ventilator."

"*On* the ventilator? Why would anyone be touching the ventilator?"

"Precisely."

"*Where* on the ventilator?"

"The cuff. Where the intubation tube connects to the ventilator's tubes."

"Are you going to tell me whose?"

"One was his wife's."

"Go on."

"The other was a young woman who runs a local

cosmetology shop. I believe her name is…" there was the sound of paper rattling.

"*Karen Black?*"

"Goddamn it, Lew. How the hell did you know that?"

"She runs a local cosmetology shop."

There was a muffled growl. "You know, sometimes…"

"Okay, okay. She was a friend of Jim's. I just had a drink with her."

"You had a *drink* with her."

"Is your hearing okay, Tim?"

"Well, tell me who she is, for God's sake."

"Jim met her in a therapy group. After his separation. They'd become friends. You know, supports for each other."

"I suppose that explains her presence in his hospital room. But not why her hands were on his ventilator."

"Good point. That's weird. So what about the third set?"

"They were on the room's door handle, from a gentleman who has enjoyed free room and board at a number of our exclusive public establishments. The ones where people aren't allowed to leave." There was more paper rustling. "He goes by the name Zeke Zorias."

"The Reverend? Oh my god."

"The Reverend? What are you talking about?"

"Jennifer at the hospital—Harve's friend—clued me into this guy. He's homeless, and crazy. He was hanging around the hospital when Jim was there. I tracked him down and talked to him."

"You *talked* to him?"

"You do need to get your hearing checked."

"Goddamn it. Fill me in."

"I suppose you could describe him as an entertaining sort. You know, the kind where you're not sure what's going to come out of his mouth, only that whatever it is will bear at best a passing resemblance to reality."

"What the hell was he doing there?"

"According to Jennifer, he'd been hanging around the hospital for reasons that aren't entirely clear, but seem to involve bestowing God's blessings on those in suffering."

"He's a Jesus freak?"

"It's more like he thinks he *is* Jesus."

"Jesus lived two thousand years ago."

"I didn't say it made any sense."

There was a pause. "Well, there was one more thing they found."

"I'm listening."

"A small buckle with a piece of leather strap in it. On the floor."

"Where on the floor?"

"Next to the ventilator. They can't think of any reason there would have been anything made of leather there. Those rooms get cleaned pretty often, so it hadn't been there long."

"Hmm."

"Oh, and there is one more bit of information I should probably share with you. Gus told me they've brought in the cops to investigate."

"Yeah, I'd heard that."

"You're kidding?" His voice held exasperation. "From who?"

"Your office mate. Don't you guys ever talk?"

"Harve has been out in the field all day. What did he tell you?"

"That they'd brought in the cops to investigate."

There was a quiet click. I called him back.

"You're a little sensitive. It's Friday night; you have a whole weekend to look forward to."

"It will start picking up when this conversation ends. So…to rephrase my question, what *else* did Harve tell you?"

"That this will give me a chance to renew my old friendships with the local men in blue?"

"That should be interesting."

"I don't dislike them, Tim. I'm just not sure how far they'll get."

"Well, you might offer them a hand. They know about the fingerprints. They're trying to find these people as we speak. Maybe you should clue *them* in."

I sighed. "Yeah. Okay."

"Try to contain your enthusiasm."

"I should probably add that Harve also mentioned they want to keep the investigation on the low down until they get things figured out."

"I've no doubt. Gus is very worried," Tim said.

"It's not just the hospital."

"Who else?"

"The cops themselves."

"Why?"

"Because they aren't likely to solve this thing?"

"Oh. Well, I suppose Harve's got a point." It seemed we shared a view of the local police force.

There was a brief pause. "Well, hey, Tim. Thanks for all the new information."

"Go to hell."

"No, I'm serious. That fingerprint stuff. The leather strap. Those seem like important clues."

"Yeah, okay. They do need looking into."

"So, have a lovely evening? You watching anything interesting?"

"Yes. The clock. Wondering when this conversation will end."

"As I recall, you called me."

"Won't happen again."

"Good night, Tim."

"Good night, Lew."

I hung up and pondered this new information. Then I jotted down a few more notes. And tried to decide if I should call the Sienna Police Department. Actually, I knew I *should* call them. I was just reluctant to help those guys when they were always exercising their bureaucratic prerogatives around me. I decided to think on it for the time being.

Earl, still lying next to me on the couch, was pawing me on the thigh, his request for petting. I ran my hand through his fur and behind his ears, and the purring started. He had a deep, reverberating voice; he would have made a good bass singer in a cat chorus.

After a while I got up and wandered out to the kitchen, looking for something more to eat. There was nothing even approaching dessert there. I made a mental note to do something about that. Then I wandered into the den.

I stared at the computer, contemplating what I might say to the one person I could think of I really wanted to reach. I sat down at the desk and let my fingers drum on the keyboard, knocking out nonsensical strings of letters. Then I erased them and started anew.

```
    Hi, Sweetie,
    Good to hear from you. It has to
be tiring, dealing with all those
little bundles of energy every
day. But you're really good at it.
Glad you enjoy them. I'm sure they
can sense it.
    I'd love to have you come up for
a few days around Easter. The
```

```
longer the better. I need some
help getting the early stuff put
into the garden. And I'd love one
of your home-cooked meals. Not to
mention a pie; you make terrific
pies. So let's plan on it.
    Have you heard from Nick lately?
I haven't had an email from him
for weeks. I trust he's okay back
there in Boston. I read their snow
is long gone and they're having
spring rains instead. Hope the two
of you are staying in touch.
    Just let me know when you're
coming. Can't wait.
    Love, Dad
```

She was wonderful, Kate. As was Nick. Just a difference between daughters and sons. She liked to stay closely in touch. Nick was just as connected, but didn't want the same frequency of communication. I loved them both more than they'd ever know, and I knew how proud Mary would be of them. And how proud I was.

How did it get down to exchanging emails, and an occasional visit, when there used to be so much energy and love contained in these four walls? The echoes from the past were still there, like the leftover radiation from the big bang that lingered through the universe. Always would be; it just got a little fainter as time passed. Adjusting to the quiet is hard. It's what happens to old people, I guess.

17

Saturday

The dawn found its way into my bedroom, casting soft shadows from the tree outside against the lowered shade. I glanced at the clock: six forty-five. Earl rested against my leg, snoring softly, still sound asleep. I had to decide whether to get up or try for more sleep, but sensed it wouldn't come, so gave up and climbed out of bed. Happens when you get old; along with a lot of other things, your ability to sleep well goes south. It can be frustrating as hell.

As I pulled my tired body out of bed I remembered the conversation with Tim, and the fact I had never quite gotten around to calling the cops. I went through the usual routine, got the paper and fixed coffee, and looked for something worth reading. As I sipped on the second cup of coffee I girded up my loins and reached for the phone. It wasn't quite seven-thirty, so I suspected the night crew was still on. A gruff female voice answered.

"Sienna Police Department."

"Hello. This is Lew Travis. I'm wondering if I could talk with an investigator?"

"An investigator?"

"An officer. I think I have some information that will be of interest. Related to a case you're working on."

"Can you be more specific?"

"I'd rather not. It's a little sensitive."

There was a momentary silence. "Okay, sir. There's no one here at the moment to help, but I can have someone call you. What was the name again?"

"Lew Travis. I'm with the paper."

"The *Sentinel*?" Apparently even the receptionist harbored skepticism on this count.

"Yes."

She sighed. "Okay. Your number?"

I gave it to her and we hung up. I wondered if they would actually call back. They liked talking to me about as much as I liked talking to them. Plus it was Saturday; they might be a little short-handed.

I wandered back upstairs, washing my face and shaving and trying to get more fully awake, then put on a flannel shirt and blue jeans. I glanced in the mirror and realized I needed to comb my hair, which I attacked with only partial success. Even that didn't function as well as it used to. Maybe its sense of independence was strengthened by the fact the ranks had thinned considerably and there were fewer fellow soldiers falling into line.

When I came back down Earl was at the back door meowing. Seemed early for his morning sojourn, but I wasn't privy to his cat logic so opened the back door and let him out. He had his own door that I'd rigged through a window in the den, but that required making his way down a little ladder to the ground. He preferred the ease and service of his personal doorman.

As I closed the door behind him the phone rang. I strode back into the kitchen and glanced at the clock—eight o'clock exactly—then looked at the phone's screen: Sienna Police Department. I picked up.

"Hello."

"Is Mr. Travis there?"

"Speaking."

"This is Tony Garcia with the Sienna Police. You asked for a callback?"

Must be my lucky morning. I liked Tony. He was the youngest guy on the police force, with more hair and less stomach than the rest.

"Hi, Tony. This is Lew. Do you remember me?"

There was a momentary silence, then a tone of recognition. "Mr. Travis. Sure. What's up?"

"I have some information I think will be of interest to you."

"Of what sort?"

"It pertains to the death of Jim Pearson. It's my understanding you found fingerprints on his ventilator. I happen to know all three people so identified; just thought you might need help tracking them down."

"We've already talked with Mrs. Pearson and Ms. Black. But we haven't yet located Mr. Zorias. Do you know his whereabouts?"

"Well, I know where he was staying a couple nights ago. I don't know if he's still there."

"All right. Where would that be?"

I gave him the address and filled him in on what I knew about the gentleman. And offered a tip. "Be careful of the dog when you go there. I thought I might be eaten whole."

"Thank you for that."

"And if he's not there, you might check the Methodist-Presbyterian church. Front pew."

"The front pew?"

"That seems to be the place where he likes to dispense his blessings."

"Sounds like you've been looking into this."

"Jim Pearson was a friend. I'm not happy about the manner in which he left us."

"What else do you know?"

"Nothing definitive. But I'm trying to learn more."

"It would be helpful if we could stay in touch if you do learn more."

"Sure, Tony. And vice versa?"

There was a brief hesitation. "Sure. And…thanks."

"No problem. I think you'll find Mr. Zorias an interesting character."

"He has quite a list of priors."

"His relationship with the real world seems a little hazy. Sometimes that goes hand in hand with scrapes with the law."

"Is he dangerous?"

"Hard to say. I think that's what we need to find out."

"Right. Well, thanks for the heads up."

"No problem."

I set the phone down carefully, wondering just how much more complicated my job had become, having to not only figure out exactly what happened to Jim, but also negotiate around the Sienna Police Department while doing so.

***

I pulled out my notes and sifted through them once more. Who did I most need additional information from? The cops should be tracking down The Reverend; now was not the time for that. There might be more from Karen Black—I was curious what she'd told the police—although I feared she might think I was the one who had given them her name. Who knew if she'd even talk to me again. There was more I wanted to learn about the Cantons, but Zane was working on that. Jennifer at the hospital had already been about as much help as anyone could ask, and I sensed she'd get in touch if anything new turned up. That left…well, one person came to mind.

As I pondered how to approach her, the phone rang. I glanced at the ID screen: an unexpected caller. "Hello, Emmett."

"Good to see you're up."

"It's nine-thirty."

"I've heard you're a late sleeper."

"From?"

"Can't say. But it relates to the reason for my call."

"You challenging me to a game of chess?"

"Nope. Not close. I believe I mentioned the other day that I've turned over a new leaf. And that it includes my social life, and I have a date tonight."

I groaned internally. I knew Emmett and Violet knew each other, and the fact they were both busy tonight was disturbing. This was not a topic I wanted to talk to Emmett about. "Yes."

"Could be big, Lew. As it happens, you know the lady in question. Who shall nevertheless go unnamed. I'm not a guy who is out to ruin a lady's reputation."

"What's your question, Emmett?"

"If I'm going to have success tonight, do you think I ought to take her to a really fancy restaurant, or some place more casual?"

Now I was really conflicted. I didn't like his use of the word 'success'. I had all too clear a sense of what that meant.

"It kind of depends how you *define* 'success', Emmett. Are you hoping this will develop into something long term, or just looking for a one-night stand?"

"I'm looking for a very hot first-night stand, to be followed by many more red-hot nights. I think this could be the one. I get the sense she's really into me."

Emmett was capable of the typical male braggadocio. On the other hand…

"Sounds like it doesn't really matter, if what you say is true. She's likely to rip your clothes off in the car and have at you right there."

There was a pause. "I was hoping for a serious response."

I sighed. "Here's my advice, Emmett. You need to tell her about yourself. Women want to feel they know a man before they get too close."

"Like what?"

I somehow couldn't help myself. "Your childhood, your past girlfriends in high school and college, your two marriages and divorces. You need to fill in the gaps in her knowledge of you."

"Really?"

"Well, I might go a little light on the sex itself. Just make it clear you're very skilled in that department."

"Skilled. Right" He sounded doubtful.

"Have you thought about what you're going to wear?"

"I wanted to ask you about that too."

"Women like their men to look good."

"Good point."

"Do you have a three-piece suit?"

He hesitated. "Well, yeah. It's a little dated."

"What style?"

"Kind of a yellow plaid."

"Sounds perfect."

"Really?"

"You asked my advice."

"Well, okay. What about the restaurant?"

"If you really want to impress her, I'd opt for the noisiest place you can find. That means it's popular. You don't want to end up in some stuffy French place with waiters draped all over you. And I'd keep the wine flowing. It may cost you a buck or two, but you don't want to skimp on that front."

"Okay."

"I think that's it. Go get 'em."

"Hey, thanks, buddy. You're a real pal."

"Why don't you give me a call in the morning, let me know how it went? We coaches like to know how our boys do."

"Okay. Wish me luck."

"Break a leg."

We hung up, and I leaned back in my chair, shaking my head. Emmett, Emmett. How could a man that old still not have learned some of these things? I chuckled to myself.

But as I sat there feeling smug, I sensed queasiness in my stomach. That was actually pretty mean. Emmett was a friend. Why had I done that?

Well, because no guy is going to help even a friend steal his woman. Say what? *'His woman'*? I didn't want other guys dating Violet, even though I hadn't been in touch with her for weeks? What kind of jerk was I? Sure, those weeks-long funks still sometimes haunted me, missing Mary. They probably always would. We'd had a long history together, one I'd never forget or stop missing; nothing was going to take that away.

But it *had* been ten years. Life goes on. And Violet was really more than I had any reason to hope for: pretty, smart, thoughtful, funny. Plus she had her own difficult history to deal with. I sat and contemplated this for a while, feeling stupid and mean.

Only gradually did my mind wander back to the case at hand. It drifted to all the questions I needed answers to, one after the other. One of which was Jim's marriage and how it had managed to go so off the rails. He and I even had some parallels that way; we'd both lost our wives and had sunk into depressions accordingly. Except Jill hadn't died. And I still didn't have a clear sense for why she'd thrown Jim out.

I finished the coffee and gathered my jacket and keys. It was time for another visit.

***

I pulled up in front of the big Victorian and glanced around. The shrubs had grown ragged around the front porch, and there were signs of missing paint here and there. From my recollection, this was not the sort of thing Jim would let go. But then he hadn't been living here for the last two years. And wasn't going to be.

I climbed the stairs to the front door and knocked. No response. I glanced at my watch; was I too early? It was nearly ten; wouldn't people be up by now, even on a Saturday? I knocked harder, and heard footsteps approaching.

The door swung open and there stood a pretty young blond woman, maybe twenty years old, in a bathrobe.

"Good morning," I said, a bit sheepishly. "Did I wake you?"

She shook her head. "No. I was up. What is it?"

"I'm Lew Travis. With the *Sentinel*? I'm putting together a story on your Dad, a retrospective. I talked to your Mom the other day, and had a few more questions. Is she around?"

"She just left on an errand. She said it wouldn't be long. Do you want to come in and wait?"

"Sure. Thanks." I stepped into the foyer and closed the door behind me. The young woman nodded to the couch in the front room, which served as a parlor.

159

"You must be Jim's daughter?"

"Yes." She held out her hand. "Rebecca."

I took it and shook. "You're in college, if memory serves?"

"I was. I'm taking a few weeks off to help out here."

"I'm so sorry about what happened."

She sighed. "It still doesn't seem real." She sounded tired. This couldn't be easy for her.

"I worked with him on some stories a few years ago. About the homeless folks in the area. He was very concerned about them."

She nodded. "Dad was concerned about everyone who needed help. That's just who he was." She blinked, her expression sad.

There was an awkward pause. I tried to think how to fill it.

"Well, since I'm looking for things for this retrospective, do you have anything you'd like to share about your Dad? Something you wouldn't mind having in the paper?"

She shrugged, then sat down on the other end of the couch and leaned her head back, rubbing her fingers over her eyes. I noticed they were moist. Then she looked at me.

"It's hard to pick just one. They're endless."

"How about something from when you were little?"

She looked away, thinking, then back. "Well, there were the suckers."

"Suckers?"

"Dad used to buy suckers. The little ones on sticks? All different flavors. And he'd hide them around the house for us to find. Everywhere. With our toys. In our clothes drawer. The pantry. We would sometimes find them under our pillow at night. I think it was his way of telling us we were always on his mind. And when he was away, it reminded us that he was thinking of us."

"Sounds like Jim."

"Yeah."

"It must have been hard, leaving for college?"

She frowned. "It was really hard. He sent me a postcard every week. Just a little note to remind me he was still there, thinking of me. And emails. He'd take pictures of things I liked here, just so I wouldn't forget. Parks. Shops we'd go to. Restaurants. He didn't want to lose touch."

I pondered whether to bring up the separation. It felt cruel given this conversation. I was saved from deciding when a noise came from the back of the house. Jill and the younger daughter appeared.

Jill looked at me and frowned. "Mr. Travis?"

"I came by to follow up on a couple things. Rebecca was nice enough to let me wait."

Jill scowled at Rebecca, who returned a look of confusion, as if asking, "Did I do something wrong?"

"You should really call before you drop by, Mr. Travis."

I nodded. "Apologies. I just happened to be in the neighborhood and…"

"What do you want to know?" Her tone was not friendly. She nodded toward Rebecca, a suggestion to leave. The younger daughter looked at Rebecca with an expression that suggested she was wondering what had gotten into her mother. They both left with a shrug and Jill sat down in a chair across from the couch, glancing at her watch.

Why you're being so difficult, I wanted to say. But I decided on discretion. "I realized I didn't really get any examples of Jim as a father, his relationship with your daughters." I glanced toward the door they'd just left through. "I remember how much he talked about them

161

when we worked together. I just thought that would be nice to include in the piece."

She rolled her eyes. "Jim was very close to the girls, yes."

"And was that not something that…?"

She scowled in apparent exasperation. "Of course it was something I approved of. Assuming that's where you were going with that." Her voice was tinged with anger.

"I'm sorry, Mrs. Pearson. I'm not trying to pry. I just thought…"

She sighed, then waved her hand dismissively. "It's fine. It's just a hard time. But yes, Jim doted on the girls. He was very attached to them."

"As I'm sure you were. Are."

"Well, yes, of course. Probably not quite as over…" She stopped. "Of course."

"The separation must have been hard on them?" This in the gentlest tone I could muster.

"I'm sure it was."

"It must have been difficult having to take care of them by yourself, when he…?"

"Not really. Rebecca was just starting college. And Adele was a junior. I think they were pretty capable of getting along without quite so much attention."

I nodded. "Was it hard for you?"

"Was what hard for me?"

"Not having Jim here?"

She exhaled in a burst. "We were separated, Mr. Travis. That has implications for how well a relationship has been going. Surely you must understand that?"

I nodded. "Of course. I didn't mean…"

"Jim left because things weren't working for us. We both needed time to get a better perspective on things."

"Uh huh."

"Of course it was a little hard on me." Her tone remained hard. "Probably harder on me than it was on him."

I cocked my head in inquiry.

"It didn't take all that long for Jim to find...other companionship."

"Ah."

"Of the sort men tend to seek out."

I frowned, with my innocent inquiring expression.

"I think you know what I mean. Don't all men? Their wives get a little older, not quite the nubile young things they married, and their fantasies turn to...I'm sure you know what I'm talking about."

"So...Jim had a girlfriend?"

"Hardly a girl."

"Are you referring to...?"

She stared at me. "Why is it men have so much trouble controlling their urges, Mr. Travis? Maybe you can clarify that for me."

"I'm not sure..."

"Any hot little number flits across their field of vision and they might as well be a kid at an ice cream parlor. They start salivating. It's like Pavlov's dogs."

I waited, not knowing how to respond.

"You may have seen Jim's girlfriend at the funeral. She was the one cozying up to his partner, now that Jim couldn't provide for her needs."

"Karen Black?"

"Oh. You *have* met her."

"I talked with her, yes."

"That must have been interesting."

I hesitated. It didn't seem like there was much point in my trying to affect her view of Karen Black.

"So, to get back to...?"

163

"Right. Jim's glorious fatherhood. Well, you name it. Dredge up any example you want of what the perfect father should be, and you'll doubtless be right."

I worked to keep my tone neutral. "Is there a particular one that comes to mind for you?"

"Presents. There were endless presents. He loved to buy them presents."

"What kind of presents?"

"All kinds. Dolls. Toys. Clothes. Jewelry. You name it, he bought it for them."

"And I sense you weren't in complete…?"

She looked at her watch again. "I think you probably have enough for your article, Mr. Travis. And I have some things I need to get to. Can we finish up here?" It was clear from her tone there was only one right answer.

"Of course." I put my notebook and pen away and stood. "Thanks for your time."

"Quite all right. Have a good day." She stood and waited for me to leave.

As I headed down the sidewalk toward the street, I couldn't get the thought out of my mind. Jim wasn't just a nice guy; in that marriage, he was a goddamn saint. He was an angel, living in his own personal hell.

18

When I got back to the house there was a phone message from Harve. As usual, it was short and simple:

```
Hey, Sherlock. Give me a call.
```

I did so, to his direct line. He picked up on the second ring.

"Walter Harvey."

"Walter Harvey? That sounds almost professional."

A pause. "That's what I get for not checking who it is before I pick up. One sentence and you've already lowered the quality of my morning."

"That was two sentences."

"What do you want?"

"You asked me to call."

"I withdraw the request. Good bye." There was a dial tone.

I called him back. "Jeez. What is it with you guys over there? Tim did the same thing to me."

"You bring that out in a person."

"My apologies, *Mr*. Harvey? Esteemed newspaper reporter. And sleuth extraordinaire."

"More like it."

"So? What have you got?"

"I've been talking with our men in blue."

"How did you manage to pull that off? They're usually taciturn around those of us from the fourth estate."

"I have a mole there."

"A mole? What do you have on him?"

"Her."

"Another one? What is it with you and women?"

"I listen to them. They find it refreshing."

"Okay. Fill me in."

"I believe Tim mentioned the fingerprints they found in Jim's room? Two on his ventilator, and a third on the doorknob?"

"Yes."

"Well, they've taken Karen Black into custody."

"Ouch. Although I guess that's not all that surprising. Those fingerprints on the ventilator cuff certainly raise questions. Have they charged her with anything?"

"No. They're questioning her. And they'd like to do the same with our messiah friend. Apparently he's been a little harder to locate."

"I provided them with two addresses."

"He doesn't seem to have regular sleeping habits."

"He wasn't at the church?"

"No. Nor the house you gave them. They're checking the homeless camps. But that brings up the main reason for my call. I think you'll find this interesting."

"Okay."

"Do you know Bob Richards? One of our photographers?"

"I've met him."

"Bob worked with Jim on one of his homelessness stories. I think it was a follow-up to the series the two of you did together. Since he'd known Jim, I mentioned Jim's death to him."

"Yeah?"

"He was of course shocked. And he started reflecting on the things they'd worked on together. Something interesting came out."

"Could we cut to the chase, Harve?"

"He has a picture of Jim talking with our friend The Reverend."

"*What?*"

"Yeah. It's in one of the homeless camps. You know Jim talked to a lot of those folks, and Bob wanted to give readers a sense for this."

"Okay."

"As we talked about this, Bob remembered a conversation Jim had with The Reverend. He was trying to reason with the man about his beliefs, to strengthen his links with reality, explaining that he couldn't really be Jesus. Apparently it did not go well. Instead of accepting Jim's logic, The Reverend took umbrage at the attempt. Bob remembers the guy yelling at Jim, his face red with anger. Like Jim was some kind of…I don't know, given the religious lens through which the guy sees everything … devil?"

"Wow."

"Bob showed me the picture. The expression on The Reverend's face is a dark angry scowl."

"Jeez, Harve. I had no idea they'd met."

"It struck me as perhaps significant, given the fact that The Reverend's fingerprints were on Jim's door handle?"

"Duh. Have you shared this with the cops?"

"Not yet, but I'm going to. I think they should know."

"Duh."

There was a pause. "I think one 'duh' is sufficient."

"Seemed like two different thoughts there, Harve."

Another pause. "Only if you're being picky."

"Just striving for clarity."

"Well, your clarifications aside, it struck me as pretty good work."

"I quite agree. You've outdone yourself, Dr."

"Dr.?"

"Watson? Sherlock's assistant?"

Another dial tone.

***

As I reflected on this development, I wondered where things stood with the police inquiry of Karen Black. I'd grown sympathetic to her, having learned what I had about her history, not to mention the way Jim had supported her. Plus Jim had needed a friend himself, and she seemed to have filled that need. Real friendships between men and women, not involving more than that, had been rare in my experience. I wondered where things stood with her interrogation.

I dialed the number of the Sienna Police Station. That gruff female voice answered.

"Is Officer Garcia in?" I asked innocently.

"Can I tell him who's calling?"

"Lew Travis."

A brief sigh. "Just a moment." I heard her shout into the room, "Is Tony around?" I couldn't hear the response. She came back on.

"He doesn't seem to be here at the moment, Mr. Travis. But there is someone else who would like to talk with you."

"Okay." I wondered who that would be.

"Mr. Travis." A male voice, clear and strong, and a bit officious. I sighed inwardly.

"Captain Christiansen. How are you?"

"I'm busy. I understand you provided some information to my staff about the whereabouts of a Mr. Zorias?"

"I did."

"We've been unable to locate him at either of the addresses you provided. I wonder if you know of any other locations we might check?"

"I learned of his whereabouts from some people at the homeless camp out on West Portal Road. You might check there."

"Some officers are checking there now. Any other suggestions?"

"Did you talk to the homeowner where he's been staying on Old Mine Road?"

"Yes, that's the first place we checked." A pause. "Appreciate the warning about the dog. He didn't seem well disposed toward police officers."

I almost felt sympathy for the guy. "Don't feel singled out."

"Any other thoughts?"

"Not really. But I do have a question."

"Yes?" Tone of irritation.

"I believe you're holding a Karen Black there?"

"Yes, we're questioning her."

"Would it be possible for me to talk with her?"

There was a long pause. "For what purpose?"

"I talked with her myself yesterday, trying to get a read on her relationship to the deceased. I think I established at least some minimal rapport. It's possible a follow-up conversation might prove helpful to your investigation."

Another pause. "I appreciate your interest in supporting our investigation, but I think we're fully capable of conducting such interviews."

"I'm not questioning that. It's just that people are sometimes more open with other people they trust. And someone in a police uniform can be intimidating. Especially when there is evidence potentially linking that person to a crime."

Still another pause. Then a grudging response. "Uh huh."

"Can I ask another question?"

A reluctant "Um hm."

"Has she asked for legal representation?"

"Yes."

"So she's already talked to a lawyer?"

"Not yet. It's being arranged."

"Would you have any objection to my talking to her? Assuming she agreed to that?"

This time the pause was protracted. "How about if my lead investigator listened in on such a conversation?"

"I couldn't agree to that if it was done without her knowledge. That would compromise my own credibility with her, were she to find out. Not to mention violate her Miranda rights. I'd in effect become an agent of the police. I'm just a friend of Jim Pearson's who is trying to figure out what happened." I paused. "But, I suppose if I learned of new clues—one's not related to Karen Black's possible involvement—I could share those."

He sighed, and there was a prolonged pause. Finally he spoke: "All right, Mr. Travis. When did you have in mind?"

"The sooner the better?"

Another sigh. "This has to be on the condition that you'll share any new relevant information with us that might help to resolve this thing. This is a police investigation, Mr. Travis, not a newspaper lead."

"Understood."

"All right. You know where we are."

We hung up and I headed out the back door.

***

170

I was ushered into a small conference room by a female police officer. Karen was sitting alone at a table, looking gloomy. She glanced up as I entered, and I noticed a slight lightening of her expression.

I sat down across from her. "Hi."

"What are you doing here?"

"They've given me permission to talk with you, if you'll agree."

"I don't think I should talk to anyone until my attorney is here."

I nodded. "That's sensible."

She frowned. "What do you want to talk about?"

"As you already know, my interest is in finding out how Jim died. It's that simple."

Her eyes narrowed. "How am I going to be any help, given the position I'm in? They seem to think I killed him."

"I understand that. I'd just like to hear your side of the story."

She stared at me, apparently gauging what to do. She glanced away for a moment, frowning, then back at me. "Can you guarantee no one else will be listening in?"

I looked at the female police officer still at the door. "Those are my instructions," she said. "This is a secure room. No one can listen in here."

"How can we be sure of that?" Karen asked, staring at the officer.

"The interrogation room where people can listen in has a large one-way mirror in it," the officer said. "So they can watch expressions also. This room has neither a window nor listening devices." Her finger made a brief circle around the four walls, then stopped palm up, indicating the obviousness of this.

Karen glanced at me inquiringly. I shrugged. I didn't

know any more than she did. But I was willing to take the woman at her word.

Finally Karen spoke. "Okay, but if that's not the case, I'll sue your asses off."

The officer nodded. "The Chief has agreed to this arrangement. You can trust him, he's an honest man."

I nodded. "I can confirm that." He *was* honest. He was just a pain in the ass.

Karen reluctantly sighed. "Okay."

The door closed and I sat down across from her.

19

Karen stared at me with an expression that was more than skeptical; accusatory, really.

I frowned. "What's that for?"

"I talk with you yesterday, opening up a little, and today I'm here being questioned as a suspect? Are you the reason I'm here?"

I leaned back, putting my hands up defensively. "No. I had nothing to do with this."

"Then why am I here?"

"You haven't heard why they picked you up?"

"All I know is that they said I needed to come down here for questioning related to Jim's death. And it wasn't a request; it was an order. They were going to arrest me if I hadn't agreed. I haven't been able to talk to my lawyer yet. I don't know why I'm under suspicion. I have a bunch of angry clients who are wondering why I'm not at my shop when they show up. What the hell is going on?"

I was surprised myself that the cops hadn't told her why she was there, and I wasn't sure, given that, whether I should either. But she was so obviously confused that it seemed unfair to me. Even a little un-American, to be held without any explanation of why.

"I don't know all the details, Karen. But I think I know what is probably their main reason for holding you." She scowled, waiting. "They've been collecting possible clues from Jim's hospital room to try to learn what happened. Where you visited him several times?"

"Three times, yes."

"And they found evidence of your presence there in a place they're suspicious about."

Her eyes narrowed. "I don't know where that could be. I sat in the visitor's chair next to him and talked with him. Well, talked *to* him; he couldn't talk back because of the tube. But he could nod and shake his head and converse that way. What's suspicious about that?"

"Did he ever touch the ventilator while you were there?"

She cocked her head to one side in a questioning gesture. "What?"

"Did Jim ever try to…adjust the ventilator?"

"Adjust it?"

"Like it was uncomfortable, not working right?"

"He didn't like it, that was pretty clear. I remember he asked a nurse—through a scribbled note—when he could get it taken out."

"What did she say?"

"It wasn't her decision, that it was up to the presiding physician. But his lungs were still pretty compromised, they weren't sure how he'd do on his own yet, so it probably wouldn't be that day."

"How did he react?"

"He didn't like it. He kind of grabbed the thing and shook it a little. Like you might something that is holding you in place that's uncomfortable."

"Did you ever touch it?"

She frowned. "I don't think so. Why?"

There was the sound of a cell phone ringing. She rolled her eyes and reached into her blue jeans pocket, pulled out her iPhone and looked at the window. She glanced back at me with a look of mild exasperation. "Give me a minute."

She turned away from the table and spoke quietly into the phone. I could only hear snatches. "…isn't a good time…at the police station…I'll explain later." She listened for a little while, then her voice took on a stronger tone. "I can't really talk here. If I get out of here I'll call you later. They think…" She appeared to have been cut off, listening again. After a bit she nodded, her eyes looking off in the distance as though she was considering something. "Well, I suppose that's a thought." She listened some more. "Yeah, okay. I'll give you a call when I get out of here." Then she nodded and ended the call.

I looked at her inquiringly.

She shook her head, waving her hand dismissively. "Not important."

I cocked my head, waited for her to say more.

"Just a friend."

I shrugged; it seemed clear she didn't want to reveal who it was.

"Where were we?" she asked.

"Talking about the ventilator. And whether you ever touched it."

She frowned, as though thinking.

"Try to remember. It might be important."

Suddenly her expression took on a look of recognition. "Oh my god."

"What?"

"That's it! He signaled for me to check the connector after the nurse left and he'd shaken it. I think he was worried about the Velcro strap, and that one of the tubes from the ventilator might have come loose."

"And?"

"I stood up and looked at it. It looked fine to me, I couldn't feel any air escaping, so I assured him it was okay."

"And when you looked at it…?"

Her eyes were wide. "Yes! I grasped it with one hand, so I could get a clear feel with my other hand whether there was air escaping. I was careful not to yank on it, but I did grasp it."

"Where on the ventilator?"

"On that connecter thing. Where the tubes come together. That's what he was worried about."

I nodded. "Well, that probably explains why you're here. They found your fingerprints on that cuff."

She leaned back, staring at me. "Wow."

"The cops haven't asked you about that themselves?"

"Not directly. Now that you've explained this, what they have asked about makes more sense. They've gone around the edges, asking me what I did while I was there, and a couple times they asked me something about the ventilator."

"Like what?"

"What I knew about ventilators, how they worked. And whether the tube was ever out of Jim's mouth while I was there. That sort of thing. Which it wasn't. But they never mentioned that my fingerprints were on the connector."

"Well, I think all you probably need to do is give this explanation to your lawyer when he gets here, and let him take it from there."

"She."

"What?"

"When she gets here."

"Ah. Apologies. Hard to adjust when you've lived seventy-two years."

She shook her head. "Forget it. You've given me a reason to feel some relief."

"As long as I'm here, can I ask you about something

else?"

Her eyes narrowed. "What?"

"Who else visited Jim while you were there?"

"I think you asked me that before. His daughters were there one of the times. I didn't stay long that time. I got the sense they weren't comfortable with my presence. I tried to explain to them I was just a friend, but they wanted to be alone with him."

"Anyone else?"

She looked away, considering the question. "No. Just the nurses."

"Did you ever see an old guy in the hallway outside Jim's room? Wearing a jacket and tie, but kind of unkempt?"

"You mean that homeless guy?"

"Yes."

"Yeah, I saw him. I couldn't understand why he was there, why the hospital let him walk around. I don't think he was completely...together."

"Why do you say that?"

"He'd be mumbling to himself, and when I passed him in the hallway, he'd look at me and put his hands into a prayer position, say 'God be with you' or something like that. He didn't seem to belong there."

"Was he outside Jim's room when you saw him?"

She shook her head. "No. He was on Jim's floor, but down the hall. Why?"

"Just curious. I'm trying to gather as many clues as I can about who was around there. Did you see anyone else?"

"There were other people in the halls, sure. Visitors of other patients. Although not very many, frankly."

"Do any in particular come to mind?"

Again she looked away, then back. "There was a little

kid, there with his mother I think. Cute little guy. He seemed really shy. I said hi to him once and he just glanced at me and kept going, like he was afraid of me."

"Do you remember which day?"

"Which day?"

"As I understand it, Jim was there three days. The day he was admitted and put on the ventilator. The next day. And the day he died."

She frowned. "I think it was the last time I visited. So it would have been the day he died."

I nodded. "Okay."

"Why does that matter?"

"Probably doesn't. But you never know. Sometimes the sequence of events is important."

"So, Lew, can I ask *you* something? You sound like you're doing more than collecting information for a retrospective on Jim's life."

I shrugged. "Maybe."

"Are you an investigator of some kind?"

"An investigative reporter."

"You seem more like a private eye. Like someone who gets paid to investigate crimes."

"No one is paying me. But I do want to find out how Jim died. He was a good man, and I think this deserves an answer."

She nodded. "Too good, sometimes."

I cocked my head, waiting for more.

"He was trying to do right by everyone he knew. He was kind of…an angel, really." Said in a wistful tone.

"Are you saying…?"

She sighed. "We kind of touched on this at the bar. He was a man I think almost any woman could feel close to. That usually leads to other things. But not with him." She looked out the window with a wistful expression, then back

178

at me. "I sensed he wanted to sometimes. I suppose he needed that as much as any guy. He just wouldn't give in to that urge. He lived on a higher plane."

"You really liked him, didn't you?"

She stared directly at me and spoke with genuine passion. "I would have done anything for that man. Anything."

***

When I got back to the house it was nearly noon. There was a phone message waiting, from a number I didn't recognize. I punched the button.

```
    Hello, Mr. Travis. This is Nancy
Wilson. You stopped by the other
day to ask about a friend of yours
who had died in the hospital. I
wonder if you could give me a
call?
```

I did so. She answered on the fourth ring, slightly breathless. "Hello."

"Nancy? This is Lew Travis. Did I call at a bad time?"

She took a couple deep breaths. "No. This is fine. Just let me catch my breath."

"You just come in or something?"

"I was outside playing catch with Jeremy. He gives me quite a workout."

"He likes baseball?"

"He *loves* baseball."

"So, what can I do for you?"

Her breathing was returning to normal. "It's kind of a hunch, more than anything."

"Okay."

"Jeremy has been having nightmares lately. Really scary ones, where he comes into my room terrified. Takes me awhile to get him calmed down enough to relax. And he refuses to go back to his room."

"Yeah?" It wasn't clear to me how this was relevant, but I was curious.

"He won't talk much about the dreams, except to say it's somebody trying to get him."

"Okay."

"When I try to get him to talk more, he clams up, like he's too afraid to talk about it."

"Kids that age can be like that. I remember my son had problems with nightmares around then. They're beginning to think of themselves as the guardians of their house, and there can be scary things out there."

"Yes. Well, you're probably wondering how this relates to you."

"Sort of."

"I think these dreams originated when I was in the hospital. He seemed different after that, more quiet and reserved. I've asked him several times about it, keep reassuring him that I'm fine, the abscess has gone away and I'm all healed. But I'm getting the sense this may not be about me."

"What do you think it is?"

"I think something happened to him in the hospital that really scared him. So much that he can't even talk about it. And I think it's what's causing these nightmares."

"Tell me again what happens."

"He won't say much when he comes in at night, just that someone mean is after him."

"Chasing him?"

"I guess. He won't say anything more."

"Do you think it would help for me to talk with him?"

"I've been trying to decide. I'm kind of thinking probably not. He doesn't know you, and he will barely talk to me. And this only happens after these nightmares."

"Well…"

"Yeah. I'm sorry. I'm probably just wasting your time."

"No, you're not wasting my time. I appreciate you thinking of me. Maybe the best thing for the time being is to see if he tells you more. And if you get a clearer sense for what might have happened at the hospital—assuming the nightmares are related—we can talk then?"

She sighed. "Yeah. Okay. I'm just so worried about him."

"I can see why. Let's hope something more comes out. And if it does, this could be really helpful, Nancy."

"So you don't think I'm crazy?"

"You said you're playing catch with him?"

"Yeah. I should get back out there, he's probably wondering what happened to me."

"Any mom who's willing to play catch with her son is as far from crazy as I've known."

She chuckled. "I should probably have my head examined. He's got a pretty good arm on him. Anyway, thanks."

20

When I hung up I decided to check email. There was the usual spam: a free vacation to Tahiti if I'd just send them a thousand dollar refundable deposit to hold the reservation; an offer to loan me a thousand dollars interest free for a year if I opened an account at the bank; and a free tote bag if I'd renew a subscription within the next two weeks. And one from Zane.

```
    mr. t. got some more info for
you. call me when you'd like to
talk.
```

He picked up on the second ring.

"Yo. Mr. T. How you doin'?"

"Hi, Zane. How'd the date go?"

"Date?"

"With your woman last night?"

"Oh, yeah. We don't 'date'; we're tight. Nothin' much happnin'. Just hung out with some friends."

"Late one?"

"Nah. Decided to call it a night early. Got to bed around midnight."

"Midnight. That's early?"

"If there's something going on, that's when things usually get started. But it was a quiet one."

"So, you said you had something for me?"

"Yeah. You asked me to look into the Canton business?"

"Right. But before you go into it, since you're putting in all this time for me, maybe we should meet somewhere so I can pay you?"

"Where did you have in mind?"

"How about that diner on Oak Street? I could use some lunch?'

"Okay."

"Do you need a ride?"

"It's not that far. I can just bike it."

"See you there."

The diner was only a few blocks away, so I decided to walk, and when I got there I noticed an old bike locked up outside. I spotted Zane already sitting at a table looking at a menu. He was wearing loose fitting khakis and a gray hoodie. He needed a haircut, and it looked like he was trying to grow a goatee.

I entered and sat down across from him. "That a beard you're growing, Zane?"

He felt the soft hairs beginning to emerge on his chin. "Has a ways to go."

"Have to start somewhere."

"So, what are you going to have, Mr. T?" He was studying the menu.

I glanced at it as a stocky middle-aged woman with a pad in one hand and pencil behind her ear headed our way. I knew this waitress; she didn't take prisoners. I quickly surveyed the options.

She strode up to the table. "Gentlemen. What's it going to be today?" She held the pencil above the pad, ready to write.

"Double bacon cheeseburger, garlic fries, and a

strawberry shake," Zane said.

She jotted this down and looked at me.

"Are you still serving breakfast?"

"All day." She nodded to a sign above the counter, her tone suggesting I might have figured this out for myself.

"How about the huevos rancheros and a cup of coffee, black?"

"You got it." She marched over to a circular device and clipped the order on it, twirling it around so the chef could see.

I turned back to Zane. "So, what have you got?"

"The Cantons; let's see. They incorporated eleven years ago. An S corporation. This protects them from liability, and can save them taxes. They started small, but grew substantially as the years went by. Last year they grossed over a million dollars."

"Impressive."

"Yeah, there's a reason so many people go into selling insurance."

"What kind of insurance do they handle?"

"Mostly home and life. They act as local brokers for big national firms. They get a percentage of every policy they sell. The bigger the policy, the more they make. They use whatever company offers the kind of coverage their customers are looking for. And the one that pays them the most, of course."

"Are you suggesting they don't try to find the best deal for their customers?"

"I didn't really look at comparison prices. But they tend to use mostly one or two firms, so I'm guessing they have things worked out with them for a better percentage."

"What kind of life insurance?"

"There are two main varieties: term and whole life. They sell mostly whole life. Which isn't just insurance; it's a form of investment. Again, I'm no expert, but they generally don't get high ratings compared with other kinds of investments. I think they're called whole life because the premiums go on for practically your whole life." He rolled his eyes. "And even though the returns are pretty modest, once a person is hooked in and has money invested, they're usually reluctant to stop. It's kind of a racket."

I nodded.

"And even that modest return isn't really guaranteed. These companies can fail. There is no FDIC standing behind such investments, just individual states, which vary in how much backing they provide. Like everything else, the people who never seem to lose are the bigwigs at the head of these companies, even if the company itself fails."

I frowned.

Zane looked suddenly uneasy. "You don't have a …?"

I shook my head. "No reason for me to have life insurance, Zane. I don't have anyone to protect, and I don't have enough money for anyone to care about bilking me. I have a car that's twenty years old and a little bungalow that's paid for. That's about it."

"Didn't want to alarm you."

"How'd you learn all this?"

"I'm taking a course called 'Practical Business" in school. It covers the kinds of stuff you need to know to function as an adult. Investments, credit cards, checking accounts, that kind of stuff."

"Wish they'd had that when I was in high school."

"It's more interesting than most the other stuff," he said. "It actually applies to your life."

"So, to get back to the Cantons. They've been making a lot of money, especially lately. What did you learn about how their firm operates?"

"Their income goes into a corporate account against

which they can both write checks. They just have to file a tax return that shows how much the business made, back out all the expenses they can come up with, and pay taxes on the profits."

"What kind of expenses?"

"Hard to believe how much traveling they do, given the fact it's a local operation. Conferences all over the place: the Caribbean, Hawaii, Florida. And food. They claim they're spending tens of thousands of dollars taking clients out for meals."

"And that's legal?"

"As long as they have receipts, and don't get audited, they can claim whatever they want. And frankly, almost no one as small as this gets audited."

"Are you saying they're cheating on their taxes?"

"Who knows? But they seem to be living a good life while paying a pretty small tax bill."

"How did you get access to all this, Zane? Sounds like you saw their actual tax return. You didn't hack into the IRS did you?"

"No way. That can get you into big trouble. Actually, it was pretty easy. They attached a draft of their return to an email they sent to their CPA. All I had to do was hack into their email account."

"How did you do that?"

He looked at me slyly. "Do you really want…?"

I waved him off. "No, forget it. Okay, let's move on. Jim was an employee. What did you learn about their employees?"

"Your friend was the only one. No secretary or receptionist, no accountant, no one else. It's almost as if they didn't want anyone else to have access to any of the company's records."

"Could you see how much Jim was making?"

"His salary was only a couple thou a month. Most of what he made must have been from his commissions. Your friend was kind of out there on his own. His income was pretty much dependent on what he could sell."

"Benefits? Health insurance?"

"If you're as small as they are, you don't have to offer any, and they didn't. Your friend had to cover those himself. There is also no retirement plan."

"Hmm."

"There's one other thing I thought you might find interesting. Roberta Canton handles all the legal arrangements. It's her signature on all of the official documents."

"She explained that to me when I talked with them. She said Bruce is the people person, handles most of the contacts with their customers, while her role is pretty much behind the scenes. Does that matter?"

"Not as long as they trust each other."

"Are you suggesting…?"

"She seems to have the power of attorney. I guess that was to simplify things for them, so he doesn't have to sign everything that comes along."

"Okay."

"And one more thing. There's a clause in there about how the firm can be dissolved, if and when that's of interest. This may be standard boilerplate, I'm not an expert on corporate law, but it struck me as a little strange."

"What does it say?"

"If either party is found guilty of a crime, all assets revert to the other party during any period of incarceration."

"I suppose that makes sense. The person who's incarcerated won't be in a position to manage the company or its assets."

"Yeah." His tone suggested he wasn't quite buying this.

"Did you find all this in their email also?"

He shook his head. "This stuff goes back to their incorporation. I had to dig it out of their attorney's records."

I stared at him. "I'm not going to ask."

He smiled. "There isn't much that's really private with electronic communication. If you're good at this."

"So what do I owe you?"

He frowned. "I never know what to charge you, Mr. T. Why don't you just pay me what you think it's worth?"

"That doesn't sound like something they taught you in that practical business course. Don't they cover sticking it to the client?"

He chuckled. "I don't really think of you as a client. You're the first person who ever hired me. And I haven't forgotten that time you bailed me out when I was at that restaurant with that girl and didn't have any money with me."

I pulled out my wallet and dug out five twenties.

He took the bills with raised eyebrows. "Wow. Thanks."

"Just want you to know how much I value your help. Want to tackle one more?"

He shrugged. "Sure."

"This one isn't about business. It's something personal."

"Okay."

"This thing I'm working on, it involves a marital separation between the dead guy I was friends with and his wife. I'd like to know more about his wife. Her name is Jill Pearson. Think you could take a look at her emails over the past while?"

"How long a while?"

"They were separated a couple years ago."

"What are you looking for? That could be a lot of email."

"The separation seems to have been pretty nasty. I'm curious what the main issues were."

"Okay."

"I'd also like to know who else she corresponds with regularly. And what kinds of things they talk about."

His eyes narrowed. "Is this about an affair, Mr. T?"

I shrugged. "I don't know. It might be. I do know she's still angry. I'm curious just how angry. And why this continues to be the case, after two years."

"I can do some quick scanning. At least see who she's most in touch with. That might be most revealing."

I nodded. "Okay."

"Can it wait just a bit?"

"More woman stuff?"

"No, I'm playing in a chess tournament this afternoon."

"Ah, chess. Aren't you president of the club or something?"

"No, I'm VP. But I want to take this guy. He bugs me."

"Why?"

"He's one of those arrogant Ivy League types. Blond, handsome. Wears fancy shirts and topsiders. Thinks he's god's gift to women."

I nodded. "Good luck."

Lunch arrived and he gobbled up his burger and fries, using the milkshake to wash it down. I'd barely started on my huevos rancheros when he'd finished. He glanced at his watch, then wiped his mouth with the paper napkin and pushed back from the table.

"I'm sorry, Mr. T. I need to get going."

"No problem. Go get 'em." I made a shooing motion.

"Thanks. I'll get back to you." And he was gone.

189

I sat there amazed at what a kid who was barely passing enough classes to make it through high school could learn when he was really interested in something, and what a business future he probably had. He should be teaching a course about computers and the Internet, something none of his teachers were probably nearly as qualified to do.

***

I was sleepy when I got back to the house. Happens these days. It's like we return to our early years when we get old. When you're a kid, you stop taking naps past a certain age. Then you start again as you wind down. I'm not complaining, it always feels good, gives you a new level of energy when you wake up. Mine were usually short.

This one was shorter than usual. I'd barely fallen asleep when the phone rang. I groggily reached for it, still lying on the couch, and glanced at the screen: *The Sentinel*. I pushed the talk button and answered in my sleep-deadened state.

There was a momentary silence. "I know you're sleeping late these days, but surely you're not still in bed?"

"They're called naps, Harve. When you actually get to take one."

"Want to call me back?"

"No. Once the edge is gone, it won't come back. What's up?" I sat up and rubbed my eyes.

"I just touched base with my contact down at police central."

"Let me guess. They're confused?"

"Karen Black's attorney arrived and got her released. Apparently whatever you talked to her about helped spring her. I'd had the sense they were about to charge her with something, but it sounds like that possibility has faded."

190

"Karen did have an explanation for her fingerprints being on Jim's ventilator which seemed legitimate. So who are they looking at now?"

"She didn't say directly, but I got the sense there is someone."

"Oh, right; she. Your female mole."

"I'm a reporter, Lew. I need contacts however I can get them. Women seem to like men who actually think they're worth talking to about serious things."

"You're a shrewd man, Harve. Do you know who the new suspect might be?"

"No. But I know they've been looking for your religious friend. That seems like a good bet."

"Assuming he's still in the area. If he's the culprit he might be on the lam."

"Maybe. But since he thinks he's the son of God, it hardly seems likely a little problem like the Sienna Police would cause him much consternation."

"Although you never know with these crazy people. Sometimes they're crazy like a fox."

"Has he impressed you as someone who's crazy like a fox?"

I considered this. "Maybe like a cow?"

He chuckled. "I think they're also talking with Jill Pearson. Based on her fingerprints being on Jim's ventilator."

"Could be the same reason Karen's were there."

"Yes. Or not."

"She does still hold a lot of vitriol for the guy."

"The majority of homicides are committed by someone close to the victim."

"I suppose no one was closer."

"What did she give you when you talked with her last?"

"Mostly hostility."

191

"Toward Jim?"

"Yeah. And me."

"Your usual charms didn't work?"

"There were absolutely no signs that whatever charms I managed to summon had the slightest effect. She just wanted me to leave."

"Well, at least you can't fault her on her judgment of character."

I hung up this time. Seemed like it was my turn.

21

I leaned back on the couch and let my head rest on a cushion, trying to think what I could do next. Somehow in spite of all the information I'd gathered I still felt like I wasn't much closer to figuring this out. I ran over the possibilities in my mind. There was Karen Black. On the one had, she seemed an unlikely suspect, she was clearly so fond of Jim. But who knows, it seemed like she'd do whatever he wanted, even if it meant ending his life. There was also that phone call that interrupted our discussion at the police station, which left me doubtful. Why had she been so coy about who had called her?

Then there was The Reverend. Knowing he'd known Jim, and had gotten into an argument with him about whether he was the voice of Jesus, something critical to his own identity, sounded a little scary. He *was* scary. It was clear that vengeance was part of his philosophy of religion, and that he seemed capable of carrying a grudge. I found people who thought they spoke for God among the creepiest on the planet.

Then there were the Cantons. While they had helped Jim succeed financially, and seemed to be saying and doing all the right things, I retained a sense of discomfort there. Sure, it was nice of Bruce to have spoken at his ceremony, and for them to have given Jill something to honor Jim's passing. Still, they had a different attitude about the

business and making money than Jim had, and there had
been some tensions around that. And then there was
Bruce's apparent crush on Karen. That could create
jealousy. Not to mention Roberta's possible jealousy
concerning Bruce's interest in Karen.

Then there was Jill herself. I'd rarely heard a woman so
angry toward a man, especially one who had just died. She
still held deep feelings of hostility toward Jim, for reasons
that weren't entirely clear to me. Karen had suggested that
this sprang from wanting more money—how had Karen put
it, she liked 'nice' things. More than one marriage had
foundered on that rock. But was there something more?
Why were her feelings so different from Jim's daughters?

And there were other possibilities, perhaps ones I
hadn't even thought of? Someone at the hospital? Some
client of Jim's? An accomplice of one of the above? Or
pure random chance? It seemed like there were endless
random killings these days, they made the news all the
time. With the easy access of guns, and a ready supply of
people going off the rails for no discernable reason, who
knew what the possibilities were?

I tried to think where I could go for more clues, ones
that would provide some definitive evidence and point in a
clear direction. The cops seemed to be hot on The
Reverend's trail; assuming they tracked him down, that
might lead somewhere. I had Zane working on Jill to see if
I could learn anything from her emails; if there were clues
there, Zane would find them. Maybe more would come out
of the hospital investigation; I hadn't heard from Tim for a
while. Where else could I turn?

As though in answer to my question, the phone rang. I
checked the caller ID: Sienna Memorial Hospital.

"Hello?"

"Mr. Travis?"

"Jennifer?"

"Do you have a minute?"

"Sure. What's up?"

"As usual, I'm on a short break here, but I just overheard two police officers talking out in the hall. It's probably not my place to be sharing their conversation with others, but I couldn't help myself."

"Okay."

"They were talking about Jim's ventilator. I think they've found another clue."

"Really?"

"If I understood—I just caught a couple snatches as I was walking past them—I heard one say, 'caught in the Velcro'."

"Caught in the Velcro?"

"Yes. And the other one clarified, 'a *blond* hair'? With emphasis on the word 'blond'."

"To which you inferred, they'd found a blond hair in the Velcro on Jim's ventilator?"

"Yes."

"That is interesting."

"And the thing that made it especially interesting for me is that we don't have any blond nurses who work this floor. We all have dark hair."

"Meaning that it must be...?"

"This is your department. I'm no investigator. But I think there was only one woman who was in there with Jim who had blond hair."

"Jill."

"Uh huh."

I took it to the obvious next step. "And the fact it was caught *in* the Velcro means the Velcro must have been unfastened."

"It seemed kind of important. That's why I called."

195

"You're a treasure, Jennifer."

"I don't know if it will make a difference, Mr. Travis. But there has to be *some* explanation for Jim's death."

"Exactly."

"Well, hey, I do need to get back to work."

"Thanks, Jennifer."

I set the phone down, contemplating this new development. When it rang again. I looked at the screen ID, then picked up.

"Harve. The reporter extraordinaire. That was quick."

"Could we at least start out this conversation without the sarcasm?"

"You're a hard guy to satisfy. If I'm sarcastic you hang up, and if I'm not, you think I am anyway."

"Maybe that's because you're *always* sarcastic."

"Consistency isn't a bad thing. Besides, it's a sign of affection. You don't say these things to someone who won't understand they're in jest."

There was a pause. "I think there was a compliment in there somewhere?"

"Your reason for calling?"

"I just got another call from my friend at the police station."

"That lady you have something on?"

"I don't...never mind. They found The Reverend."

"Really? Are they learning anything?"

"No, because he won't stop hurling angry epithets at them, mostly taken from the Bible."

"He does know his Bible."

"Well, she wondered if maybe I'd ask you if you'd consider coming down to talk to him?"

"Me? Why?"

"Well, you know him."

"Not really."

"Actually, I think they're desperate. They can't get him to shut up."

"And they think I can?"

"Maybe better than them. As you pointed out with Karen Black, you don't wear a police uniform, which might make you less threatening."

"You're serious? They want me to come down there and try to get information from this whack job?"

"That seemed to be her gist. I told her I didn't think it was a good idea."

"Wait a minute. Why not?"

"I should get back to work."

"Harve?"

A dial tone came on the line.

***

I reluctantly headed out to the garage and down to the station, trying to think what I could possibly say to The Reverend that would do any good. As I walked into the station I could hear the shouts coming from the lockup in back.

"God is a wrathful God! He that believeth not the Son shall not see life! The wrath of God will be upon the children of disobedience! There can be no compromise with wickedness! He will cast the evildoers from his kingdom! There will be fire and brimstone cast down from the heavens upon the likes of you! Great is the wrath of the Lord!"

Even out in the reception area it was loud. The young woman who greeted me there rolled her eyes as I approached.

"Hi, Mr. Travis." It was a warmer greeting than I was used to here.

197

"I understand you would like me to try to have a conversation with someone you have in custody?"

She nodded. "Yes." In an exasperated tone. "I believe the chief would like to talk with you first. Let me call him." She punched a button and spoke quietly into the phone.

I waited, and in a moment John Christiansen appeared from in back and strode up to the counter. "Hello, Mr. Travis. Please come on back." His voice held irritation.

I followed him to a small conference room, the one where I had talked with Karen. We sat down across from each other.

"Your colleague at the paper tells us you know this...gentleman?"

I nodded.

"Well, we're not having much luck talking with him. He seems more interested in shouting his...thoughts to us, than in answering our questions. I know this is a little irregular—especially twice in one day—but we'd be appreciative if you would make an attempt."

"I can try. But I make no promises. He wasn't exactly what you would call evidence-based in his conversation with me either. I wouldn't get my hopes up."

"That's understood. But we'd appreciate any attempt you could make. We're going to take him into the official interrogation room so we can listen in, if you have no objection."

"Has he been advised of his rights?"

"Of course. He's declined attorney assistance. Says God will be his judge."

I nodded, still reluctant. "I still don't think you should listen in. Again, that in effect makes me an arm of the police. But I will offer to share anything relevant that comes up, assuming it doesn't obviously implicate him."

Christiansen frowned. It was clear he didn't like these

conditions. But what choice did he have? He glanced toward the lockup in back as another fusillade of oaths issued forth, then nodded reluctantly: "You drive a hard bargain, Travis. But okay."

I sat down and waited. The shouts grew louder as he approached, until a female officer opened the door and gently nudged him in. He looked at me with a frightened expression, his eyes wide and hair flying in all directions.

"Hello, Reverend," I said. I held out my hand.

He stared at me for a moment, then seemed to ease, edging into the room while watching me guardedly. He finally reached out and took my hand, then put his other hand over mine, in what would normally be a comforting gesture, looking me in the eye. "How are you, my son?"

"I'm all right. Thank you, Father. Would you like a seat?" I nodded to the chairs across the table.

He looked around warily, then cautiously found his way to the other side and sat down. "What is it you wish to talk to me about, my son?"

"I come seeking your help, Father."

He cocked his head to one side in a listening gesture. "Yes?"

"You may recall our conversation yesterday? How I recently lost a close friend?"

"I do indeed. Have you found solace in the Lord?"

"Yes. That has helped. Thank you for your guidance."

"I am but the messenger. I have no power but in the Lord."

"But you carry His thoughts to us mere mortals, and give solace to those in need. That is a gift."

"Yes, I have been granted this gift."

I nodded, letting my eyes widen a bit in a questioning gesture. "I do wonder, how do you find those on whom to bestow this gift?"

"I go wherever I find pain. It is all around us."

"Does this include the sick?"

"That is where the greatest pain often lies. The Son is a miracle worker among the sick, as the Bible tells us."

"Such as those in our clinics and hospitals? You must wish to help them?"

He nodded. "I bestow His strength on those in need. Man's healing is weak in comparison with God's. Only God offers true healing."

"My friend was in great pain, even though he was in the hands of trained doctors. I wish you could have helped him."

"I do sometimes minister to those under medical care."

"Then you may remember him. His name was James. He was on a ventilator. He could not even breathe without help. But alas, even this could not save him."

His expression took on a guarded look. "We must accept God's will. He is all knowing. He takes all men at the appointed time."

"Is this something you hear in God's messages? When those appointed times arrive?"

He looked at me skeptically. "I hear His word in all matters."

"Does He sometimes ask your help?"

He nodded.

"Do you remember helping such a person? A man struggling to breathe and on a ventilator?"

His face darkened. "The Lord would not wish me to speak of this. It is not given to man to understand God's wishes. We must accept His all-knowing wisdom."

"But might He choose to call someone to Him at an appointed time?"

"Of course."

"And might He share this with you when such a time

arrived?"

He nodded beatifically.

"And is it possible He might ask your assistance in such a matter?"

"I try to be of service in whatever way I can."

"And how do you know what to do in a situation such as this, where God perhaps asks something"—I hesitated, seeking the right phrasing—"that might be seen in another light in the court of human judgment."

He hesitated. "You remember His answer when asked if one should pay taxes? He said, 'Give unto Caesar the things that are Caesar's, and unto God the things that are God's'. You speak of man's laws and man's understanding. These are nothing in comparison with God's. It is His word we must obey."

"I see. So if he had asked your help…"

He frowned. "I have tried to answer your questions as best I can. Let us not dwell further on this, my son."

I nodded, sensing I would not get any more from him, and wondering just what kind of crazy The Reverend was. "Well, I thank you."

He smiled, placing his hand on my head. "You may go in peace, my son."

There was a soft knock at the door; I wondered if someone had been listening. The female officer peeked in. "May we offer you some sustenance, sir?" she said, speaking to The Reverend.

He cocked his head to the side, seeming to give this some thought, and finally nodded slightly. "We are mere mortals. We must give our bodies the things they need, so that we may serve the Lord."

She nodded toward the hallway. "Please follow me. We'll try to provide for your needs."

He looked back toward me. "The Lord is your

shepherd, my son. Follow His guidance in all things." He stood and followed her out.

I waited and Christiansen came back in and sat down across from me, rubbing his eyes. "Well?"

"I can't say I learned anything conclusive. When I tried to pin him down about 'helping' Jim, he just dodged the question with some gobble-de-gook about following God's wisdom. As far as I can tell, he pretty much lives in his own delusionary world, and it's hard to know what he's capable of if he thinks that's what God is telling him to do. And he can be crafty."

Christiansen looked tired. "Well, at least it stopped the infernal shouting."

I nodded. "So, I guess I'll be on my way?"

He stood and held the door open for me, then followed me toward the front of the building. As we reached the front desk, the young receptionist spoke to him.

"Captain, there's an officer trying to reach you from the hospital. I think he has some interesting information."

Christiansen took the phone from her. He mouthed a 'thanks' to me and turned away. I pushed out through the front door, pretty sure I knew what that information was.

22

I climbed back into Old Blue and leaned back in the seat, rubbing my eyes with the base of my palms as a wave of fatigue passed over me. It had been a long day. I glanced at my watch: nearly six. Weren't Saturdays supposed to be a day off? This one felt like it was never going to end.

I turned the key and felt the engine come alive, pulled out and headed home. Maybe a nice quiet dinner by myself and an evening at home with Earl would help. I tried to think what was in the house to eat. As usual, I couldn't come up with much.

Earl was waiting at the back door when I arrived. For the umpteenth time I explained to him that he had his own door he could use if he just wanted to exert himself a little. This was greeted by what could only be described as a cat harrumph: one short half-meow half-growl that was quite clear—shut up and open the damn door.

He quickly went to his favorite spot, his food dish in the corner of the kitchen, then looked at me with an equally clear expression and another harrumph at the lack of offerings there.

"Okay, okay. It's been a long day, Earl. Give me a minute."

I pulled his bag of kibble out of the cupboard as he restlessly paced back and forth in front of his dish, offering up additional expressions of impatience. Cats might not know actual words, but they could certainly communicate clearly. I shook a generous portion of kibble into his bowl and he went to work. Then I turned my attention to my own dinner.

Too tired to much care what I ate as long as it stopped the hunger pangs, I hunted through the refrigerator for something of interest. There were a couple onion bagels stuck at the very back of the freezer compartment, left over from some long-forgotten visit by Kate. I reached back and pulled them out for an examination. What the hell; they'd been frozen. Didn't frozen foods last pretty much forever?

I pulled one out, nuked it until I could get a knife through it, and popped it in the toaster. Then I fished around in the cheese drawer for something to put on it. There was an old container of cream cheese, but when I pulled back the foil I was greeted with a wide swath of blue mold. I tossed it in the garbage. This left butter; it would have to do.

And of course there was the more important component of the repast. I got out a large glass, half filled it with ice, pulled down the bottle of gin, and filled it half full. Then I added tonic and a splash of orange juice. Still waiting for the bagel to pop up, I swallowed a large gulp and felt the relaxation beginning.

By the time I made it into the living room the news was mostly over. I surfed through a bunch of other channels, finally landing on a preview of the upcoming Giants game. They were now one and three, and about to play a night game against the Dodgers, who had picked up an impressive new pitcher and power hitter in the off-season. It already wasn't looking like a great year, but it was refreshing just to see the team taking the field and going through the ancient rituals. Baseball was a rite of spring, a harbinger of warmer days and longer evenings. In fact, baseball felt like a national pastime that had passed; it belonged to an earlier era. Which was a big part of what made it appealing.

***

The knock at the front door awoke me from a nap. I glanced at the TV; it was the fourth inning and the Giants were already three runs down. I shook myself, trying to wake up enough to answer the door. I took a deep breath, dropped my feet to the floor, sat there for a minute for my head to clear, and carefully stood as a second round of knocks sounded. Who the hell would be coming over unannounced on a Saturday night?

I half stumbled to the front door and opened it cautiously, looking out into the dusk. Two attractive young blond women stood there, nicely dressed and looking at me expectantly. I tried to make sense of it: Jehovah's Witnesses? Avon ladies? Was I just having a dream?

"Hello, Mr. Travis," one said. "We're sorry to bother you at home." She turned to the other young woman. "This is my sister Adele."

Finally my brain started to kick in; I knew that voice. Jill's daughter. Jill's daughters, to be more precise.

"Hi, Rebecca. What can I do for you?"

"We need to talk to someone, and we couldn't think who else. We should have called but didn't know how to get your number."

"That's probably because it's unlisted. Keeps the robo calls down." I hesitated. "How did you know my address?"

Rebecca looked down and blushed slightly. "I'm not sure I should tell you."

"You hacked into some account?"

"No. We called the paper. I talked to some nice lady

there who asked why we needed it. When I explained she said she understood and thought you might like a little company tonight."

I looked at her askance. "Her name wouldn't have been Violet by any chance, would it?"

She shrugged. "She didn't say. But she seemed to know you."

"Hmm. I thought she was busy tonight. Anyway, what can I do for you?"

Her expression darkened. "Did you know that our Mom has been taken in by the police?" Her voice conveyed distress.

"Really?" I wasn't surprised, but wasn't sure I should convey this.

"Yes, late this afternoon. We don't know what to do."

The realization came to me they were still standing on my front porch, and it had cooled off considerably. Also that an opportunity to perhaps learn something from a new source had just fallen into my lap. I swung the door open wider and stepped back. "Come in. I'm not sure how I can help, but come in and tell me more."

They followed me into the living room, where I straightened the pillows on the couch I'd been sleeping on, motioned for them to have a seat, turned off the game, and sat down across the coffee table from them in my old worn armchair. I realized my bagel plate and gin and tonic glass were still on the table and set them off on the floor beside my chair, brushing away the crumbs on the table.

"So, your Mom was taken in by the police?"

They took turns talking, but it seemed there was little to explain. The three of them had been having a pre-dinner snack when two officers had come to the front door with an official-looking paper and told Jill she had to go with them. When she'd asked why, they just said for questioning.

When she asked if it was about Jim's death, they kind of hemmed and hawed but said they were just told to bring her in, that she'd learn what she was being questioned about when she got to the station. When she asked how long she'd be there, they said they didn't know.

I nodded. "Well, I might have a clue here. It seems the police found a blond hair on your father's ventilator. Actually, on the connector between the ventilator and the esophageal tube, the one that went into his mouth. They think someone may have tampered with it."

They stared at me in apparent disbelief. "*Mom? No!* That's not possible." This from Adele.

I responded with a sympathetic expression, hoping it looked genuine. "I guess they felt they had to question her."

Her tone turned to anger. "Well, that's just ridiculous. There is no way Mom would do something like that. It's absurd."

"Well, your Mom and Dad *were* separated, and there appeared to be some pretty hard feelings still between them."

"Well, yes. But that's not the same as wanting to kill someone."

Again I nodded sympathetically. "Your Mom seemed pretty angry the last time I talked with her," I said, in as gentle a tone as I could muster.

"She *was* angry. Who wouldn't be when their husband, who they loved, took up with another woman? But she didn't want to *kill* him. She wanted him back."

"Really? She wanted your Dad back?"

"*Yes.* She couldn't believe what he'd done, but she hadn't stopped hoping he'd come to his senses and come home. It was practically the only thing she talked about."

"When you say 'took up with another woman'…could you explain that?"

Rebecca jumped in. "It was that hair dresser. That…*woman*…who he met in some therapy group."

"Karen Black?"

They both nodded.

"And your Mom thought they were having an affair?"

"They *were* having an affair."

I leaned back in my chair. "Well, not according to Karen."

They scowled in unison. "What do you mean?" Adele said.

"I've had a couple conversations with Karen Black. According to her, it was just a friendship. Your Dad wouldn't let it become more than that."

"She's lying!" This from Rebecca.

"How do you know?"

She hesitated. "Well, she *has* to be. They were together all the time."

"How do you know that?"

"Well, Mom said…" Her voice trailed off.

I waited for a moment. Then I tried a different tact. "Something I've been trying to understand as I've been looking into this is what caused their separation in the first place. What were the problems they had? Before Karen Black was ever on the scene."

They glanced at each other. Rebecca spoke, somewhat reluctantly. "There *were* problems. They'd been there for a long time. Mom thought Dad was too focused on other people's problems, rather than those our own family had."

"How do you mean?"

"Dad always tried to help those he saw in need. That's just the way he was. Like, he never passed panhandlers without giving them money. He was really concerned about homeless people."

"And this bothered your Mom?"

"It drove her crazy. She must have said a hundred times, 'We have our own problems; can't you focus on those for a change'?"

"And did you? Have your own problems?"

"I suppose. Mom always thought we had to skimp on things. She hated seeing Dad spending money to help total strangers when we didn't have all the things we needed ourselves."

"How did he respond?"

"He said we had an awful lot, compared to people who didn't have enough to eat or a place to stay. We needed to share what we had with the less fortunate."

I leaned back, watching their expressions. "Who was right?"

They looked at each other, shrugging, then back at me. Adele spoke. "They both had their points. We tried not to take sides."

I nodded. "Did you stay in touch with your Dad? After the separation?"

"Actually, Mom had custody and didn't want us to. She felt he was in the wrong and needed to apologize, and that until he did, one way to punish him was to not let him see us."

"How often *did* you see him?"

"He used to email us pretty often, ask us how things were going with school, sports, boyfriends," Rebecca said. "Mom couldn't really control that. But in person? Not very often, actually. She just wouldn't let it happen."

"Did that seem fair to you?"

She frowned. "From her viewpoint it was. I guess from Dad's it wasn't. It's hard as a kid when you get caught between your parents. You want to be fair to both."

"Did you get a sense he missed you?"

"Oh, definitely. He missed us a lot. But he didn't seem

to want to make up with Mom."

"Any idea why?"

"I think he didn't think he'd done anything wrong. He didn't really understand why he'd had to leave in the first place. He said he wasn't having an affair with anyone, just trying to help other people who really needed it."

"But your Mom was convinced he was?"

They both nodded.

"And it sounds like you agreed with her?"

"There was no doubt in *her* mind."

"But not before she made him leave?"

"No. That was about not being home enough, spending time in those homeless camps, giving part of his income away to help those people. That sort of thing."

"Did you ever meet Karen Black?"

The both shook their heads.

"But you're sure your Mom would not have done anything to hurt your Dad? Even though she threw him out of the house and wouldn't let you see him?"

"No," Adele said doubtfully. "Mom's not a…killer." She said "killer" as though it was a question.

I nodded. "Well, I'm doing everything I can to try to figure out exactly what happened to your Dad. I thought a lot of him. And just so you're clear, there are several other people the police are questioning also. I don't think they're ready to bring any charges."

"Does that mean Mom will be coming home tonight?"

"That I don't know. They may want to keep her there overnight for questioning. I believe they have twenty-four hours they can keep her before they have to either charge her with something or let her go."

"So she probably won't be back tonight?"

"The only way you could find that out would be to talk with the police. But they might not even know themselves.

It may depend on how the questioning goes."

They looked at each other with woebegone expressions, on the verge of tears. I wasn't sure what to do, but sensed I needed to say something. "I understand it's really hard to be in your position. But don't despair. Your Mom will be back, if not tonight probably in the morning. And that may be it; they may decide that they have no reason to be suspicious of her. You'll just have to be brave tonight and hope for the best."

They nodded, unconvincingly.

"Would you like…I don't know…a cup of coffee? Tea?"

They both shook their heads. Rebecca spoke. "We should get home in case they do release her. But thanks for talking to us. At least we know why they took her in. And that there are other suspects."

"Okay."

"Thanks for telling us about Dad, also. Maybe he wasn't having an affair. That puts a different light on things. Mom was just so sure…"

"It's easy to jump to that conclusion in her situation."

"We really miss him, even though we haven't been able to see him much for a while. He was a great Dad. We can't believe he's gone." There was a slight tremor in her voice.

"I don't know one person he knew who didn't think highly of him. He was a fine man."

They stood and reached out their hands. "Thank you, Mr. Travis."

As I gently shook each hand, I said, "Call me Lew. And if I learn anything more, I'll be glad to share it with you."

"That would be great." They turned and headed for the door.

***

When they'd left I wandered back into the living room, picked up my plate and glass, and returned to the kitchen. Then I poured myself another gin and tonic, reflecting on what had just transpired. It was painful to see the effects of a separation on kids. Caught in the middle, having to be the adults in the room, when they needed their parents there, working as a team.

Not all that different from the death of a parent, really. Mary had been the perfect Mom: energetic, patient, joyful, supportive, able to provide guidance and counsel when needed. Kate and Nick had had to face their own struggles when she died. None of us would ever be able to completely fill the vacuum that was left.

I'd barely made it through the first long valley, the depression that overwhelmed me for nearly a year, my endless attempts to dull the pain, my self-destructive consumption of far too much gin. Only gradually had I pulled myself out of that hole, aware that I was damaging not just myself, but my kids. I was their only living parent, they needed me, and I owed them better.

And in spite of my continuing struggles, I'd come to realize that depression is ultimately selfish. It is a cousin of self-pity. While there may be a genuine cause, and it may be overwhelming, it is nevertheless destructive not only to the one depressed but to those around him. And while there may be medical help, which can make a difference, ultimately no one else can pull you out; you have to battle it with every resource at your command and find your way to a better place.

With this thought in mind, I decided it was time to get off a missive to Nick. It had been too long. I hadn't seen him face-to-face in almost a year, but that was more under his control than mine, living in Boston. At least I could shoot him an email.

I sat down in front of the computer and clicked on email, trying to think what might be of interest to him. When I noticed an email waiting there from Kate.

> Hi, Dad,
> Okay, it's set. I'm driving up next Thursday evening. We get Friday off, and the whole next week. Kind of a combined spring and Easter vacation. So get those garden tools out and tuned up; I'm ready for some serious digging and planting.
> Not to mention getting caught up on lots of fronts. You're going to like some of the stories about my little monsters; I've got some pretty amusing ones this year. And I want to hear about what's going on with you. Working on any good stories for the paper these days?
> I also have a little surprise for you. It involves someone else who's going to join us for a bit. Seems someone has a business trip scheduled to the Bay Area at that time. I don't want to give it away, but his initials are NT.
> Love, Kate

23

Sunday

The night was a restless one: dreams of wild-haired preachers shouting their warnings of doom and destruction to those unconverted; attractive young women under siege from dirty old men; desolate children unable to find their parents. I awoke with a bad taste in my mouth, glanced at the clock, and saw it was still early: six-thirty. I needed more sleep, I was still tired, but as had too often become the case these days, the sleep gods had abandoned me. I threw back the covers and rolled out of bed, plodding into the bathroom and going through the usual routine. Earl stood at the door watching, with occasional complaints about my sluggish pace.

I glanced out the front door when I'd made it downstairs, remembering there was no Sunday edition of the local rag. If I wanted to learn the latest bad news it was going to require a trip to the local store, which didn't open until seven. I fixed myself a strong cup of coffee and put away the bottle of gin, listening to Earl crunch away on his breakfast. Again the thought crossed my mind that there could be a lot worse things than being a cat. As far as I could tell, Earl had few worries beyond getting his next meal and exploring the neighborhood for whatever tidbits of interest it might offer. Sure enough, he completed his repast and headed for the back door, making the usual demands for doorman attention. I complied and watched him head off to who knew where.

After a second cup of coffee I girded up my loins and headed out to a little local market that stocked Sunday newspapers. It was another lovely spring morning, the sun just up and the air crisp. The five-minute walk provided a slight boost to my mood. The store was empty of other customers, but the old lady who ran the place was there behind the counter as usual. She nodded at the fresh-baked offerings as I plopped the San Francisco Chronicle down on the counter.

"They just arrived, Lew. Really. You're not going to try to resist that aroma, are you?"

"Velma, you're an evil woman. The health column in the paper warms you against eating sweetened doughy things. Don't these qualify?"

"Absolutely. That's the main reason to eat them. We're too old to violate most of the other rules of good behavior. We need some vestige of rebellion to fall back on. What else is life about?"

"You're a silver-tongued devil. Don't you know that kind of talk will wind you up in the place you don't want to be?"

"I hear the company is pretty good down there."

I nodded. "Will you be running your store there, urging evil things on people?"

"That's my plan."

"Okay. As long as I have that to look forward to, give me a couple of those big glazed things."

"Only two?"

I stared at her. "Make it three."

She pulled out a paper bag and tossed three giant bear claws into it, adding a couple napkins on top. "It'll make your morning, Lew."

"Something needs to." I paid her and headed for the door, the Chronicle under my arm, taking a bite from one of the bear claws. As I pulled open the door I stopped and looked back at her: "These *are* good, Velma. Keep up your evil ways. I'll need company down there."

"Have a good day, Lew."

Somehow the walk home felt better. Bear claws and a Sunday paper; life could be worse.

***

As usual the most interesting section of the paper was the green one, otherwise known as the sports pages. The Giants had finally won another game, having beaten their arch rival, the Dodgers. It was a three-game series, so there would be a game this afternoon as well. But the Dodgers had their ace pitching the game, so the odds would be in their favor. Meanwhile, the Warriors were cruising through their last few regular season games, playing mostly backups while awaiting their first playoff series.

By the time I finished reading the paper it was after nine. I was headed out to the kitchen to fix another cup of coffee when the phone rang. On Sunday morning? I picked it up and checked the screen ID. Really?

"Zane?"

"Yo. Mr. T."

"You're up early. I thought you young guys slept late on weekends."

"Usually do. Just couldn't make it past eight-thirty this morning. Is this too early…?"

"Been up for hours. What's up?"

"Thought maybe you'd like an update on things."

"By all means. What have you got, Zane?"

"Well, as you'll recall, I've been seeing what I could

216

learn about Mr. Pearson's wife, Jill. "

"And?"

"She buys a lot of stuff."

"What do you mean?"

"Amazon, eBay, Nordstrom, Macy's; you name it."

"What kind of stuff?"

"Clothes, cosmetics, shoes. She must average a couple packages a week."

"Actually, that pretty much jibes with what I'd heard elsewhere. Anything else?"

"Yeah, didn't mean to go there first, I was just kind of amazed. But there is some other stuff."

"Yes?"

"She emails a lot also."

"With whom?"

"Mostly girlfriends. There is one guy, however. His name is Don Drambowski. He lives in Florida, has a boat there. He keeps inviting her to come and spend some time with him. She keeps saying she can't."

"Who is he?"

"An old high school boyfriend she's reconnected with on Facebook. There's a bunch of stuff about other friends they knew, the crazy stuff they used to do together."

"Does this have anything to do with Jim?"

"She mentions him some."

"And?"

"She talks about how he's having this wild affair with some hot young thing. She has friends who see them together here and there. She sounds pretty hurt."

"Do you get a sense for *how* hurt?"

"Hard to say. She remembers how he used to dote on her when she was younger and more attractive. Sounds like he was a good father, but stopped focusing on her so much after the girls arrived. She even harbors some hard feelings toward them. And there's other stuff."

"What kind of other stuff?"

"She mentions his involvement with homeless people. She really has no use for them, sees them as worthless and lazy, thinks they should get jobs and provide for themselves. She really resents the time and money he spends on them."

"That's also consistent with what else I've learned. Anything else?"

"She talks about his job. How he changed when he started working for the insurance company. He made more money, but got really unhappy. He'd come home after work and withdraw into himself. He stopped being a companion. She felt like she didn't know him anymore."

"It sounds like this Don guy was kind of a sounding board for her?"

"Yeah. Plus they seemed to share common views on things. He doesn't have much use for homeless people either, says they're blots on society. He wonders what has happened to good old American grit. And there was some suggestive stuff, like he was trying to rekindle an old romance. I couldn't really tell how serious it was. Do you want me to go into that?"

"That's okay, Zane. It sounds like he was giving her what she needed to feel attractive still."

"Yeah, exactly. He also kept asking her why she didn't just abandon Jim altogether."

"And?"

"She mentioned the girls. And the fact that Adele was still living at home. Plus she was worried it would also look bad, Jim doing all this good Samaritan stuff and she leaves the scene."

"Hmm."

"And there was one I thought you might find especially

interesting, Mr. T."

"Because?"

"She said the only way she could leave would be if something 'happened' to Jim. She didn't put 'happened' in quotation marks, but that's how I read it. And here's the kicker: she said if something did, at least money would be no object."

I hesitated, trying to interpret this. "How did you take that, Zane?"

"Two thoughts. One, maybe they had a lot of money invested that would then be under her control?"

"Which makes no sense, since Jim took the insurance job because they didn't have enough money."

"Right. Well, the other seems pretty obvious. He *was* working at an insurance firm."

"A life insurance policy!"

"That's how I took it."

"And of course Jim would want to make sure Jill and the girls were well taken care of, so it was probably for a healthy sum."

"Frankly, it sounded a little creepy."

Creepy indeed. "Is she still communicating with this guy?"

"No. The last email, which was just after Jim died, said something awful had happened and she couldn't write to him for awhile."

"But she didn't say what?"

"No. He kept asking, but she wouldn't say. Just that something too awful to talk about had taken place and she had to deal with things at home for awhile."

"Can you forward these to me?"

"Not really. They're in her email. Stealing them is another step into questionable territory. It would make it easier for someone to track me down if I passed them on to someone else. I need to stay under the radar."

"Okay, understood. And much appreciated."

"Oh, I forgot, one other thing."

"Yeah?"

"When she talked about Jim's work, she mentioned that she wondered if these insurance people were on the up and up. She said she got the sense that the reason Jim didn't like to talk when he got home from work was that maybe there were things going on there that weren't quite right."

"Did she give any examples?"

"No. Just that he wasn't happy there, he didn't like these people, and he seemed troubled by what he had to do."

"Okay. Well, thanks a bunch, Zane. That's all very helpful. If anything else comes up, let me know."

"Will do, Mr. T."

24

I sat there contemplating this new information. While it was just one piece in the puzzle, it put Jill's situation in a little different light. While it might have gotten me a step closer to figuring this thing out, there were still some important things I didn't know.

I looked over my list, sifting the options. Then I decided a call to Harve was in order. He wasn't the religious type so I figured he wouldn't mind a call on a Sunday morning. I dialed his home number.

The phone rang four times before a sleepy female voice answered. "Hello."

I hesitated. Maybe this hadn't been such a good idea. "Is Harve there?"

"Can I tell him who's calling?"

"Lew Travis." I felt a little sheepish.

"Just a minute."

There were voices in the background, but I couldn't make out what they said. After a moment Harve got on.

"You're hard to figure out, old man. One morning you sleep late, the next you call me at the crack of dawn."

"It's almost eleven, Harve."

"Okay, the crack of eleven."

"And while it's none of my business, it appears your ability to listen to women has its rewards."

"I try to be understanding. What can I do for you?"

"I was wondering if you'd had any more chats with your woman friend at the police station."

"As a matter of fact, something turned up last night."

"To wit?"

"It appears they've found what may be incriminating evidence in Jim's room."

"You mean the blond hair caught in the Velcro?"

There was a pause. "How did you know that?"

"Your nurse friend called yesterday afternoon. She overheard two police officers talking at the hospital."

"Well, you're half right."

"What does that mean?"

"You did say blond *hair*, right? As in the singular form of the noun?"

"I believe that's what hair means, yes."

"There were actually *two* hairs found. The one caught in the ventilator's Velcro. And a second one found on Jim's blanket. They did not appear to be from the same head."

"How could they tell?"

"The first was relatively short and neatly cut."

"Jim was blond himself. Couldn't that have been his?"

"Apparently it was longer that that. Plus it was caught in the Velcro on the ventilator he was breathing through. Which makes that doubtful."

"Unless he was trying to…"

"They thought of that. The problem is the Velcro was reattached as it should be. It would be hard for him to do that after expiring."

"And the other?"

"Long and wispy, with split ends."

"To which they concluded?"

"I believe they're questioning two different suspects."

"Jill and The Reverend."

"Lew. I'm impressed."

"Any sense for who they're leaning toward?"

"I think they see the Velcro hair as pretty clear evidence of tampering. But they can't explain the other one. No one at the hospital saw The Reverend in Jim's room. That was verboten. Somehow he snuck in unobserved. Given their history and his penchant for vengeance, they're not letting either of them go."

"Interesting."

"Not bad for a Sunday morning, eh?"

"Well, before you break your arm patting yourself on the back, those *are* both examples of circumstantial evidence. Nobody saw either of them actually committing a crime."

He hesitated. "True. But those are both pretty damn incriminating."

"Okay, I'll give you a B, Harve."

"A B?"

"You only get an A when there's conclusive proof."

He sighed. "It's Sunday, Lew. It's not even a work day."

"I sensed that when the phone was answered."

"To my point. Some of us have other interests in our lives."

"I've noticed. You seem to have several."

"Goodbye, Lew." A dial tone came on the line.

***

By now the sun was in full bloom, pouring in through my 'office' window. I sat in front of my old Mac drumming my fingers on the keys, wondering how Jill was doing after a night at the police station. And how her daughters were doing at home, worried about her. My thoughts were interrupted by the ringing of the phone.

I looked at the screen: Emmett. I'd forgotten; I'd asked him to give me a report on his date. I picked up cautiously; I was no longer entirely sure of my footing on this front.

"Good morning, Lothario."

"Eat your heart out, old man."

I experienced a sinking sensation. "You sound chipper."

"Just wanted to thank you for your advice. It worked like a charm."

"She liked the suit?"

"She stared at it all night."

"I'm impressed you could still get into it."

"It took a little doing. I couldn't actually zip the pants all the way. But it still looked good."

"How did you keep them up?"

"I have one of those big wide belts with a giant buckle. It'll hold anything up."

"Did you have a good tie to go with it?"

"Absolutely. A Disneyland special: Donald Duck, Mickey Mouse, and Goofy all prominently displayed. It was a little challenge to get it tied; the shirt was really tight around the neck. I couldn't quite get the vest buttoned either. But it didn't matter. I don't think she even noticed."

"And the restaurant?"

"We had to shout at the top of our lungs to talk. Just like the kids at a rock concert. She ate it up."

"What did you have?"

"I decided I might as well go for broke, like you suggested. I had the bouillabaisse. It was a little messy, but they had those big plastic bibs, so it worked fine."

"And the wine?"

"We went through an entire bottle. Of the best stuff they had."

"Sounds expensive."

"Yeah. But you were right, my friend. You have to show a lady a good time if you want her to like you."

I girded up my loins and asked the question I'd been holding back. "I trust she showed her appreciation?"

"She just kept smiling at me the whole night. She was charmed."

"And after dinner?"

"Well, I actually ate a little more than I should have. So I had to spend a little time in the bathroom. But I recovered."

I needed to get to the chase. "I trust she showed her appreciation when you took her home?"

"Definitely."

"Oh?"

"A *serious* peck on the cheek."

"Ah."

"It *was* a first date, Lew."

"No. Probably good that you didn't push it."

"Hey, I'm not that kind of guy. I was worried she might just shake hands, but it was a definite peck."

"Sounds like a perfect night."

"Eat your heart out, my man."

"So your New Year's resolutions are paying off."

"Big time. How about that game of chess?"

"Anytime, Emmett."

He hesitated. "Actually, I can't do it today. I'm a little busy. But let's get it on the calendar soon."

"Just let me know what works for you."

"You got it, pal. Eat my dust."

***

I had barely hung up when the phone rang again. I figured it was Emmett calling back to add some additional tidbit about his wild success, so answered without even checking the ID.

"Hello, Emmett."

"Emmett? You are losing it."

"Timothy. I believe the usual words of greeting are more something like 'good morning'."

"There is a little screen in your phone, Lew. If you look at it before picking up it tells you who's calling. I know these new fangled devices are a little hard for you to master."

"I did sleep pretty well. Thanks for asking."

"At least it's reassuring you're up. We do worry about you, Lew."

"We?"

"Harve. Me."

"Ah. And you worry because…?"

"You old people have a way of kicking off."

"You put it so delicately. Was there a reason for your call, other than insults about my age?"

"I thought I ought to check on how the story is coming."

"The story?"

"That you're writing. For the paper. As our investigative reporter. The reason we pay you."

"Ah. So this is a work call. On a Sunday morning."

"Your religious inclinations make that objectionable, do they?"

"No, it's more my lifestyle inclinations. Like not being hounded by bosses on weekends."

"You don't have any bosses, Lew. We've all given up. You've managed to carve out a role that leaves you full independence. I'm just calling out of curiosity."

"In that case, proceed."

"Well, since Harve and I seem to have given you most

of the leads you've managed to obtain, I was just curious: you *are* going to write a story about this, aren't you? That retrospective on Jim's life?"

"Of course. And I do owe you and Harve a note of gratitude. You have been helpful, and I give you credit."

"Thank you. So?"

"I've gained a lot of background information on Jim's life. I think that part of the story is coming along well."

"Do I sense a 'but' coming?"

"It seems to me that before I submit the piece it might be useful to know how the story ends?"

"We sort of know how it ends, don't we? Jim died."

"Good, Tim. I see why you're an editor. I was referring more to the why."

"Well, what have you been doing?"

"Wracking my brain. The situation is a little complicated, actually."

"Wracked brains can cause problems. I'd be careful, given your age."

"You know *you* haven't kicked in any new information for awhile. Harve is well ahead of you. He's provided leads from the hospital *and* the police department."

"He's one of our best reporters."

"And you have nothing to contribute at this point?"

"Since you seem stuck, I do have one small bit of information that might be of interest."

"I'm listening."

"It actually comes from someone at the paper who, strangely enough, seems to like you. And who has taken an interest in this matter herself."

"*Her*self? A female reporter?"

"Not exactly a reporter. You may remember that Violet has excellent research skills. She's a very sharp lady."

"I'm aware of that."

"With a small gap in her judgment relating to her taste in men."

"Could we get to the point?"

"Violet got wind of the suspects the police were questioning. She decided maybe a little more background information on one of them might be useful."

"The Reverend?"

"Try again."

"Jill Pearson."

"Keep trying."

"I give up, Tim. Who are you talking about?"

"Karen Black."

"Really? Why Karen?"

"Because Karen knew Jim well, and knows his employers, and she visited Jim at the hospital several times."

"Okay."

"Did you know Karen Black has a police record?"

"What?"

"She was arrested for grand larceny, found guilty, spent three months in jail, and is still on probation."

"What did she steal?"

"A car."

"Wow. Tim. How did Violet learn this?"

"Police records. They do cooperate with us, as long as we're circumspect in the use of their information. It's a reciprocal arrangement."

"And this was recently?"

"It was a couple years ago. But the probation was for three years."

"Has Violet talked with Karen?"

"I don't think she wants that kind of involvement. But she knows you have."

"How did she find that out?"

"She seems to have her ways."

"No wonder the cops were interested in Karen as a suspect."

"Yeah. Since you know her, I thought you might want to inquire about this."

"I'm still a little unclear. How does this relate to Jim's death?"

"It's just a tidbit about a potential suspect. I thought it was worth sharing."

"Well, Tim. I take back all the nasty things I've been saying about you."

There was a pause. "I'm going to take that as a thank you."

25

This flurry of phone conversations left me somehow hungry, and for something more than a bear claw. As tasty as they were, they were a little lacking in protein. I considered my options. There was an all-day breakfast café I could walk to, but it was always so busy on Sunday you had to wait in line, sometimes for an hour. There were also the chains, but somehow IHOP and Denny's didn't appeal. Finally I decided on an out-of-the-way place with an outdoor patio called Flynn's. It was a little cool, but a beautiful spring day, and I could wear a jacket. I grabbed my keys and headed for the garage.

Even Flynn's was busy—spring seemed to have that effect on people, tired of the long winter rains and occasional snow at this 2,500-feet-above-sea-level locale. But the wait was short and the coffee arrived quickly. I ordered my usual, huevos rancheros—the combination of runny yolk with cheese and refried beans, avocado on top, hash browns on the side, had a unique appeal—and settled back to wait, sipping on a glass of fresh-squeezed orange juice. The place buzzed with waiters hurrying this way and that, young people talking animatedly, and busboys cleaning tables as soon as they were free to prepare for the seemingly endless flow of new arrivals.

Someone had left a couple sections of the Sunday *New York Times* on an adjoining table so I reached over and grabbed them. I was in luck; one of the sections was Arts and Leisure, and the other the magazine section, where the crossword appears. To the uninitiated, New York Times' Sunday crosswords were the ultimate test. Actually, they're easier than the Friday and Saturday versions, just bigger, and usually with a 'shtick' of some sort, a theme or trick associated with the longer words or phrases. Figuring out the shtick was a key to solving the puzzle.

I was just getting underway when my breakfast arrived. I set the puzzle beside my plate so I could continue working on it as I began taking bites of that delicious combination of tastes, letting each bite linger for a bit to reap the full enjoyment, and sipping the aromatic coffee between bites. I was making good progress on the puzzle by the time I'd finished, although still had a ways to go. The cute dark-haired waitress came by with a pot of coffee and gave me a refill. As she disappeared inside another couple emerged, looking around for a table. I did something of a double take: it was Bruce Canton, accompanied by Karen Black.

I quickly grabbed the Arts and Leisure section of the paper and raised it in front of me, pretending to be engrossed. Only after a minute did I lower it enough to see where they were being seated. It was the table furthest away, with enough people in between I didn't think they'd spot me. Bruce held Karen's chair, then sat down next to her.

I watched them surreptiously as they studied their menus, and as the waitress arrived and took their order. Then Bruce leaned over and put his arm around Karen's shoulders. She smiled at him but made no move to lean closer. He gave her a peck on the forehead and put his arm back down, whispering something in her ear as he did so, and she nodded without facial expression. What could this mean? There she was, having breakfast on a Sunday morning with Bruce Canton.

I waited until their food arrived before making my escape, figuring they'd be looking down at their plates. Sure enough, they both dug in. But as I wound between other tables to leave I noticed them having an animated conversation, with Karen mostly listening and nodding from time to time, clearly engaged. Neither of them showed any awareness of my presence.

When I was back in Old Blue I sat in the driver's seat for a few minutes without starting the car, trying to think what this implied. It seemed clear that Bruce was interested in Karen in other than a business sense. She had confirmed this when I'd talked with her, although somewhat dismissively. However, here she was out having breakfast with him on a Sunday morning. I wondered whether, given the loss of Jim, Karen had turned to Bruce to fill that vacuum. Or whether perhaps this had been going on before Jim's death, which suggested other possibilities.

I headed home, to be greeted by Earl at the back door, making his usual demands for door service. I complied, and knowing his next stop, sprinkled a little kibble in his bowl. He gave out one short meow, which I took as a thank you. It was as close as he came. Then I checked for phone messages. Just one.

```
    Hi, Lew.  I don't think we've
made meeting plans yet, have we?
Could you give me a call?
```

There was no name given, and none needed.

I dialed her number. That lovely soft voice answered. "Hi, Lew."

"Hey. Sorry I missed your call. Just out getting a little breakfast."

"*Two* meals out today. Impressive."

I waited two seconds. "Oh, was tonight the night we agreed on?"

There was a pause. "Would you prefer to reschedule?" Her tone was ironic. You couldn't get a lot past Violet.

"When's a good time for you?"

"Six?"

"Did you have a place in mind? I haven't made any reservations yet."

"I'm easy. Do *you* have a place in mind?"

"Maybe someplace kind of low key and casual. I'm not really in the mood for a big meal. Like you might have, say, on a *Saturday night*." I waited to see if she picked up on the cue.

Apparently she didn't want to give me the satisfaction. "That sounds good. Why don't you pick out the place?"

"Or maybe we can just figure something out when I pick you up, without a reservation?"

"That's fine too. Shouldn't be all that busy on a Sunday night."

"While I've got you here, can I ask you about something else?"

"Sure."

"Tim called a while ago. He mentioned your sleuthing efforts with regard to Karen Black."

There was a pause. "Okay."

"Can you share what you learned?"

"That was kind of the point, Lew. How much did Tim tell you?"

"That she stole a car, was charged with grand larceny, was found guilty, and was sentenced to ninety days in jail and three years probation."

"Actually, the term used in California is grand theft, but otherwise that's correct. What else did you want to know?"

233

"Details?"

"Well, it was an old car that belonged to her then boyfriend. It's estimated value was about $2,000."

"Your phrasing sounds like you're a little skeptical of the charge?"

"Court records show she said she borrowed the car to get to work, and that he'd given her permission. He said she took it without permission. Apparently she didn't have funds to hire a lawyer, and he won the case."

"Doesn't sound like a very strong case."

"Under California law, any theft over $950 is considered grand theft. As opposed to petty theft, for amounts less than that. There is apparently a fair amount of discretion on the judge's part about which to use. The boyfriend claimed blue book value on the car, but it was fourteen years old and had some dents. Unfortunately, she had a prior conviction, so the judge apparently felt some jail time was called for."

"A prior conviction?"

"She was caught selling weed."

"When was that?"

"In high school."

"Wasn't she a minor?"

"She was eighteen; it was her senior year."

"How much weed are we talking about?"

"The court docs didn't say exactly, just that it was 'small amounts'. Probably a few joints."

"And for that she got a felony conviction?"

"Selling is regarded quite differently from using. Even small amounts."

"I thought weed had been legalized in California."

"It has now. It wasn't then. And it's still illegal under federal law. As is dealing, even in California."

"So she has two strikes?"

"Uh huh. For selling some joints to a friend, and in her testimony, borrowing her boyfriend's car."

"Jeez."

"Still doesn't mean she's an innocent."

"Why do you say that?"

"The law may have been hard on her, but in both cases the decision went against her. Presumably the judges involved looked at all the evidence and made what they thought were fair judgments. And ninety days in jail for a second felony conviction is actually a light sentence. It's often several years. You could argue she got off easy."

"Still."

"I agree. On the surface it seems unfair. She was eighteen the first time and twenty-three the second. Actually, she's still on probation. She has another year to go."

"Did you know I've had a couple chats with her?"

"Yeah, Tim mentioned that. What have *you* learned?"

"Nothing about this. But she had a rough childhood. She's an attractive young lady, and had an uncle who sexually abused her when she was thirteen. Plus she apparently used her attractiveness in the way young women are sometimes wont to do, especially those not getting a lot of love at home, and wound up having to get an abortion."

"You sound sympathetic to her yourself, Lew."

"I should probably temper that by admitting all my information came from her. There may be another side to the story."

"There usually is."

"And while we're on the topic, I happened to see her out with Bruce Canton at breakfast this morning."

"The insurance agent?"

"Yeah, the one Jim Pearson worked for. She led me to think he was making unwanted advances toward her, but that doesn't seem to square with her going out to breakfast with him. So who knows?"

"How's your investigation going in other respects?"

"My investigative *reporting*, you mean?"

"Uh huh." Her skepticism dripped.

"Violet." Innocent hurt tone.

"So your sole interest is the story, Lew?"

"Can I fill you in on the details over dinner?"

"What a lovely dinner topic. A murder investigation. You old sweet talker."

"See you at six?"

"I'll be here."

We hung up and I leaned back in my chair. There was nothing more appealing than an intelligent woman. Especially one who, for whatever reason, seemed willing to put up with me.

***

I was going over my now copious notes when the phone rang yet again. This was getting ridiculous. I looked at the caller ID. Hmmm.

"Hello?"

"Mr. Travis?"

"Yes."

"This is Rebecca Pearson."

"Hi, Rebecca. How are you doing over there?"

"Not so well. It's been a long night and morning. And Mom still isn't back."

"Well, as I said, it could be a full day before they release her."

"We're afraid they're not going to. We're really scared."

"I'm sure they're taking good care of your Mom."

"It's not that. We've been talking all night, and we're not as certain as we were about whether she might actually have done something. It still seems unlikely, she's our Mom, and we love her. You can't imagine this of your mother. But she was really angry."

"Really? You think she might have been capable of…?"

She hesitated. "We don't know. But we're really worried. And the fact the police are questioning her for so long…" Her voice trailed off.

"I think we just have to wait and see. The police aren't going to accuse her of something unless they have solid evidence."

There was a long pause. Finally she spoke, in a doubtful tone. "Could I maybe ask you for one more favor?" I waited. "Could you maybe talk to her at the police station?"

I frowned internally. "I'm not sure they'd let me."

"Could you try?"

"What do you think I could say?"

"We don't know. We're just really worried. Half that Mom might really have done something, and half that the police won't listen to her they're so desperate to find someone to charge with Dad's death. And they won't have anyone else who looks like as good a candidate."

I hesitated. "As I said, Rebecca, they won't charge her without clear evidence."

"But isn't that hair pretty clear evidence?"

"Well, it's evidence of something. But it's circumstantial evidence. No one actually saw your Mom do anything wrong. They'll probably send it off to a DNA lab for testing, and the results will determine if it's hers. But there could be other explanations for it even if it is hers."

"That's what we're worried about, that there is another explanation and the police won't listen to her."

She had a point. The police were anxious to charge

someone, and all the pieces fit. Jill had the motive, the opportunity, and now there was evidence to explain the method. She might well be about to be charged with Jim's murder.

I sighed. I had no doubt the police were tired of me talking to their suspects. But I could hear the desperation in Rebecca's voice. It was hard to say no, especially knowing this was Jim's daughter, and he would have wanted me to try to help if I could.

"Let me see what I can do, Rebecca. I can't promise anything, this is a police matter and they have no obligation to let me talk to your Mom. But I'll give them a call and see what they say."

The gratitude in her voice was palpable. "Thank you, Mr. Travis."

"Sure."

"Can you let us know what happens?"

"Sure."

26

As I expected, the conversation with Christiansen had not been easy. He was not in a great mood, and even on the phone I could hear The Reverend shouting his damnations in the background. I actually felt some sympathy for the guy. I could tell he was feeling beleaguered, knowing there was growing pressure to charge *someone* with this crime and not having clear proof yet who it was. In the end he agreed, even with the condition this had to be a private conversation.

When I arrived at the station there was still another issue: Jill herself. She was in a terrible mood, having slept barely at all, outraged that she'd been held overnight, and demanding to be released. It was only the fact I'd been talking with Rebecca and Adele, and was there at their urging, that she agreed to talk with me.

I was ushered into the small meeting room again. She was sitting slumped in a chair, looking tired and angry. I closed the door behind me, quietly pulled up a chair across from her, and sat down.

"Hello?"

She stared at me with a look of contempt. "I can't believe those SOBs kept me here overnight. With no evidence at all."

"Well, that's actually not quite true. Did they tell you about the hair?"

She scowled. "What hair?"

"So you don't know?"

"Know *what*?" She glared at me.

I explained to her about the blond hair they'd found in the Velcro on Jim's ventilator. At first she continued scowling. Then her eyes widened, as though she remembered something.

"Oh my god."

I cocked my head in a listening gesture.

"That damn ventilator. It looked like it came from World War II. Doesn't that hospital have funds to buy up-to-date equipment?"

"What do you mean?"

"I was sitting there with Jim, trying to reassure him. And the damn thing sounded like it was hissing."

"Do you mean the little whoosh it had?"

"No. I was used to that. That just meant it was going. But every once in awhile it emitted a little hiss. It was a different sound. Like it was leaking air."

I remembered Karen's experience; it sounded similar. "So you thought it was leaking?"

"I think *Jim* thought it was leaking. He pointed to it with a worried look."

"And...?"

"Yes. I checked it. I actually loosened the damn Velcro and re-wrapped it so it was tight. And the hiss stopped. That must be when that hair got in."

I watched her expression carefully as she said this, and listened to her tone. I was usually pretty good at detecting lies. But I wasn't sure.

"What day was that?"

"The day he died. It was that morning."

"Did anyone see you do this?"

"Who would see me? I was there alone with him."

"How did Jim react?"

"He nodded his thanks. How would you expect him to react?"

"Did you report this problem to anyone at the hospital?"

She frowned. "No. It actually didn't even occur to me. I guess I just thought that if they had to use equipment that old there wasn't much point. They must not have a newer ventilator. But now that you ask, I probably should have." Her tone had softened.

I hesitated. "It sounds like you were pretty worried about Jim?"

She scowled, her tone incredulous. "What do you mean? Of course I was worried. He was lying there in a hospital bed with a damn tube down his throat so he could breathe. Who wouldn't be worried?"

I waited a moment, studying her expression. "You sounded pretty angry at him when we last talked."

Her scowl deepened. "Yeah, I was angry with him. I still am. But that doesn't mean I wasn't worried about him."

"Really? Those don't always go hand in hand."

"He was my *husband*, for god's sake."

"Who you had thrown out of the house. And wouldn't let see your daughters."

Her scowl turned to a frown, like she was trying to make sense of this. "I was really mad at him. Everyone knows that. But that doesn't mean I didn't care about him. You don't get mad at people you don't care about."

"You don't?"

"*No*. You ignore them."

"So you did still care about Jim?"

"*Yes*. Of course! I wanted him to come to his senses and come home."

"Come to his senses?"

"Oh, he was off on one of those flings with a younger woman that middle-aged men go on. You know, a mid-life crisis thing. And he was trying to save the damn world. He'd become obsessed with helping those worthless homeless people."

"Then why did you throw him out? Why didn't you try to work out your differences?"

She rolled her eyes, sighing. Her tone softened again. "I probably shouldn't have done that. I mean, looking back, I can see it was mean. I just thought it would jar him into his senses. But it didn't work."

"And by that you mean spending more time with you and the girls?"

She ran her hands over her face. A sad tone entered her voice. "I was worried he'd stopped loving me. I guess…well, I was middle-aged, too. And I know how men think. I wanted to always be the ingénue he'd married. I wanted to be young and beautiful and the object of his fantasies. And I wasn't anymore."

"Is that why you bought all the clothes and cosmetics?"

She looked taken aback. "How did you know about that?"

I waved my hand. "Doesn't matter. Is that right?"

She rolled her eyes again. "Yes. I was doing everything I could think of to get him back. Really back, wanting me, like he used to. But his concerns had gone elsewhere. He just wanted to help those poor people out there without a place to live. That had become his whole focus. And that trollop he found."

Her whole manner had changed. She now sounded miserable. I noticed there was even a slight moistness in her eyes. "It was stupid," she said, "looking back. Somehow we kind of locked horns; we're both stubborn as hell. He didn't want to apologize, and I didn't want to give in until he had." She was shaking her head.

"Can I ask you about something else?"

She blinked away tears, nodding.

"He changed jobs. He left the paper and moved to the insurance firm so he could earn more money. Right?"

She nodded.

"And that seemed to make things worse. Not financially, but in other respects?"

She wiped her eyes with the back of her hand. "Yeah. How did you know that?"

"I've been talking with people for the retrospective I'm writing."

She sighed, shaking her head. "It turned out to be a mistake. He hated that job."

"Why?"

"The kind of work it involved. Selling insurance. Jim hated trying to sell things. It just wasn't who he was. And his salary mostly depended on how many policies he sold."

"And he didn't sell many?"

"Actually, he sold quite a few. But he just wouldn't push people to buy a policy. He was careful about learning their actual needs, and tailoring the policy to those needs, so they didn't end up paying more than they needed to."

"Was that the company policy?"

She rolled her eyes. "Hardly. Those people? They were vultures. They didn't care about anything but making money."

"Really?"

"They're awful. Which made it even harder for Jim. I frankly don't know how he stood it. And I have to admit, it was half my fault. I urged him to try it. He wasn't making a lot at the paper." She hesitated. "As you probably know, small town newspapers just don't have the funds to pay good salaries."

I nodded.

"And he was worried about putting the girls through college. They're not cheap these days. But it was still a mistake."

"Tell me more about the Cantons."

"What do you want to know?"

"When you say they were vultures, can you give me examples?"

"I don't know all the details of their operation. Jim didn't like to talk about it. But they made a lot of money. And it wasn't all legitimate."

"How so?"

"They'd sell people big policies they didn't need, and then badger them if they didn't keep up the payments. Or threaten to cancel them if they didn't increase the value of their policy. And those whole life insurance policies they sold people? They're just a racket. They're terrible investments. But they didn't care if it made money for them."

"Did Jim complain to them?"

"He tried, when he started out. But he figured out pretty quickly it wouldn't do any good. That's why they were in the business." She sighed. "It's why he hated it so much."

"Why didn't he leave?"

"He felt he needed the money. And after awhile, I think he felt trapped."

"Trapped?"

She hesitated. "Like I said, he didn't like to talk about it. But I think they had something on him."

"You mean they blackmailed him?"

She nodded. "Yeah."

"With what?"

She shrugged. "If you're part of an illegal operation, I

guess you're seen as guilty, even if you don't like it and try to avoid doing that stuff yourself."

"That's kind of a serious charge, Jill."

"I didn't talk with Jim much, but I did have one conversation in which he said he was putting together a dossier on their illegal activities. He said it was time to bring a stop to them."

"He was going to the police?"

"That's what it sounded like."

"Do you think there's any chance they…." I stopped myself. This was not a question for her. But it was for me.

I switched gears. "Was it more one of them than the other? That Jim hated."

"He didn't like either of them. But they had different roles. Bruce was the front man; he did most of the interacting with clients. He had an outgoing way, was good at selling policies. Roberta was more the brains behind the operation, so to speak. She kept the books, did the financial planning, that sort of stuff."

I was struck at how this jibed with what Karen had told me. "So he disliked them equally?"

She cocked her head to one side, as though considering this. "You know, I think he actually had a little sympathy for Bruce. Like he was being pushed by Roberta. He really hated her. She was vile."

"Really?"

She leaned back, looking me directly in the eye. "That woman is one piece of work."

"How do you mean?"

"Have you met her? I only did a couple times. But I would not want to run across her in a dark alley. She could stab you in the back as fast as you could say hello."

I nodded, amazed at the strength of her venom. I wouldn't have wanted to run into *her* in a dark alley either.

I waited for her to say more. When she didn't, I prompted: "Is there anything else you can add to that? Or that I should ask?"

"You might ask the pigs out there when I can leave."

"I think they either have to charge you by late this afternoon or let you go. So you'll know before too long."

"*Charge* me? With killing Jim?" Her tone dripped with sarcasm.

I nodded. "You need to explain to them about the hair in the Velcro. I think that will help."

"If they'd told me that was their reason for bringing me in in the first place this would have been a lot easier."

I nodded. "And it could be argued that you did have a motive to do him in."

She scowled contemptuously. "Like what?"

I wanted to see how she'd react. "The life insurance policy."

Her eyes widened and her jaw dropped. "How did you know about that?"

***

I talked briefly with Christiansen before leaving. While it wasn't really my place, I conveyed Jill's explanation for her hair in the Velcro.

"Do you believe her?" he asked.

I frowned. "That's a tough call. I don't have anything beyond her word to go on. You need to talk to her and form your own opinion."

He nodded. "We'll probably have to release her soon; I don't think we have enough to charge her with murder with just the circumstantial evidence from that one hair."

"Well, if nothing else her daughters will be appreciative."

He nodded. Then he winced as another fusillade of invectives issued forth from the back of the station. I had to admit, it was impressive the number of ways The Reverend could find to bring down the wrath of God on those he disapproved of. I only heard a few as I started to leave.

"The hour of judgment will be upon you! The wrath of God comes down on those with iniquity! His wrath shall be poured out like fire! He will rebuke thee 'til the sea runs dry! The day is coming when God's righteous judgment will be revealed!"

Not being a student of the Bible, I had no idea whether these were accurate quotes. But it was apparently quite clear to The Reverend. Christiansen rolled his eyes with a glance toward the back.

"He does know how to hurl hate at others, doesn't he?" I said.

"Yeah. We don't have anything firm on him either, but the fact he was in Pearson's hospital room—his fingerprints on the door handle and that hair on his bed—and seems capable of doing him harm…. Since he doesn't even have a residence to release him to, we're inclined to provide him with free public housing for the time being."

I couldn't disagree. We shook hands and I left.

The drive home was short. When I arrived, I called Rebecca and Adele and told them what Christiansen had said about the probable release of their Mom soon. Their relief was palpable, even over the phone. I didn't mention the life insurance policy.

Then I noticed that the message light was on. Really?

27

I listened to the message. Then, as requested, I called her back. She picked up on the second ring.

"Mr. Travis?"

"Hi, Mrs. Wilson. How are you?"

"I'm…okay. Sorry to call on a Sunday."

"No problem. What's up?"

"I'm wondering if we could maybe talk again?"

"Sure."

"I mean here. Not over the phone."

"Is there a reason?"

"I'd like to have you talk to me and Jeremy together."

"Is he still having nightmares?"

"Yes, and they're getting worse. I'm seriously worried about him."

"And you think I can help?" I probably sounded skeptical; this didn't make a lot of sense to me.

"I don't know, I was hoping so." I sensed the pleading in her voice.

"How?"

"You remember how I thought maybe something had happened at the hospital that scared him? And that he's afraid to tell me? Well, I'm pretty sure of it now. I thought maybe if you were here—another male, who he might feel could give him some protection—it might help to bring him out."

"Well...okay. Can you give me any clues?"

"Not about what he saw; he just won't tell me. But his nightmares keep getting worse. Last night he came into my room screaming in fear, saying Mom, Mom, over and over. It was several minutes before he stopped shaking. I don't think he's going to be okay again until he gets this out." She paused. "I realize this may be an unfair request. I just don't know where else to turn." There was desperation in her voice.

"Have you thought of seeing a therapist?"

"I can't afford a therapist, Mr. Travis."

"Right. Well, okay. What time is good for you?"

"Frankly, the sooner the better. This afternoon would be good, while he's not in school and I'm not at work. I can't tell you how much I'd appreciate it."

"Okay. I'll head over."

"You just don't know how much I've worried. I've got to do something."

"I can't promise I'll do any good. But I'll see you in a little while."

We hung up and I leaned back in my chair, wondering what this could mean.

***

I pulled up in front of their little house and parked. The front yard looked as shabby as ever, but there were two gloves and a baseball lying there, and a youth bat a little ways away. Nancy Wilson was a trooper. I got out and walked up to the front door, knocking lightly. It opened almost immediately.

"Hi. Come in." Again, that desperate tone, mixed with gratitude.

I stepped in and she closed the door behind me. We

made our way into the living room and she motioned me toward the chair across from the couch. "Let me get Jeremy."

They emerged from the hallway, Jeremy's eyes big, like he wasn't sure what to expect. She nudged him toward the couch where he sat down cautiously, his eyes never leaving me. She sat down next to him and put her arm around his shoulders.

"You remember Mr. Travis, don't you, Jeremy?"

He nodded.

"He's the man from the newspaper who's writing a story about the life of the man who died in the hospital."

His eyes strayed to her, then back at me.

"I thought it might be good for you to have a chance to talk to him about that. He's been looking into things and might be able to tell us more about what happened."

I waited, but that was all she said. She lowered her arm from Jeremy's shoulders and put her hands in her lap. Finally, I said, "Is there something you'd like to ask me, Jeremy?"

He looked at his Mom, then at me, his eyes big and fearful. It was pretty clear, even to an untrained eye, that he was keeping something in. He shook his head.

"I've been talking to other people about what happened at the hospital, " I said. "The doctor who is the chief medical officer. A very nice nurse named Jennifer, who you might remember. The people who visited my friend at the hospital. Even officers at the police station who are trying to figure out what happened."

His eyes narrowed. "Policemen?"

I nodded.

"Why are they...?" His voice trailed off.

"I think they're suspicious that something happened there that shouldn't have. They don't know what, but just like me, they're trying to find out."

He glanced at his mother, who nodded reassuringly.

"Your Mom thinks that maybe something happened there that scared you, Jeremy? Is that true?"

His face turned dark and he hunched his shoulders. He said nothing.

"She said you're having nightmares that are scaring you?" I was using my gentlest tone, hoping he'd say something, anything.

He glanced at his Mom again, then shook his head.

"You're not having nightmares?"

He hunched his shoulders further, like a turtle pulling his head into his shell.

A thought occurred to me. "Could we maybe talk about something else?"

His expression lightened slightly.

"Have you watched any Giants games yet this season?"

He nodded.

"Do you remember what ones?"

Nancy intervened. "We watched last night's game, didn't we?" she said, looking down at him.

He nodded.

"And we beat the ol' Dodgers, eh?" I said.

A slight smile touched the corners of his mouth.

"Do you have a favorite Giant?"

"Buster Posey."

"The catcher?"

He nodded.

"He's a very good catcher, isn't he?"

"And hitter." Thank god; words.

"Yeah. I've forgotten; what is his batting average so far?"

"Two eighty-five. He has two homers already."

"Right. Including one last night?"

His expression had eased considerably. "He's going to be the MVP again."

"You think so?" I nodded in encouragement.

"If he doesn't get injured."

"Yeah. That's always a danger. Especially for a catcher."

"He broke his leg once."

"I remember that. Almost like your Mom and her leg."

He frowned.

"But he got better, didn't he? Just like your Mom."

He nodded, his expression reflective.

"People do get over things. It just takes time."

He looked away, seeming to consider this.

"Things aren't always quite as bad as they might seem at first."

His look turned to a frown.

"So, could we maybe get back to the hospital? I'd like to tell you what I know. Would that be okay?"

He looked doubtful, but nodded slightly.

"Mr. Pearson—the man who died—was a wonderful man. He did all kinds of good things for other people. He has two daughters. One is in college and the other in high school. He was a wonderful father to them. And he tried to help other people who didn't have as much as he did. Like homeless people?"

He nodded, seemingly not sure where I was going with this. Nor, to be honest, was I; I was winging it. I let my instincts guide me.

"This is why we're trying to figure out what happened to him. He wasn't very old. The doctors don't think it was his illness that killed him. They expected him to get better."

He continued to watch me, his expression guarded.

"They think it must have been something else. So we're doing everything we can to try to figure out what that was.

That's why I'm talking to all these different people."

He'd stopped frowning. He was listening and taking all this in.

"I don't know if you remember, but he was getting help breathing. He had an illness called pneumonia, which affects your lungs. There was a machine that was pushing air into his lungs for him, and pulling it back out. It's called a ventilator."

He nodded. "The whooshing noise."

"Yes. Exactly. So you must have heard it?"

He nodded. "When I went to the bathroom."

"Of course. Past his room."

He nodded.

"It wasn't all that loud, but you could hear it?"

"Uh huh."

"And it went all the time. You could hear it every time you went past."

His expression darkened.

"No?"

He scowled.

"It's okay, Jeremy. I'm just curious. You didn't hear it every time?"

His scowl deepened, and he looked down at the floor. Finally, after what seemed an age, there was the slightest shaking of his head.

"Okay. So there were times you *didn't* hear it?"

"One time."

"One time?"

He nodded, still scowling. I glanced at Nancy, her expression a mix of concern and wonder, apparently at the fact Jeremy was actually talking about this.

"On your way to the bathroom?"

He nodded.

"And back?"

He shook his head.

"Not on the way back?"

"No." His voice was so soft it was barely audible.

"So, it was not going when you went to the bathroom, but it was going again when you returned to your Mom's room?"

He nodded.

I stared at Nancy in confusion. What could this mean?

"You're sure?"

He nodded again.

"Did you go into his room?"

He shook his head vigorously.

"Did you see anyone else go in?"

He closed his eyes and his lips began to quiver.

"You saw someone else go in?"

He shook his head, ever so slightly.

I pondered this. Why was he so frightened if he hadn't seen anyone else there? Then a thought struck me.

"Jeremy, did you see anyone *leaving* the room?"

His eyes welled up and he put his hands over his face. His shoulders began to shake.

I waited for him to regain his composure. It took several moments. Then I tried again.

"Okay. You don't have to say anything. Just nod, okay? You saw someone leaving the room?"

Immediately he was back into full shaking and crying mode. The sobs were awful, and his expression was pure misery. I waited again, saying nothing. Finally, still shaking, tears pouring down his face, he said through gritted teeth, "I can't tell you."

I looked at Nancy, who had a baffled expression. "Okay, Jeremy. You don't have to tell us. That's okay."

He began to calm, and I waited again. Nancy now had her arm around his shoulders and was running her hand through his hair. "It's okay. It's okay."

Finally I said, "Is there anything else you *can* tell us?"

His lower lip began to quiver again, the look of misery clear. "I don't think so."

"I get the idea that there was someone who came out, but you can't tell us who. Is that right?"

He nodded slightly. I glanced at Nancy. At least this was progress. A thought occurred to me.

"Okay. Let's try this. I'm going to guess, okay? You don't have to say."

He looked at me with fear in his eyes.

I spoke in the gentlest voice I had. "Is it because he said he was going to hurt you if you told anyone?"

The sobs again became full throttle, tortured, from deep inside. This went on for several moments. Finally, as it eased just a bit, he uttered something nearly indiscernible. It was barely a whisper. "And Mom."

Again I glanced at Nancy. Her expression too was now tortured. She pulled Jeremy's head into her chest and ran her fingers through his hair, over and over, looking at me with pain in her eyes.

Again I waited for him to calm. Finally he began to dry his eyes with his sleeve, and looked up with a tormented expression. "He said he would kill me and Mom if I told anyone I'd seen him." And the full-throttle tortured sobs resumed.

I leaned back in the chair. "It's okay, Jeremy. He's not going to be able to do that, because we're going to catch him. Okay?"

His lips trembled, his face was soaked, his fear was palpable.

"He's a bad guy. Sometimes we run across bad guys. But that's why we have police. If we can tell the police who the bad guys are, they'll catch them and put them in

255

jail."

He nodded, his face a picture of misery.

"But I need you to tell me just a little more. Okay?"

He blinked, again drying his eyes with his sleeve, saying nothing but waiting for me to speak.

"To catch him, we need to know what he looks like. Does that make sense?"

He nodded slightly.

Nancy said, "Jeremy, do you understand what Mr. Travis is asking?"

He nodded.

"So, can you tell us what this man looked like?"

He turned his face to her. "Will he come after us if I do?"

"No. Mr. Travis just explained that. And think about it, Jeremy. Is that man here?"

He looked confused for a minute, then shook his head.

"So he won't know what you've told us. He can't possibly know. He's not God, just a man. He has no way of knowing what you're saying."

His brows furrowed as he considered this. Finally, frowning, he nodded.

"So, can you tell us what he looked like?"

He looked away, as though trying to remember. Then he looked back, directly at me. "He was big."

"A big man? Was he fat?" I asked.

He shook his head.

"Tall?"

He nodded.

"Do you remember what color his hair was?"

He looked at me in confusion.

"For example, did he have long blond hair? Almost white?"

He shook he head.

"Dark hair?"

He nodded.

"Did he have a beard?"

He shook his head.

"So he was a tall man with dark hair and no beard?"

He nodded.

"Okay, good. That helps a lot. Anything else?"

"He was mean."

"A tall dark-haired mean man?"

He nodded, wiping his nose on his sleeve. "He was putting something in his pocket."

"In his pocket? How big was it?"

His brow wrinkled in a thinking gesture. "Kind of the size of his hand, I think."

"It didn't look like"…I stopped, wondering if I should mention this, then thought better of it. The last thing he needed was the image of a gun in his mind.

He looked at me, waiting for me to finish. I shook my head. "Just an idea that I realized didn't make any sense."

"His face was really close to mine," he said.

"Okay. What you've told me is a big help, Jeremy. Now I'm going to call the police and tell them what you've told me. And they will begin looking for him. Okay?"

He nodded.

"It's not okay for grown men to say they'll hurt boys if they say anything. He was a bad man. The police will know that. And they'll protect you. Okay?"

He nodded again. The torture seemed finally to be starting to lift.

"They may also want to talk to you, just to get as clear a picture as they can of what he looks like. But that's up to you. I will tell them everything you've told me. So it's really only if you can think of other things that might help us to find him that you need to say more. Okay?"

Again he nodded.

I pulled the cell phone out of my pocket, stood and walked out of the room, and put in a call to the police station. As it happened, Christiansen was still there; I shared what I had just learned. He said there would be a car on the way shortly, and he'd be in it.

I walked back into the living room and explained this to Nancy and Jeremy, saying I'd wait until they got there. Nancy was wiping tears from her eyes. She came over and put her arms around me, half sobbing.

"You're a godsend, Lew. There is no way to thank you enough."

I hugged her back, but gently. I didn't want to mention that we still had a ways to go. We hadn't yet found this man, nor captured him. That still needed to happen. In fact, we weren't even certain who it was. But I had a pretty good idea.

28

Christiansen arrived as promised and I filled him in in more detail about what I'd learned. He was particularly interested in the description of the man, tall and dark-haired. And what he might have been putting in his pocket. He spent some time going over the same territory with Jeremy that I had, and I had to admit, he did it carefully and gently. But no new details emerged.

When he was finished, he spoke to the deputy who had come with him, asking him to stay and provide a guard on the house. Then he phoned the station and explained the situation to someone there, arranging for a 24-hour guard. Christiansen might not be the sharpest knife in the drawer, but his heart was in the right place. I knew there was little chance Jeremy and his mother were in any real danger; he was stationing a guard there solely for their emotional well-being.

There seemed no point in my hanging around any longer, so I took my leave and headed out to Old Blue. I sat there for a while at the curb, going over the information Jeremy had provided. It raised new questions. Apparently the ventilator had been turned off for a while. How that had happened without the nurses getting a signal? How long had it been off; that seemed crucial. It provided a logical explanation for how Jim could have died. And of course, the critical question: who was the tall dark-haired man leaving Jim's room, presumably after having just killed him. Why else would he be so concerned about Jeremy saying anything to anyone? And what was he putting in his pocket?

***

I glanced at the clock in Old Blue: two-thirty. There were two places I wanted to visit. And as I reflected, I decided on the order in which to hit them.

I found my way to the dodgy neighborhood where Karen Black's shop was located and pulled up in front. I didn't expect to find her there—it was Sunday after all—but I thought I might find something else.

I got out and walked up to the front door, and sure enough, there it was. A note hanging in the glass, in large print:

```
    Apologies. Away temporarily.
    Will reschedule all missed
            appointments.
```

I walked back to Old Blue and headed for the second stop, in a better part of town, on Cedar Street. I didn't expect to find anyone there either, but again, thought there might be a similar note. I parked across the street and walked through the little parking lot in front of Canton's Insurance office.

There was no note in the window here, and there was a light on inside. I looked through the window and saw someone sitting behind one of the desks. Someone I recognized: Roberta Eileen Canton, bent over her desk, studying something.

I decided I had nothing to lose by having a chat with her. I knocked on the front door and she looked up with a surprised expression. I tried the door but it was locked. She got up and unlocked it.

"Mr. Travis? To what do we owe this surprise on a lovely Sunday afternoon?" She nodded to a chair in front of her desk. "Come in and have a seat?"

I tried to gauge her tone; it felt falsely friendly. But then so did all salespeople, especially insurance salespeople. I stepped in and sat down.

"I had a few more questions for my article, just came by on the off chance someone might be here."

"Can I answer them for you?"

"Actually, I was hoping to talk with Bruce. Is he around?"

Her expression darkened. "No."

"Do you happen to know where I might find him?" I kept my voice even.

She sighed and leaned back in her chair. "Actually, I don't know where he is. And if I may be open with you"…she paused and waited for a response, and I nodded an 'of course'…"I'm a little worried about him."

"Oh? Why?"

She looked out the window, seeming to consider whether—or perhaps how—to continue. Then she looked directly at me.

"I'm going to be entirely honest with you, Lew. Can I call you Lew?"

I nodded.

"Lew, Bruce has disappeared. I don't know where he is, and haven't been able to get in touch with him. I'm frankly worried."

"Disappeared?"

She frowned. "Yes. It's never happened before. He's a very reliable man. I'm confused and worried. I fear something has happened to him."

261

"How long has he been missing?"

"Just today. He left to have breakfast with a client and never returned."

"Does he usually work on Sundays?"

"We work whenever clients are available; weekends are often our busiest time. That's not unusual. But he's never failed to return before."

"And you've tried his cell phone?"

"Repeatedly. I've tried calling and texting. He seems to have simply vanished. I was sitting here trying to decide what to do when you knocked."

"Have you considered contacting the police?"

She nodded. "It seemed a little premature, but actually, I think that's a good idea." She glanced at the phone on her desk. "Would you mind?"

"Not at all. Proceed." I was curious exactly what she'd do.

She lifted the phone and dialed a number. I could just make out the voice on the other end of the line: "Sienna Police Department".

"Yes, this is Roberta Eileen Canton. My husband has disappeared and I'm quite worried about him. Is there someone there I could report this to?"

I could just make out the voice on the other end. "Yes, Mrs. Canton. The chief just returned from the field. Let me get him."

She looked up at me, mouthing the words: "They're getting the chief of police."

I nodded, and waited. Sure enough, I could hear his voice: "Hello. This is Christensen. What can I do for you?"

She proceeded to tell him exactly what she'd just told me, waiting a couple times for Christiansen to take notes. He asked a few sensible questions: When and where she'd last seen Bruce; what he'd been wearing; what kind of car he drove and its license number; what client he'd been meeting with; where the meeting had taken place. She provided all the right answers. I took note of Bruce's car; a white Jeep Cherokee. The call ended with Christiansen saying they'd get on it and let her know when they'd learned anything.

She hung up the phone and looked at me. "Frankly, I don't know what more to do." She sounded genuinely distressed. "Do you have any other suggestions, Lew?"

I shrugged. "Not really."

"It's just not like Bruce." She rolled her eyes, sighed deeply. "Could you excuse me for just a moment, Lew. This is a little embarrassing, but I need to visit the bathroom."

"Sure."

She shuffled some papers on her desk as though covering something up, then strode through a door at the back of the office, closing it behind her. I decided to take the opportunity to have a look at what the papers on her desk were.

There were several pages of charts laid out, covering almost all her desk, none of which made any sense to me. Then I noticed a picture in one corner, the only thing not covered by charts, scotch-taped to the top of the desk. It had been taken from the deck of a cabin in the woods, the railing visible at the bottom but out of focus, looking down toward a small lake. Bruce was waving to the camera from below, smiling and walking up from the lake, carrying a large trout in one hand.

I recognized that lake: Loon Lake. It was only a few miles outside of town. I could even get a rough sense of where the cabin must be located from the boat ramp I could just make out on the far side. I made a mental note and returned to my chair in front of the desk.

Roberta took her time, but eventually returned from the bathroom and sat down again, running her hands through her hair in a gesture of desperation. "I just don't know what to do, Lew. I'm so worried."

"I think you've done what you can. Why don't you let the police do their work and see what they come up with? I know it's hard, but I think you just have to give them some time."

She nodded, her brow furrowed. "Good advice, I've no doubt. It's just not easy."

"No." I hesitated; I wanted to leave. I now had another place I wanted to go. "I should probably be on my way."

"Sure, Lew. Thanks for your help. I hope they find him." She held out her hand in a gesture of appreciation, which I shook briefly.

I edged myself out the front door, heading for Old Blue. I glanced back at the office as I pulled out; Roberta was standing in the window, staring out at me with an expression I couldn't interpret.

***

It was only a fifteen-minute drive to Loon Lake, on a remote country lane, and another five-minute drive around to the side where I had gauged from the picture the Canton cabin must be. I drove slowly, keeping an eye on the spot where I estimated it was as I made my way along the forested one-lane road, with patches of broken pavement and potholes here and there. I got a couple glimpses of the cabin as I did so; it was set back from the shoreline a couple hundred feet. I slowed as I approached the spot, and stopped just short of a rustic gate, where I sat and thought for a moment. Then I pulled Old Blue ahead around a curve and over to the side as far as possible, enough so another car could get by. I got out and walked back to the gate.

It was made of heavy metal pipework, and padlocked shut. But it was only about four feet high, so I hoisted myself over it and eased down on the other side. I started down the dirt driveway, hoping there would be no dog. As I rounded a gentle curve, there it was: a cedar-shingled one-story cabin with steps leading up to a narrow deck along the back and down one side, connecting to a larger deck in front. A white Jeep Cherokee was parked behind the cabin. An entry door and two windows looked out on the back deck, one window small and frosted, apparently for a bathroom, and a larger clear one, probably either a bedroom or kitchen. I waited and watched for a few moments to see whether there was any sign of movement inside, but all seemed quiet.

I approached slowly, carefully making my way up the steps, which creaked as I did so, and onto the narrow back deck. Here I could look through the clear glass window, which turned out to be in the kitchen. I could see through to the front and a large window that looked out onto the lake. Still I saw no sign of movement. The lake was also quiet; there was just one small craft on one end, a canoe or kayak. I tried the door but it was locked. Cautiously I edged along the side deck and peeked around to the front. Still no sign of life.

I stepped around the corner onto the broad front deck, when, much to my surprise and consternation, my phone rang.

29

Quickly I pulled it out of my pocket and checked the ID: Violet. I punched the talk icon and whispered, "Violet?"

"Hi, Lew. I had a thought about tonight."

I spoke in the softest voice possible that was still audible. "Hey, I'm in kind of a delicate spot at the moment. Can I call you back?"

She hesitated. "Sure. Where are you?"

"Loon Lake. I'm snooping around somewhere I probably shouldn't be."

"Lew, you're a damn fool!"

"That's not exactly headline news."

"What the hell are you doing?"

"Collecting evidence?"

"Well…."

"So, can I call you back?"

"I was just going to invite you over for a drink before we go out to dinner."

"Invitation accepted."

"What the hell am I going to…." Her voice trailed off.

"See you there?"

"Sweet Jesus. You're going to get yourself killed one of these days."

"Let's hope it's not today."

I pushed the end call icon and looked out on the lake

from my perch on the deck. There was a canoe just easing into shore, with two people in it: a tall dark-haired man, and an auburn-haired young woman.

I considered my options. It didn't appear they'd spotted me; I still had time to reverse course and escape. But I hadn't learned anything more than I already knew. It occurred to me that this was actually an ideal setup: I'd found them and now all I had to do to learn more was to find a place where I could eavesdrop on their conversation.

I looked around the deck for such a spot. There were a couple wooden Adirondack chairs and a round glass-topped table with four rattan chairs. None seemed adequate to provide cover. But the entry door in back had been locked. Then I noticed the sliding glass door from the deck into the living room. I tried it and sure enough, it was unlocked. I quietly slid it open enough to slip in, watching the two canoeists get out of the craft and pull it up on shore. They began to make their way up toward the cabin.

I looked around for a good place to hide. It was not a very big room, all one open space. The living room area contained a couch against a wall and a couple of easy chairs on the other side of a coffee table. There was a dining area in front of the kitchen with a rectangular wooden table and four chairs. The kitchen was small with no furniture. None of these seemed adequate for hiding.

A hall led toward the back. I quietly found my way down this to a single door on the left. I opened this and peeked in. It was a bedroom with one large bed, a bureau on one wall, and a closet on another. A window faced out the far side. There was also a door leading into a bathroom at the back of the cabin.

I stepped into the bedroom and closed the door behind me, looking around for the best hiding place. The only real option seemed to be the closet; I slid the door open and looked in. Fortunately, it was not very full. I pushed some hangers aside and crunched down inside, sliding the door shut behind me. And waited.

In just a few moments I heard a key in the entry door at the back, and voices.

"Pretty nice spot, eh?" Bruce said.

"It is nice. I love the outdoors, woods and lakes. It was a nice canoe ride."

"I'm going to fix us a little something."

"Like?"

"Just a couple of drinks."

"I don't really want anything alcoholic, Bruce. Maybe some coffee?"

"Aw, come on. Here, I'll make you one and you can just ignore it if you don't want it."

I heard ice being dropped into glasses and the sound of liquids being poured. Then the two glasses were being set down somewhere, probably the coffee table in the living room.

"Come on back in; it's just a simple gin and tonic." Bruce's voice.

Her voice was fainter: "I like it out here. It's a pretty view."

"Okay, I'll bring them out there." Annoyance had crept into his tone.

Both their voices became faint and I stepped out of the closet and over to the door, opening it a crack so I could hear.

"I really don't want a drink. You said we were just going for a canoe ride."

"We went for a canoe ride. This is just to relax afterward."

"Uh huh."

"Come on. One drink isn't going to kill you."

"I told you, I don't want a drink."

"It's four in the afternoon. It's time for a late afternoon quaff."

"You go ahead."

"Jeez, Karen, you're not making this easy."

"Not making *what* easy?" Her tone held annoyance.

"I'm just trying to be friends."

"It feels like maybe you have more than friendship on your mind."

"And would that be so bad? It just means I find you attractive. You didn't seem to have any trouble having drinks with Jim Pearson."

"Jim's intentions were always clear. We were just friends."

"Didn't look that way from my perspective."

"Well your perspective was wrong."

"Jesus. One sip, for God's sake."

"I think it's time for me to leave."

There was a moment of silence. Then Bruce's voice. "What makes you think you can?"

"What the hell does that mean?" There was now clear anger in her voice.

"Let me put it to you straight. You're a convicted felon. With two strikes. And as it happens, I have a picture of you smoking a joint. That's a probation violation."

Again a moment of silence. "You're threatening to turn me in for smoking a joint?"

"Not if you're...nice to me."

"God damn it Bruce, no." I heard a chair move and the scuffling of feet. Then some steps. And in a muffled voice: "Let go of me. God damn it, Bruce. *NO!*"

I was about to push the door open the rest of the way and enter the fray when I heard another noise, a key in the back door. Apparently they heard it also, as the scuffling noises stopped. I pulled the bedroom door quietly shut.

The back door creaked slightly as it swung open. A new voice spoke. "Well, hello, you two." It was a female voice I knew, and it was not friendly. "I thought I'd find you here."

"What the hell are you doing here, Roberta?" Bruce sounded livid.

"Oh, I just thought I ought to swing by and see what you're up to."

"How did you know we were here?"

"You're very predictable, Bruce. Pretty girl? Where else would you take her?"

"She's none of your business."

"Oh, really? Have you forgotten we're married? I believe somewhere it's written that adultery does affect married partners."

"There hasn't been any adultery."

"I'm sure not because of your lack of trying."

Karen's voice chimed in. "Actually, I was just leaving."

"What's the hurry, sweetie. I think it might be nice for the three of us to have a little chat."

"About what?" Karen asked.

"The fact you're cavorting with a murderer."

"*What?*"

Bruce's angry voice cut in. "All right, that's enough, Roberta. We're both leaving."

There was a brief silence. Then: "I don't believe you are, Bruce dear."

"My God, Roberta. What are you doing with a gun?"

"Pointing it at you. Making sure you hang out here until the police arrive."

"*What?*"

"Yes, dear. While you've been trying to make it with this…this little whore, I've been sharing the details of your crime with the men in blue."

270

"What do you mean, *my* crime? *You* planned it?"

"Who's going to believe that, sweetie? I was nowhere near the scene. I had no idea what you were doing. You're the murderer. With a clear motive: replacing Jim in the affections of this young trollop. I think her presence here will support my story quite nicely."

"But…but…you said we were partners. That it was a way to keep Jim from going to the cops with the evidence he had of our illegal business practices. I did that for *us*."

"Illegal business practices? Where did you ever get that idea?"

There was some unintelligible mumbling.

"There is no evidence of anything like that in our records, dear. You see, I happen to be the one who keeps them. It's a shame you never took the trouble to look at them."

"But…but that's what you told me."

"I would never say anything like that."

"God damn it, Roberta. I can't believe this."

"Believe it, dear."

There was a moment of silence. "You won't get away with this, Roberta. It's your word against mine."

"*Your* word, Bruce? The word of a killer?"

"They can't prove that."

"Oh, but they can. With the evidence I've already given them."

"*What* evidence?"

"Well, for openers, the step-by-step description of how you did it. Unplugging the ventilator. Which disarmed its alarm. Then holding Jim down while he struggled to breathe. Until he didn't struggle anymore. It took what, about five minutes? Then plugging the ventilator back in. So it appeared nothing was ever amiss."

"That's just a story. It's not evidence."

"Oh, but the broken leather strap they found below the ventilator is. Which as it happens, is a perfect match for the one missing from one of your gloves."

"What? How?"

"You're really not very smart, dear. Leaving such obvious clues. I don't think a jury will have any trouble reaching a verdict."

"Why…why are you doing this? We were in this together. It was your idea."

"Oh, it might have something to do with that little clause in our incorporation. The one that points out if one of the partners is convicted of a felony they forfeit all rights to the corporation's assets or profits while incarcerated. There's a tidy little sum there. Should provide quite a nice retirement for me, on my tropical island of choice."

There was more shuffling, and then a shot rang out. "*God damn it!* You just shot me in the foot. *Shit!*"

"Yes, well, I promised the police I'd keep you here until they arrived. Should be any time now."

"*Ah! Ah! Shit!*"

Then there was a softer female voice—Karen's. "Why are you saying all this in my presence? Aren't you worried I'll tell the police?"

"Not unless you want to do some serious time in prison, dear. You see, I know about your two previous convictions also. And Bruce dear left the picture of you smoking that joint in his desk. Which he doesn't lock, silly man. Shouldn't be very hard for the police to find your stash. Of course, should you choose to keep your mouth shut, I'd have no reason to mention this. And really, when you think about it, why would you want to? All that's going to happen is this disgusting man, who by now you must have come to hate as much as I do, will wind up paying the price for killing your dear Jim."

There was no response. But now there were faint sirens in the distance.

"Well, here they are now. How convenient. It certainly does give one solace, knowing those men in blue are there to protect us."

The sirens grew louder, then stopped. Male voices could be heard outside the cabin, then someone knocking.

"Karen, dear, why don't you let them in? I don't want to take my eyes off this killer. Who knows what he might try?"

There were footsteps in the hallway, the sound of the back door creaking open, then an exchange of comments between Christiansen and Roberta, Bruce interrupting with angry shouts.

"He's just implicating himself further," she said. "All this lying."

"We appreciate your help, Mrs. Canton," Christiansen said.

"Happy to be of service, chief. Just glad the thought finally occurred to me. This seemed like the place he must be." She paused. "I've always had a deep admiration for our men in blue."

"Much appreciated, ma'am."

"I'm sorry about his foot. He tried to get away, and I didn't know how else to stop him."

"Doesn't look too serious. We'll take care of it."

There were some clicks, presumably handcuffs going on, with more shouting from Bruce, and then steps out the back and the door closing. I heard nothing from Karen, although it seemed apparent they had taken her in also. And then I was alone.

Except for one other person. Who, as far as I could tell, still had that gun.

30

I listened intently for signs of movement. There were steps going into the kitchen, the clink of ice in a glass, then steps back into the living room. She was muttering to herself, which was hard to decipher. I opened the bedroom door a crack and put my ear in the opening.

"Damn fools. Even left me a drink to celebrate. What an idiot that man is. I can't believe I ever married him. Good riddance."

The ice clinked in the glass, accompanied by a slurp.

"Damn stupid cops fell for the whole thing. The world is full of morons. I just hope that damn trollop keeps her mouth shut. But what the hell, if she doesn't, I'll get her locked up too."

There was a pause in this monologue; I waited.

"I'm surprised that old coot isn't here, though. I thought sure he'd see that picture and come out and investigate. Must not be as smart as I thought."

Again a pause.

"Unless...." I could hear her take another slurp and then set the glass down.

Shit. I looked around, surveying my options. There wasn't time to get into the hallway and out the back door without her seeing me. The only other door in the room went into the bathroom, where there was just the small frosted window I'd seen from the outside. Then my eyes fell on the bedroom window. It was a sideways slider, and easily large enough for me to fit through. I tiptoed over to it, slid it open, popped out the screen, and looked down.

The cabin was built on a hillside, so that the front deck was a full story above the ground. But the bedroom was near the back of the house, where the drop was only about five feet. I climbed to a sitting position on the window frame, twisted quickly onto my stomach, and let myself slide down, grasping the frame as I did so to ease the drop. My last glimpse was of Roberta opening the bedroom door, her gun leading the way.

The ground was soft; I made little sound when I hit. But I knew she'd notice the open window. I scrambled down the hillside and headed for the area under the front deck. I looked back as I rounded the corner; she was just poking her head out the window, again gun first. I was pretty sure she'd spotted me. I tried to think what to do next.

One option was to head for the water, but it wouldn't take her long to get back out to the deck, and it wouldn't take a great shot to hit me at the distance I could make in that short time. Another possibility was to scramble along the hillside laterally, get as far away from the cabin as I could. There were a few trees and bushes on both sides, but not enough to provide reliable coverage. It felt chancy. A third possibility was to sit tight, just stay under the deck. But as I looked up, there were spaces between the floorboards. They weren't very wide—it wasn't clear she could aim a gun through them—but it was a definite risk. She would be at very close range.

I looked around in desperation. To my relief, there was one more option: a door in the siding beneath the deck that must lead to a storage area underneath the cabin. I tried the door; it was unlocked. I yanked it open and stepped into the dark, closing it behind me. I felt along the wall for a switch, which I flipped up. A single light bulb sprang to life. I looked around: it was a small room, containing a furnace, hot water heater, and stacks of boxes on shelves along one wall.

I looked at the doorknob and noticed it was lockable. It probably had been left open by accident, although it occurred to me that Roberta probably had a key to it. Nevertheless, I switched it to the locked position and made a more careful inspection. There were several life vests hanging along a second wall, two old canoe paddles, and some tools hanging on hooks. Leaning against the wall were a pickaxe, a wood-splitting mall, and a crowbar. I picked up the crowbar and wedged it against the door at an angle. Then another thought occurred.

I pulled out my cell phone. Was there someone I could call for help? Or at least let know of my predicament. The cops? Would they come back? It seemed worth a try.

I tried to remember their number, reached to dial, when, much to my amazement, the phone rang. I looked at the ID. Violet? Again? At the worst possible moment.

I punched the answer icon, not quite believing it, fearing it was going to be my last conversation ever.

"Violet?" I said, in a hushed whisper.

"We're behind the cabin, Lew. Thank God you're still alive."

"What? How?"

"You mentioned Loon Lake. There aren't many cabins out here. We found your car, figured this had to be the place."

"We?"

"I've got Tim and Harve with me. They're the only ones I figured would believe what kind of trouble you could get yourself into. Where are you?"

"Jesus, Violet. There's a woman in the house with a

gun. She's trying to find me. I'm underneath in a storage room. Be careful!"

"Wow. Really? A gun? You do get yourself into some messes, Lew. I'm impressed."

"Hey, this is no time for humor. This woman's crazy."

"Okay, okay. What should we do?"

I tried to think. What *should* they do? "Maybe you could distract her? Get her confused?"

"How?"

"Well, how about throwing some rocks."

"What?"

"If you start throwing rocks out to one side of the house, she'll hear them and look that way. That might give you a chance to sneak up on her from the other side."

"Sounds a little harebrained."

"Well, what's *your* idea?"

"I'm thinking."

"Where are Tim and Harve?"

"Here. With me. Where do you think?"

"Okay. Here's another idea. Do you see the white Jeep Cherokee out there?"

"Yeah, we're standing next to it."

"Is it locked?"

There were some clicking noises. "No."

"Okay. There's a door at the back of the cabin. It's the main entrance. If you blow the horn on the car, maybe she'll come out that door. If Harve and Tim are waiting there behind the cabin door, maybe they can grab her when she comes out?"

"That's a better idea."

"Thanks."

"Except for who's blowing the horn? I guess that would be me?"

"Let's see, subtract two from three and you get...."

"Okay, now *you're* getting silly. What if they don't grab her before she gets a shot off?"

I stared up at the ceiling, hesitating. I couldn't quite believe I was having this conversation. We were talking about someone shooting at Violet? Not to mention Tim and Harve? It didn't feel real. But it was.

"That's a good point. It sounds too dangerous. Forget it."

"No. I just explained it to them; they like the idea. We're doing it. They're creeping up to the door now."

"Well, Jesus, Violet, don't let her see you when you blow the horn. Duck down out of sight, under the dash."

"Yeah, that occurred to me. No point in offering her an obvious target. Especially when it's me."

"Tell me when you're ready. I'm going to try to help."

"How?"

"When she heads for the back door, I'll get out of here and scramble up the hill outside as fast as I can."

"Okay. Get ready. Here goes."

Sure enough, a door slammed and there was a loud blast of a horn. Then footsteps above as Roberta hurried to the back door. I pulled the crowbar out of the way, yanked the door open, ran for the corner of the house, and scrambled up the side as fast as I could, hoping not to hear a shot. There was the sound of scuffling on the back deck, but no shots rang out. And then the scuffling stopped, replaced by muffled female shouts.

I reached the top of the hill and looked at the deck. It presented quite a picture. Harve was sitting on top of Roberta, holding her hands behind her back. Tim was standing next to him with the gun, pointing it toward her. Roberta was swearing a blue streak. And Violet was just getting out of the Jeep, looking at me with an expression that asked: Did it work?

I let out a long sigh. I nodded toward Tim and Harve. "Thanks, gentlemen."

"You do owe us one," Harve said. "This is still Sunday, you know."

"Hey, I livened up what can be a pretty dull day for a lot of people," I offered.

"Normal people view it as a day of rest," Tim said. "This isn't my idea of restful." He glanced at Roberta, still pointing the gun her way.

"Will you %&7@#*&$! idiots shut up," she screamed. She squirmed violently under Harve, who rode on her back like a rodeo cowboy on a bucking bronco.

"You're not bad at that, Harve," I said. "Do you have experience in this arena?"

"Dealing with %@&^%*# idiots? Yes. Would you like me to provide an example?"

***

It was decided I should be the one to put in the call to the police station. I dialed the number and waited. That gruff female voice answered.

"This is Lew Travis. Could I speak to an officer?"

"The captain just arrived with two prisoners. Let me get him."

"Great."

There was a moment of silence, and then Christiansen's voice came on. "Travis?"

"Yeah. Hi."

"What can I do for you?" His voice sounded more relaxed than it had in days.

"I have in my custody someone I think you'll want to take in."

"What are you talking about? We just brought in the

279

person we've been looking for. He's already in custody. We've solved this one."

"Yes. Well, unfortunately, he had an accomplice. Actually, the brains of the operation."

"What are you talking about?"

"He didn't commit the murder entirely of his own volition."

"What? Who?" He was sputtering.

"We have the accomplice here?"

"Here? Where are you, Travis?" Annoyance had entered his voice.

"At a little cabin on Loon Lake. You may remember it?"

"That's where we just *came* from. When did you get there?" Annoyance had turned to confusion.

"I've been here all along."

"No you weren't."

"I was in the bedroom."

There was a sigh. "Okay, Travis, let's take it from the top. What the hell are you talking about?"

I explained the whole situation to him, including the current circumstances. Roberta could be heard swearing through muffled lips in the background. When I had finished, there was a pause. He seemed to be considering the plausibility of all this.

"Is that her I hear shouting?" Christiansen asked.

"Yes."

"She has quite a mouth on her, doesn't she?"

"She does."

There was a long pause. His tone had now gone to resignation. He sighed. "Okay. We'll come back out there. I can't believe this day isn't over."

31

I spent a while at the police station, providing chapter and verse of what I'd heard. Which, along with Jeremy's account from his experience at the hospital, provided about all the evidence needed to convict Bruce Canton and send him up for a very long time. Not to mention the corroborating evidence of the broken leather strap from his glove, which he'd worn to prevent fingerprints, and was what Jeremy had seen him putting in his pocket. When Karen added her story, including details of the conversation between Bruce and Roberta at the cabin, and we both agreed to testify at their trial, there wasn't much doubt Roberta would be accompanying her husband to similar public accommodations, also for a very long time. Meanwhile, Jill was released from jail with apologies, and The Reverend was sent to a mental rehab facility for examination and treatment.

After we'd finished with the explanations I asked Christiansen for a brief private meeting. We walked back into that little conference room.

He rubbed his eyes, obviously exhausted. "This better be short."

"What do you see happening to Karen Black?"

"You talking about that picture of her smoking weed?"

"So they did tell you about that?"

"Yeah. That woman would turn in her own mother out

of vengeance."

"So?"

"So what?"

"So…are you going to charge her?"

"From a picture of someone smoking something that we can't identify? And what if it is weed, it's legal now in California. She can smoke as much of it as she damn pleases. I didn't see her trying to sell it to anyone in the picture."

I smiled. "Okay."

"That it?"

I nodded.

He reached out his hand. "Thanks for the help, Travis. You're an annoying old son of a bitch, but I've got to admit…"

"Coming from you, chief, I regard that as a serious compliment."

***

When I got home I called Nancy Wilson and relayed the news. I could feel the sense of relief, even over the phone. She asked if she could put Jeremy on to hear it directly. I made it short and to the point: the bad man had been caught and locked up. There was nothing more to fear. There was a moment of silence, then muffled sobs of relief.

Nancy got back on. "Know what Jeremy asked me a little while ago?"

"No."

"He wondered if you could come over and throw the ball around with us. You know, it's a little hard with just the two of us."

"That's a nice offer. Tell him I accept. When the dust settles here, let's figure out a time."

Next I called Jennifer Sanchez at the hospital and provided the same news, with the same effect. As with Nancy, I could sense the relief in her voice. She thanked me profusely and said she'd spread the word there. They had all been praying Jim's killer would be found.

Finally I put in a call to Zane.

"Yo. Mr. T."

"Hi, Zane."

"What's up?"

"I thought you'd be interested to learn that there is one less insurance firm doing business in town."

"Say what?"

I filled him in on developments.

"Whoa."

"And thanks for your assistance. It was a big help."

"I'm just a cog in the wheel, Mr. T. You're the one who figures these things out."

"Which requires the kind of information you come up with."

There was a brief pause, then Zane spoke in a reflective tone. "So it was the Cantons who killed your friend. I guess greed can be a real motivator."

"Greed on Roberta's part, and jealousy on Bruce's."

"Of who?"

"Jim Pearson. Karen loved him, and Bruce couldn't stand it. He wanted her for himself."

"Men can be heinous."

"Yeah. But not all of them."

"Who you talking about?"

"Jim Pearson. He just wanted to do right. By his family, by Karen Black, by folks with no place to call home. When Jill threw him out and he couldn't see his girls, and he took on that awful insurance job, he lived in a kind of hell. But the man was an angel."

"We need more of them."

"Yeah." I hesitated. "Kind of gives you a reason to try harder."

"How do you mean?"

"Oh, nothing. Anyway, thanks."

"Sure thing, Mr. T. You take it easy."

"Bye, Zane."

After I'd hung up I sat there thinking.

***

Not knowing how long the questioning would take, nor whatever else I needed to do before thinking about food, Violet had suggested eating in. At her place. Which, as ridiculous as I knew it was, I'd never actually set foot in. It had always seemed like a step I wasn't quite ready for.

I knocked gently on her door. She opened it and looked out, then glanced at her watch. "Wasn't sure you were going to make it, Lew. It's after nine."

"I had a few things to attend to."

"Like putting on some fresh clothes, I see."

"I needed a shower anyway, figured I might as well."

"You look very nice."

"You don't look so bad yourself."

She smiled. "Thank you." She opened the door wide and ushered me in. Her place was decorated as I'd expected, tastefully and comfortably. There was a table set for two in the dining area, with two candles lit and an open bottle of petit syrah, my favorite.

"Wow."

"I figured you could use a little something to relax you. That was quite an afternoon."

"Speak for yourself. You played a crucial role."

"It was kind of fun, actually."

"You have a strange idea of fun."

"There are other things I like also." Spoken coyly.

"You make an old guy nervous."

She smiled. "I was talking about going for a ride."

"A ride?"

"Don't you have an old motorcycle stashed away somewhere?"

I frowned. "Yeah. But I haven't had it out in years."

"Don't you think it might be time? I haven't been on the back of one of those in thirty years."

"You talking about this evening?"

"I was thinking more in the morning. After we get up."

Charles Dayton

Acknowledgements

I'd like to thank the following people for their thoughtful reviews and helpful feedback: Elizabeth Compton, who in spite of caring for two small children took time to carefully read the draft and provide her usual insightful feedback and suggestions; Jay Egan, whose shrewd insights and unique wit caught several potential glitches and added color as always; Jon Fichthorn, whose discerning suggestions contributed meaningfully to the motivation of key characters; Roger Jones, who was instrumental in initiating the publication of the Lew Travis Mystery series and again offered his always astute editing suggestions; and finally Laurie Harrison, my wife, whose tolerance and support for this work, as well as her thoughtful and perceptive suggestions, proved once again that I may be the luckiest man in the world.

Let me also acknowledge that any omissions or errors are purely my own.

About the Author

Charles Dayton lives with his wife Laurie in the foothills of the Sierra Nevada Mountains of Northern California. He grew up in Western New York, moved to California in his late twenties, and worked at several jobs including at a national research institute and UC Berkeley. He divides his time among writing, traveling, spending time with his two grown children (and two grandchildren) in San Francisco, and hanging out with Laurie and assorted friends.